P9-DUW-621

3 7814 00011 1469

DISCARDED
BAKER CO. PUBLIC LIBRARY

DEC 1 1976

McBain
Guns

BAKER COUNTY
PUBLIC LIBRARY
BAKER, OREGON

25¢ fine charged
for cards missing
from book pocket

87th Precinct Mysteries by Ed McBain

Cop Hater * The Mugger * The Pusher * The Con Man * Killer's
Choice * Killer's Payoff * Lady Killer * Killer's Wedge * Til Death
* King's Ransom * Give the Boys a Great Big Hand * The Heckler *
See Them Die * The Empty Hours * Lady, Lady, I Did It! * Like
Love * Ten Plus One * He Who Hesitates * Eighty Million Eyes *
Hail, Hail, the Gang's All Here! * Sadie When She Died * Let's Hear
It for the Deaf Man * Hail to the Chief * Blood Relatives * So Long
as You Both Shall Live

and

Ax * Bread * Doll * Fuzz * Jigsaw * Shotgun

Benjamin Smoke Mysteries by Ed McBain

Where There's Smoke

Other Novels by Ed McBain

The Sentries * Guns

GUNS

GUNS

a novel by

Ed "McBain"

Random House • New York

BAKER COUNTY
PUBLIC LIBRARY
BAKER, OREGON

Copyright © 1976 by HUI Corporation

All rights reserved under International and Pan-American Copyright
Conventions.
Published in the United States by Random House, Inc., New York,
and simultaneously
in Canada by Random House of Canada Limited, Toronto.

A portion of this book originally appeared in *Mystery Monthly.*

Library of Congress Cataloging in Publication Data
Hunter, Evan, 1926–
Guns.
I. Title.
PZ4.H945Gu   PS3515.U585   813'.5'4   76-12435
ISBN 0-394-40679-6

Manufactured in the United States of America
2 4 6 8 9 7 5 3
First Edition

This is for
DICK *and* BARBARA COATS

DEC 1 1976

GUNS

ONE

The night of the liquor-store job, you could fry eggs on the sidewalk. It was seven o'clock already, and outside it was still an oven. Colley was all for calling off the job. Even there inside the cafeteria, with the air conditioner going, he was sweating.

"No," Jocko said. "I think we're primed for it, we should go ahead."

"Because when it's this hot," Colley said, "things could go wrong."

"Nothin'll go wrong, don't worry."

"Guys lose their temper, guys take stupid chances," Colley said.

"Only one guy in the store," Jocko said, "and he won't take no chances, don't worry."

"Or lose his temper or something, this heat," Colley said.

"Only heat he's gonna know is the gun I stick in his face," Jocko said. "I'll tell him up front he opens his mouth, his brains are on the wall."

"Same as always," Teddy said, and shrugged.

Colley looked at him. Teddy shrugged again. He was their driver, what the hell did *he* care if something happened inside the store? If something started in there, he'd throw her in gear and ride off into the sunset, the hell with the two dopes inside with guns in their hands. With heat like this, you never knew what was going to happen. When you got a guy on a cold winter day, he'd open the register without a peep. But on a day like today, when his underwear was creeping up his behind, or he maybe had an argument with a delivery man, who knew what might happen? When it was hot like this, you told him to open the register, he was liable to take a swing at you. So then you'd have to use the gun.

"Look," Colley said, "have I ever backed off a job before?"

"No," Jocko said. "What's right is right."

"I just got a thing about heat."

"I can understand that," Jocko said. "But there's nothing to worry about here."

"People act unpredictable when it's hot," Colley said. "I myself, I find myself getting irritated sitting here with you guys and trying to convince you to call this job off."

"It ain't hot in here," Teddy said.

"It's nice and cool in here," Jocko said.

"To me it's hot, and to me I'm getting irritated. This heat's been building here in the city for the past five days. We're gonna get a storm soon, *I* say we do the job *after* the storm. When everybody's cooled off, then we go in there and show the pieces and the old man does just what we tell him to do without no fuss."

"How you know when this heat's gonna break?" Jocko asked.

"They said any day now."

"Who's *they*?"

"The guy on television. What the hell's his name? The one used to do the weather for Con Ed."

"I don't know his name," Jocko said.

"Him. He said the heat'll break soon."

"The one with the mustache?" Teddy said.

"Yeah, him."

"We postpone the job, we have to wait another week," Jocko said. "Cause that's when there's the biggest take in there. We have to wait till next Saturday night."

"So what's so bad about that?"

"Okay, suppose we postpone, okay? And it rains. And then by next Saturday it's hot again. This is New York, this is August, it rains, it gets hot, it's up and down all the time. Also, how do we know that old fart ain't planning to go on vacation or something? We go back next Saturday, we find grilles up all over the place, the guy went to the mountains for a week. Here's what I say, Colley . . ."

"Yeah, I *know* what you say."

"I say you plan a job, then you go through with it for when it's planned."

"That's right," Teddy said.

"Otherwise, it's amateur night in Dixie."

"I'm saying you got to bend with the wind," Colley said.

"There ain't no wind," Teddy said, and laughed. "That's exactly your beef, ain't it, Nicholas?"

"Lay off the Nicholas shit," Colley said, and gave him a look that was supposed to be full of menace and threat. Teddy only shrugged again. They knew each other too long, that was it. The three of them had done twelve jobs together in the past eight months, that was a long time for guys to be together.

The funny thing was they hadn't known each other from a hole in the wall before Christmas, when Colley met Jocko in a bar on Eighth Avenue. Jocko had his hand under this black hooker's skirt. They struck up a conversation across the hooker. She was sitting in the middle, Jocko on one side, Colley on the other, they started talking across her about various cops they had known. The hooker had her legs spread on the stool there, Jocko was exploring under her skirt, and meanwhile telling Colley about the Texas Rangers and what sons of bitches they were. Colley'd never been to Texas in his life. He was born and raised in New York, he'd never been further west than New Jersey, went there to see the burlesque in Union City; that was when he was only seventeen, before the whole city opened up with skin flicks and body-rub joints and topless dancers and whatever the hell you wanted. If you couldn't find what you wanted in New York City, then, man, you just weren't looking. Jocko was telling him the Texas Rangers just *enjoyed* being mean sons of bitches. Not only to niggers. To white guys like you and me, Colley. Is that your name? Colley?

The black girl was looking at Jocko because he used the word nigger in her presence. He had his hand halfway to Yugoslavia, but that didn't upset her. What did upset her was he said nigger. She kept looking at him. Jocko didn't even know he'd said anything to upset her. He kept going on about the Texas Rangers. By that time the hooker was beginning to realize she didn't have a true john here, all she had was a honky telling Texas Ranger stories and feeling her up freebies. So she got up off the stool and wandered over to where a live nine-to-fiver was sitting there nursing a beer, and she started pitching at him— Good *rid*dance, Jocko said.

That's when they got down to straight talking.

It turned out Jocko had been in it a long time, done his first robbery when he was eighteen, well, almost nineteen. That was in Waco, Texas, held up a supermarket down there, came away with close to a thousand in cash. He was Texan by birth, six feet two inches tall, weighing two hundred and twenty pounds, hair as red as fire, pale-blue eyes, freckles all over his face. He had a baby face, Jocko, but he was built like a gorilla and there was a mean streak running through him that showed in the slight curl of his lip and the cold, flat look in his eyes. Colley was a little scared of him; big men like that always scared him. He himself was five-ten, which wasn't short, but he was built narrow and the idea that Jocko could pick him up and throw him against the wall if he wanted to . . . well, that scared him a little. He told Jocko he'd done a few things in his life, too; he didn't want to tell him *too* much, he hardly knew the guy.

They sat there drinking, and before you knew it Jocko was sounding him about a job he'd been casing for a couple of weeks. Pawnshop on Lenox and a Hun' Twelfth, up in nigger Harlem. Jocko had himself a wheel man, but he still needed a fall partner to go in there with him, keep the place pure while he was cleaning out the register. Colley said he might be interested, depended on who the driver was, and also on whether or not he could get himself a gun. He had to tell Jocko, then, that he'd only been out of jail a little more than a month, that he'd taken a fall for armed robbery four years ago, and just got out after doing three and a bit more. That was why he didn't have a piece yet; he was on parole, he wasn't organized yet. Well, Jocko said, what you need to do is meet some people who'll help you get organized, that's all.

The people Jocko had in mind, or what it looked like at first, were two girls in his apartment up in the Bronx. Colley thought they were maybe hookers, but he wasn't sure. They were both in their early twenties, one of them a skinny blonde, the other one a skinny brunette. The blonde had pimples all over her face; maybe she was younger than Colley had guessed. They both came into the apartment wearing fake furs. It was snowing outside, but neither one of them was wearing stockings. Just the fake furs, and short skirts, and boots.

Teddy came in a little while later.

"This is Teddy Stein," Jocko said. "This is the driver I was telling you about. Teddy, meet Colley Donato."

"Hey, how you doin?" Teddy said, and took Colley's hand. "Colley, huh? I never heard that name before. Is it short for something?"

"It's short for cauliflower," the blonde with the pimples said, and laughed.

"It's short for Nicholas," Colley said.

"Colley, huh?"

"That's right. Colley Donato."

"How come they don't call you Nick?" the brunette said.

"How come they don't call *you* Abigail?" Colley said.

"What do you mean? My name's Ginny, why should they call me Abigail?"

"Forget it," Colley said.

"Why don't you and Teddy talk a little?" Jocko said. "Girls, come on in the other room."

"What's so special in the other room?" the blonde asked, and laughed. But she and the brunette went out with Jocko.

"So you interested in this job, huh?" Teddy said. He was a little shorter than Colley, and a little stouter. He wore eyeglasses, and he was going bald at the back of his head. Colley guessed he was in his late thirties, which was old for a guy doing robberies. Then again, he was only a driver. In this business, Colley found it important to separate the dudes with heart from the ones who only *thought* they had heart. The dude sitting behind the wheel might kid himself into thinking he was at the center of the action, but he wasn't. The dude who went in there with the gun, *he* was the one calling the tune, man.

"I'm *maybe* interested," Colley said. "It depends on how it's set up."

"Well, I thought Jocko told you all about it," Teddy said.

"No, all Jocko told me was he's got a pawnshop picked out, and somebody to drive a car."

"So what do you want to know?"

"Has this pawnshop been cased good?"

"Yeah, Jocko done that himself."

"When?"

"Two, three weeks ago."

"How many of us will be on the job?"

"Just the three of us. If you come in."

"No lookout, huh?"

"Not outside the shop, no. The way Jocko figures it, that'll be your job. He'll be at the register, you'll be at the door, blow the whistle you see any trouble coming."

"Mm," Colley said.

"So how does it look?" Teddy said.

"Who's runnin the show, you or Jocko?"

"It's Jocko's job."

"What's the split?"

"You got to talk to Jocko about that."

"You ever do a job together before?"

"No, this'll be the first one."

"What's he promised you?"

"Well, you talk to Jocko about that, okay?"

"If he wants me in on it, I get the same as him," Colley said.

"That's up to him."

"No, that's up to *me*. Cause otherwise, I ain't interested."

"If the split's okay, you think you might be interested?"

"It sounds like he done his homework," Colley admitted.

"Oh, yeah, he's a very thorough guy. He's got it all worked out so smooth, it's almost boring."

"Boring, huh? You in this for thrills or money?" Colley asked.

"Well, money, sure. What I meant—"

"You ever been busted?"

"Only once."

"What for?"

"Hanging paper."

"How'd you get from *that* to *this*?"

"I figured if I got caught passing queer checks, then maybe I wasn't so good at it."

"How do you know you're good at driving?"

"I don't. There's always a first time, though, am I right?"

"Yeah," Colley said, and thought Who the hell wants to be with an amateur his first time out? "What about Jocko? He ever done time?"

"Twice. In Texas."

"What for?"

"Robbery both times."

Great, Colley thought. I got a punk who never drove before, and I also got a mastermind who's so good at plotting robberies he's already been busted twice. This is certainly the job for me.

"I'll think about it," he said to Teddy.

That night they fixed him up with the blonde, who was not too bad in bed once you got past the pimples. And the next morning, which was three days before Christmas, Jocko came around with a Colt Detective Special and said it was a present. Counting the blonde, that was the *second* present. They went out for breakfast together, and Jocko said, "Well, Colley, what do you think? Are you coming in with us or what?" Colley spooned cornflakes into his mouth, and said, "Only if I get the same action you get." Jocko nodded and held out his hand across the table.

So that was it, that was how it all started. Twelve jobs counting that first one on Christmas Eve, and all of them exactly the same, all of them coming off without a hitch, knock wood. But today the heat was bothering Colley. And besides, this was the thirteenth job. He debated mentioning this.

"This is number thirteen, you know," he said.

Jocko looked at him and smiled. "Always got to be a number thirteen," he said. "Less you want to retire after number twelve."

"I'm only saying . . ."

"He's superstitious," Teddy said.

"I'm not. All I'm saying is if we got to do number thirteen, then for Christ's sake let's do it when it ain't so fuckin hot!"

"Colley, I'm going to tell you something," Jocko said. There was no menace in his voice, he spoke softly and reasonably. It was just that you could read meanness behind his pale-blue eyes and in the telltale curl of his lip. If Jocko hadn't become an armed robber, he'd have made a good

Texas Ranger. "I'm going to tell you why we have to do this job *tonight,* okay, Colley? Now, after I finish telling you, you're free to do what you like. If Teddy and me has to do it just the two of us, him outside and me going in there alone, why then, that's what we'll have to do, and no hard feelings, I mean it."

"Well, you know I wouldn't let you—"

"I mean it, Colley, there'd be no hard feelings. Man has to do what he wants to do, and that's that. But let me explain why I feel it's essential that we go in there tonight. Never mind that we'd have to wait another whole week, we don't do it now. So we'll *wait* another week, so what, waiting a week ain't important one way or the other. Except, of course, the man may go away on vacation, this is August, remember. But here's the *real* reason, Colley; I am being as honest with you as I know how to be. The *real* reason I want to do this job tonight is because I am stone dead broke. That is the real reason. I am down to the bare soles of my feet, Colley, and I need to get in there and come out with some bread. That's the long and the short of it."

"I can lend you some money," Colley said.

"Colley, I don't borrow from nobody," Jocko said, and grinned. "Hell, man, reason I *started* stealing was cause I'm too proud to borrow."

Teddy laughed. "That's a good one," he said.

"Ever since Jeanine come up from Dallas," Jocko said, "my expenses have gone sky-high, I don't have to tell you. She's a good woman, a good wife, but man, she *does* enjoy clothes and whiskey and having herself a gay old time. So what can I tell you?" Jocko said, and shrugged. "I *got* to do that job tonight, I got to get me some bread. I'll tell you the truth, Colley, was you to back out, was Teddy to back out, I'd do it all by my lonesome, that's the truth, I'm that hard up for cash. Jeanine was telling me only this morning she was thinking of maybe taking a job in one of them massage parlors, help out a little, you know: Well now, man, *you* know and *I* know that those massage-parlor girls ain't nothing but whores, am I right? I told Jeanine I'd kick her ass clean around the block she even mention such a idea to me again. Point is, she's worried, and she's got reason to be. Woman has a right to expect her man to provide. I *got* to go in there tonight, and that's that." Jocko shrugged. "With you or without you, Colley, I'm goin in. Besides, it sounds to me like maybe all this business about it being hot and all is *really* cause this is number thirteen and that's somehow got you spooked."

"No, it's just it's so hot," Colley said.

"Well, either way, the choice is yours, friend."

"You'd go in there alone, huh?"

"That's right."

"End up in jail before the night's out," Colley said.

"Ain't nobody ever going to bust me again," Jocko said. "You don't have to worry about that, I can take care of myself." He spread his hands wide, said, "So that's it," and looked at his watch. "It's quarter past seven now, the liquor store closes nine o'clock on Saturday nights. I want to go in about five to, what do you say, Colley?"

"Well, I can't let you go in there alone."

"I told you that's no worry of yours."

"If I *don't* go in with you," Colley said, "I guess that's the end of us three, huh?"

"I guess so," Jocko said.

"End of the Three Musketeers," Teddy said.

"Well, I can't let you go in alone."

"Then you still with us?"

"I'm still with you," Colley said.

"Good," Jocko said.

"Good," Teddy said.

In the movies, it was always a caper. The movies made it sound like somebody dancing a jig in the street. A caper. Fun and games. Mastermind plots it down to the last detail, everybody rehearses it, gets everything down like clockwork, the day of the job something goes wrong. Crime does not pay. The thing that goes wrong is something the mastermind never thought of in a million years. Or else it's something about one of the characters. A flaw in his character, like he digs girls in boots. The day of the job a girl in boots marches by, he takes his eyes off the bank guard, watches the girl, there goes the caper.

Those two girls in boots that night in Jocko's apartment. Ginny and whoever—the blonde was the one whose name he'd forgotten, and the blonde was the one he'd gone to bed with. Surprised she didn't keep her goddamn boots on in the sack. Took off everything *but* the boots, went parading around the room for the longest time, tiny tits, narrow hips tufted blond crotch hair, looked like a teenager in a kinky English movie. Colley finally asked her was she going to march around the room all night long. The blonde said she was loosening up. He told her to come get in bed, he'd loosen her up. If it hadn't been for the blonde, he probably wouldn't have thrown in with Teddy and Jocko. Well, the gun, too. Jocko bringing him that gun, must've cost him a good two-fifty on the street, *that* was what decided him. He began to feel like himself again, hefting that gun in his hand. Yeah. That was the part they forgot to mention in all the movies. The gun. Well sure, how could they? Do a thing that's about a *caper,* all the guys talking about a fuckin *caper* instead of a *job,* then the gun becomes a minor part of it. The *major* part is the clockwork timing and the breathless suspense that's going to lead up to that girl in boots walking by at just the crucial moment— *Alice,* that was her name.

They forgot to mention the gun.

They forgot to mention what it felt like to have that big mother gun in your hand, to know that when you went in there and shoved that piece in somebody's face, why, that person was going to look at that gun, and his eyes were going to go wide, and you were going to smell the stink of fear on him, man, and from *that* minute on, from the minute you yanked that piece out of your coat and saw his eyes bug with fright, *you* were the boss. And from that minute on, you knew the man there was going to get off his money and hand it to you nice and peaceful.

Here's your caper movie, Colley thought; here's tonight's job the way it would be in a caper movie. We go in, right? I've been bitching about the heat all day long, so at the very last minute I wipe sweat out of my eyes and I miss seeing the cop on the beat who's coming around shaking doors. The cop barges in the liquor store with his gun blazing, shoots Jocko in the back, and is putting the cuffs on me even before I'm finished wiping away the sweat. End of caper.

Or else how about this, yeah, this would be even better. We go in the store, right? Jocko does his number with the old man, I'm standing watching the outside, everything goes off without a hitch. The old man opens the register, nobody comes anywhere near the store, we're home free and are running to where Teddy's waiting with the car. But right at the crucial moment, a black cat crosses my path. And since I've been worried about this being number thirteen and all, why, naturally I panic and shoot the fuckin cat and we get the whole damn precinct up there down on our asses in ten seconds flat. *Also* end of caper.

In real life, nothing like that ever happens. In real life, a job ends only one of three ways. You get the money and you get away; or you *don't* get the money, but you get away; or you don't get the money, and you get busted besides. Usually, if there's trouble, it's because somebody blows his cool. Now, unless you're dealing with amateurs, the person who blows his cool is *not* one of *your* people. A dude holding a gun has nothing to worry about, he's the one in control of the situation. What causes the trouble, usually, is some fat lady beginning to yell at the top of her lungs, or the guy who owns the store all of a sudden deciding to become John Wayne, or even just a passer-by outside seeing the action in there and marching in to make a citizen's arrest. Blow your cool when somebody's holding a gun on you, and you're forcing that man to use the gun. And that's trouble.

A man going in someplace with a gun had to be ready to use it, of course, but Colley hardly knew any robbers at all who actually *wanted* to use it. You found some kooks, yes, who enjoyed blowing a man's brains out, but they were in the wrong racket, they should have been hiring out to do contracts instead. Your armed robber was a man who showed face, don't forget; he went into a place unmasked, usually, and one reason for his sticking a gun under a man's nose was to scare the guy not only for now but for later, too. If you scared him enough, he wouldn't be so quick to identify you if you happened to get picked up later. The chances of getting picked up, unless it was right at the scene, were pretty slim anyway. What's the guy going to do, wade through hundreds of mug shots of armed robbers? *That* was for the movies, too. Guy sitting at a desk with patient, kind detective. "That's the man, Officer! I'd recognize him anywhere!" Bullshit.

You shove a gun in a man's face, he suddenly loses his mind, his memory, his courage, and ten pounds of weight. *"See this, mister? I'll shoot your face off you don't open the register fast. Now do it!"* Colley had heard Jocko using that same line a total of twelve times now. He said it the same way each time. Each time the man opened the register. Fast. There was something in Jocko's voice that told the man he meant business. Jocko *would* use the gun if he had to. The man knew it, and the man didn't want to get shot. That was simple arithmetic.

In one of the holdups—this was a Mom and Pop grocery store in Queens, they hit it on a Friday night in April, gorgeous spring night, this was about six o'clock the place was just closing. Teddy was outside in the car, it was a car he'd boosted that afternoon, they always used a stolen car on their jobs. Jocko went in, walked straight to the counter, Colley came in behind him, was closing the door when he heard

Jocko doing his monster routine. "See this, mister? I'll shoot your face off you don't open the register fast. Now do it!" This was Colley's cue to take his own gun from his pocket, keep it low, under the glass panel of the door, but have it ready to bring it up if there was trouble of any kind. The old ginzo behind the counter was opening the register almost before Jocko got the words out of his mouth. This store had been hit four times already by two different gangs, that's why Jocko had picked it, cause it was an easy mark. The guy's wife was standing right alongside him. She looked a little like Colley's Aunt Anna, big fat Italian lady wearing a black dress, faint black mustache over her lip. She was scared but at the same time angry, and you could see she was thinking her husband was a coward for not *doing* something. This was the fifth holdup here, and all the guy did was open the cash register each time. Which he was also doing this time.

Colley was at the door, half watching the action at the counter, half watching the street outside. It was stickball time, you could hear kids up the street yelling. Nice April noises. City noises. He loved this fuckin city. Outside, a woman came up to the door, she was talking to somebody over her shoulder, she didn't even look at the knob. She'd been coming here maybe half her life, she could find the place and the doorknob blindfolded. She grabbed the knob, she walked in, she saw Colley's gun. Nice Italian lady, also like one of his aunts, but not as fat as most of them. Ready to scream down the whole neighborhood.

Colley lifted the gun so the muzzle was pointing up at her head; that hole in the muzzle could look mighty big when it was pointing up at you. He slitted his eyes. He made his voice a rasp. In Italian, he said, *"Signora, sta zitta."* That meant, "Lady, cool it." He didn't have to say another word. The lady went over near the shelves where the macaroni was, and she started saying a novena. Forty Hail Marys and a few dozen Our Fathers Who Art in Heaven while Jocko was cleaning out the register. When Jocko started for the door, the lady fell to her knees because she knew from television and the movies that the two bad guys were going to kill her now. *"Signora,"* Colley said, *"è finita, la commedia."* That meant, "Lady, the comedy is finished." It was a famous line from something. Colley's grandfather, who used to go to the Brooklyn Academy of Music for the operas there, was always quoting that line. Colley figured it was from an opera. The lady looked up at him. She *still* thought she was going to get shot. Colley started laughing. Jocko thought Colley had lost his marbles, and began tugging on his sleeve, trying to get him out of the store. The lady meanwhile thought Colley was Richard Widmark in that picture where he threw a lady just like herself down the stairs. She was shaking so hard she was knocking La Rosa boxes off the shelf. Jocko finally got Colley to put the gun away, and they both went outside, the guns back in their pockets now, two gentlemen out for an evening stroll. Behind them, a real-life opera started in the grocery store. Teddy threw open the car doors. Colley was still laughing.

He was really worried about the hot weather. And about this being the thirteenth job. But he'd given them his word on it, said he was going along with them, so the only thing to do now was shut up and go along. Still, he was worried. His grandmother wouldn't even go out of the house on the thirteenth of each month. "Hoodoo jinx of a day," she'd say, sounding more like an Irish washerwoman than a lady who'd been born in Naples. His grandmother was dead now. Cancer when he was twenty-five. That was four years ago. Hoodoo jinx of a day, she used to call the thirteenth, and refused to budge from the house on that day. Even when her brother Jerry died in New Jersey, she wouldn't go to the funeral because it took place on the thirteenth of the month. Well, this had nothing to do with a *day,* of course. But still, it *was* the thirteenth *job,* wasn't it? Well, that was stupid, that really was being superstitious. Teddy was right. And Jocko was right, too. There *had* to be a number thirteen unless you wanted to retire after number twelve.

Colley wasn't nervous, he was never nervous before a job. But he was worried that this time somebody who was irritated by the heat would do something dumb. He didn't know what. Just something that would force one or the other of them to use the gun. He had never had to use the gun. Jocko had once used the gun in Texas. He had blinded a man in a gas station. Shot him in the eye when the guy told him he didn't have the combination to the safe. "See this, mister? I'll shoot your face off . . ." and that's just what he'd done. Bam, right in the eye. Jocko got busted; that was the second fall he'd taken. If you used the gun, there was always the chance of fuzz descending. Very dangerous. Also, you got into much heavier raps once you used the gun. On top of the robbery-one charge, you got felonious assault added. Or homicide, God forbid. Jesus, he would never want to kill anybody. Never. In his nightmares he used the gun and killed somebody.

"This is a nice heap," Teddy said. "It handles nice."

The car was a 1974 Ford station wagon. Teddy had boosted it that afternoon in Brooklyn. There was no need to put on different license plates or anything like that. If you boosted a car that morning, it didn't show up on the police department's hot-car sheets till sometime the next day. The police wouldn't be looking for it till maybe two, three days after it got stolen. Besides, nobody in the police department went around constantly checking license plates against the numbers in their little black books. The only time they checked out a plate was if they saw something suspicious. Three guys sitting in a car watching the street, that's suspicious. The cop on the beat'll check out the license-plate numbers in his book, just on the off chance he's got a stolen vehicle there. Wants to know what he's going up against. Are those three guys just sitting there watching the girls go by, or are they thieves casing a joint they're going to make in the next five minutes, or are they junkies waiting for the man to show with their dope? These are all considerations for the cop on the beat. He doesn't want to rap on a closed car window with his stick and all of a sudden three guys are shooting at him. So he checks out the plate first. If the car is stolen, he calls back to the ranch for help.

Another time he'll check a plate is if something accidentally rings a bell. At muster, the sergeant will read off the hot-car sheet, and all the patrolmen'll make notes, and maybe something'll stick in the guy's head—red and white Buick with a smashed right headlight, something like that. So while he's walking the beat he'll see a red and white Buick with a smashed right headlight, it doesn't take a mastermind to figure that maybe this is the car that was stolen. Out comes the book, and he checks the numbers. Thing is, your professional car thief is a man who doesn't steal a car in the Bronx, for example, and then drive it all over the Bronx so every cop on the beat can get a good look at it. If he steals it in the Bronx, he's usually from Brooklyn. And the cop on the Brooklyn beat couldn't care less what the hell was stolen in the Bronx.

"Don't you think it rides nice?" Teddy said.

"Yeah, it rides nice," Colley said.

"I grabbed it outside a supermarket. Lady must've been inside doing her shopping."

"Comes out, finds her wagon gone," Jocko said.

"That's life," Teddy said.

"She leave the keys in it?"

"No, but it was unlocked. I opened the door and got at the hood latch. Thing that always amazes me, I can be working on a car four, five minutes, hood up, crossing the wires so I can start it, nobody'll say boo to me. I once had a *cop* come over, would you believe it, stood there on the sidewalk with his hands behind his back, watching me while I crossed the wires. He nodded when I got the job finished. Nice work, he was telling me. You fixed whatever was wrong with it."

The men laughed. The sense of familiarity in the car was beginning to dispel whatever worries Colley had about the heat or the hoodoo jinx number thirteen. They had done this a dozen times before, they had talked easily and casually on the way to one job or another. Teddy, in fact, had probably told that very same story on the way to each and every job, and they had laughed genuinely each time he told it. He would now explain that he had rigged a switch . . .

"What I done," he said, "was rig a switch here on the dash. So I can start it without going under the hood each time."

"Yeah, good," Jocko said.

"Is that clock right?" Colley said. He was sitting alone in the back, and he leaned forward toward the front seat.

Jocko checked the dashboard clock against his wristwatch. "I've got a quarter to," he said.

"That's what I've got," Colley said.

"I never had a car in my life the clock worked," Teddy said. "I stole Cadillacs, Mercedes-Benzes, Continentals, you name it. The clock never works."

"They build them so they won't work," Jocko said.

"What do you mean?"

"They don't want them to work."

"Why wouldn't they want them to work?" Teddy asked.

"If they wanted them to work, don't you think they could *build* them so they worked? Man, they build a machine costs fifteen thousand dollars, whatever, everything all precision-made, you mean to tell me if they *wanted* that old clock to work, it wouldn't work?"

"I guess they could make it work if they wanted to," Teddy said.

"Sure," Jocko said.

"Then why don't they?"

"Who knows *what* their motive is?" Jocko said. "These big companies are all screwed up." Abruptly, his voice and his manner changed. "Listen, I just want to go over this one more time, Teddy. After we come out, you're going cross-town to Jerome Avenue, and we'll ditch the car someplace near Yankee Stadium, wherever you find a good spot."

"Yeah, I got it."

"Then we go our separate ways, and meet tomorrow morning at my place."

"Right," Teddy said.

"Colley?"

"Fine."

"You still worried?"

"No, no."

"Just make believe it's number fourteen. One after this *will* be fourteen, so just make believe it's *this* one instead."

"That don't bother me no more," Colley said.

"Or make believe it's a baker's dozen," Teddy said.

"What's that, a baker's dozen?"

"That's thirteen," Teddy said.

"So how does *that* change anything? If a baker's dozen is thirteen, I *think* of it as thirteen, it's *still* thirteen, ain't it?"

"Yeah, I guess so," Teddy said.

"Jesus," Colley said.

"Don't think about it at *all,*" Jocko said. "That's the best way."

"I'm *not* thinking about it," Colley said. "I'm hot, that's all. I can't stand this kind of weather, that's all."

"Probably cool off later tonight," Teddy said.

"Won't cool off till we get some rain," Colley said.

"Jeanine likes this kind of weather," Jocko said. "She's from Fort Myers originally—you ever been down that part of Florida?"

"I never been to Florida, period," Colley said.

"Gets mighty hot down there in the summer. July and August, it's a blast furnace down there."

"Sounds like just the place for me," Colley said.

"Yeah," Jocko said, and laughed. "Jeanine loves it. A day like today, that's a little too brisk for her."

"Yeah, it sure is brisk," Colley said.

"You want to take a right when we get to the corner," Jocko said.

"Yeah," Teddy said.

"Then it's four blocks up."

"Yeah."

Jocko reached in under the blue poplin windbreaker he was wearing and pulled from the pocket of his trousers a Colt Cobra. The gun was almost identical to the Detective Special that Colley was carrying, except that it was partially made of aluminum and was lighter—fifteen ounces to twenty-one ounces for Colley's gun. Both pistols were snub-nosed revolvers, with fixed sights and walnut stocks. Each gun carried six .38 Special cartridges. Jocko rolled out the cylinder now, idly glanced at the cartridges, nodded briefly, flipped the cylinder back into position, and put the gun in his pocket again. Teddy had made the turn onto the avenue now, and was heading north toward the liquor store.

Neither Colley nor Jocko had permits or licenses for the guns they were carrying; both guns had been purchased from receivers of stolen goods. If a cop stopped and searched them and found the pieces on them, they would both be charged with violation of Section 265.05 of the Penal Law—Possession of Weapons and Dangerous Instruments and Appliances. Colley practically knew the Penal Law by heart. Possession of a loaded firearm was a Class D Felony, punishable by a minimum of three and a maximum of seven. Teddy was driving very carefully. No one wanted the fuzz coming down on them for a bullshit gun violation. Get busted holding up a store, okay, that was a legitimate beef. But get stopped for passing a traffic light and then spend seven in jail on a gun rap—no way.

The Penal Law sections on robbery were very clear, with none of the fine print that existed in the burglary sections, where the degree of the crime was figured by whether the breaking and entry had been done in the daytime or in the

night, in a dwelling or in a building, with a gun or without
—man wanted to become a burglar, he first had to become
a lawyer so he'd know what crime he was about to commit!
But the robbery sections were in straightforward, almost
blunt English, starting right off with the definition: ROB-
BERY IS FORCEFUL STEALING. You couldn't make it plainer
than that. The various degrees of robbery were also plain to
understand:

Robbery 3rd Degree: Forcibly stealing property.

Robbery 2nd Degree: Forcibly stealing property
when aided by another person
actually present.

Robbery 1st Degree: Forcibly stealing property and,
in the course of the commission
of the crime or of immediate
flight therefrom, the actor or
another participant in the
crime:
1: Causes serious physical injury to any person who is not a
participant in the crime; or
2: Is armed with a deadly
weapon; or
3: Uses or threatens the immediate use of a dangerous
weapon.

Any kind of robbery was a felony. For robbery three, you
could get a maximum of seven years in prison; for robbery
two, you could get fifteen; for robbery one, which was a Class
B felony and nothing to sneeze at, you could get twenty-five.
The three of them were about to commit, by definition, robbery one.

"There it is," Jocko said. "Just up ahead."

The crime itself began for them the moment Jocko said those words; until then there had been only the preparation for the crime. Until then the atmosphere had been relaxed and informal; now it became charged and tense. They had done this a dozen times before, and each time the risk was the same. Each time Colley and Teddy gambled whatever was in the cash register or safe against a possible twenty-five years in prison. Jocko gambled a possible life sentence; he had already taken two falls, another bust would be his third. He was twenty-seven years old and had already spent fourteen years of his life in detention centers, county jails, adolescent correctional facilities and hard-ass prisons. Colley had been sentenced to seven for the robbery-two fall, and had got out on parole after serving a little more than three. That had been shortly before last Christmas. He was twenty-eight at the time.

He had gone home to pick up his clothes and then had moved in with a girl he knew, a go-go dancer in one of the joints on Forty-ninth, just off Broadway. That had lasted about a week and a half, a total bummer. She kicked him out at the end of that time, called him a freeloader, said he wasn't even any good in bed. He was living in a fleabag on Forty-seventh when he ran into Jocko in the bar that night. Only reason he'd sat down next to him was because he was hoping to make time with the black hooker. The next day he was holding a gun in his hand again. And two days after that, on Christmas Eve, he committed another robbery.

They knew just how to do it, they had done it together often enough and they expected to do it exactly the same way tonight. There was something athletic about their performance—an end running wide, perhaps, to receive a quarterback's pass, a guard taking out the sole opposing tackle; or a smooth double-play combination, Tinkers to Evers to Chance—Teddy swiftly pulling the stolen automobile in toward the curb and cutting the engine, Jocko and Colley getting out on the curb side and beginning to walk purposefully but not too swiftly toward the front door of the liquor store. There was something theatrical in their performance as well—Teddy looking bored at the wheel of the car as he lit a cigarette and let out a long stream of smoke, Colley and Jocko making small talk as they approached the store, some bullshit about Jeanine's mother having come down with a summer cold, those were the worst kind, each of them responding to every hem and haw, every pause, every lifting of the eyebrow while robbery drummed in their heads, robbery hummed in their blood, robbery propelled them to the front of the liquor store.

And finally, there was something sexual in the way they worked together, a trio that had in the short space of eight months learned each other's skills and shortcomings, and moved now to supplement or correct, the thrill of what they were doing undeniable; Teddy confessed one night that he always waited at the wheel of the car with an erection. There was for Colley and Jocko—Teddy never experienced this, or at least mentioned it—the feeling that they were on dope. That everything was being slowed down by a fix. Not all the way down to slow motion, but somewhere much slower than what the real tempo was.

Colley saw Jocko's hand reach out in the shimmering August neon, saw clearly and precisely the small heart-shaped tattoo on the ball of the hand where thumb and forefinger joined, saw the fingers grasping the brass knob, and turning the knob, and easing the door open, slowly, slowly—everything moved so slowly when the juices ran high. He heard the tinkling of the bell over the door as though it were coming from a distant lush valley, and he moved into the store behind Jocko, moved on feet that seemed cushioned—he was somehow in sneakers again, though he was wearing black-leather loafers, he was running in high-topped Keds, he was ten years old and going for a base that had been chalked onto the asphalt, running in slow motion, Go, Colley, they are yelling at him. Go.

He closes the door behind Jocko. Jocko is moving across the store. The bottles are catching light and reflecting it; brilliant color explodes from the shelves and the stacked displays, bourbon browns and Scotch ambers, sauterne yellows and burgundy reds, crème de menthe greens. Jocko is walking toward the counter and Colley watches him and sees him moving through a stained-glass window toward an altar where a baldheaded priest stands in a brilliant red surplice: the counterman wearing a red cotton jacket, the pocket of it embroidered in white with the words *Carlisle Liquors*. Colley wonders if this is Mr. Carlisle himself, he wears the name so proudly, *Carlisle Liquors,* it might easily be a family crest, a proud and ancient family name, like Donato is a proud and ancient family name if your grandmother happens to come from a slum in Naples. Or is Carlisle the man's first name? Is he perhaps Carlisle Abernathy the Third, standing there beaming behind the counter as Jocko takes forever to cross the stained-glass room.

Colley closes the door.

Has it taken him all this time to close the door? He hears the snug whisper of the door easing into the jamb, hears a tiny ear-shattering click as the strike plate engages the bolt. There is a shade on the door, he wonders if he should pull down the shade. He has never had a door with a shade before. Never on any of the dozen jobs they pulled. He wonders now if the shade on the door is the big mistake the mastermind made. Is the shade on the door the thing that is going to wreck the caper? But this is not a caper. This is a job. The job is armed robbery. You fuck up on this job, mister, you go to jail for twenty-five years.

Is Jocko at the counter yet? Colley turns from the door, glances toward the counter for just a moment, sees that the baldheaded man in the red cotton jacket is looking suspiciously at Jocko as he approaches, the smile more tentative now: Is this a holdup here? Are these two guys together, the one coming toward the counter and the other one standing over there near the door? They *have* to be together, otherwise why doesn't the one near the door either start looking at the wine bottles on the rack there to the left, or else come toward the counter himself to state what sort of alcoholic beverage he wishes to purchase here in *Carlisle Liquors,* a proud and ancient family name ... the gun is coming out of Jocko's pants.

He holds the gun like a huge cock, waving it in the bald guy's face. Colley suppresses a sudden urge to giggle, and looks out at the street. People are moving past slowly in the stifling heat, cool here in the store, though, air conditioner humming, no chance of anybody doing anything stupid in here, too cool in here for anything stupid. Behind him he hears the words he's heard a dozen times before, spoken exactly the same way, the same voice-level and tone, the same inflection, "See this, mister? I'll shoot your face off you don't open the register fast. Now do it!"

There is another voice.

Colley ignores the words at first; they are too loaded with everything he has feared since he woke up this morning. He *hears* the words, of course, and he *knows* what they mean, but he chooses to react instead to the fact that there is another voice in the store, an unexpected voice that follows so quickly upon Jocko's set opening speech that it seems like an altar boy's response to a priest's litany, and makes suddenly valid the image of the counterman-priest in his stained-glass store.

Colley is suddenly trapped inside a movie. It is a caper movie, and everything is going wrong. It is the next-to-the-last scene in the picture, where everything goes wrong. The mastermind forgot something. Or a character flaw exposes itself. In the instant before he turns toward the counter, he tries to think what it is that possibly could have gone wrong, knowing full well what it is because he has heard the words and understood them, but refuses to accept the words and the meaning of the words until he can see for himself that what the voice claims is actually so. He knows, too, that he cannot do anything to change this situation. This is the scene where everything goes wrong, and there is nothing that anyone can ever do to change it.

This is the hoodoo-jinx scene; it cannot be changed because it was filmed too long ago. Jocko said his lines a long time ago, and they were recorded on film, just as the other voice was recorded. The movie is playing here in this liquor store for the first time anywhere, folks, it is a world premiere. But it really all happened a long time ago, when it was being filmed, and nothing the actors can do or say now will change a frame of what has been frozen for posterity. Colley knows the Penal Law, he now thinks, "the actor or another participant in the crime," and he thinks yes, Jocko has said his lines, the scene is progressing nicely. The voice that answers Jocko raps into the store with machine-gun authority. Jocko knows his lines because he's said them so often, and the man responding on cue has surely said his lines at least as often— oh, the scene is going beautifully. If only Colley wasn't so scared shitless, he could maybe eat his popcorn and enjoy the rest of the movie. He is scared only because of what the other voice has just said, even though he has not yet turned toward the counter to make sure this isn't merely old bald *Carlisle Liquors* making his voice big and barrel-chested; there are some short guys like that who can find a voice deep in the soles of their feet someplace and imitate wrestling champs.

"Police officers!" the voice says. "Don't move!"

Instead of not moving, Colley moves. He turns from the door, where he has been watching the street, which suddenly seems like a foolish occupation, since the thing that is going wrong is not coming from the street but from inside the store. At first he thinks he has made a mistake. Nothing seems to be changed there at the counter. Jocko is still holding a gun in his fist, the barrel pointed up at *Carlisle Liquors'* face, and the old man is looking into the muzzle, nothing has changed, it is all a mistake. Not *the* mistake, not the big blunder that fucks up the caper, but simply an *auditory* mistake. Colley didn't *really* hear anybody saying anything about cops, all he *really* heard was the counterman saying "Yes, sir, I will open the register in a jiffy," and somehow, probably because of the shitty acoustics, *thought* he heard "Police officers! Don't move!"

But no, this is number thirteen, this hoodoo jinx of a movie was shot a long, long time ago—probably when his grandmother was a teenager walking the streets of Naples and refusing to meet a neighbor's glance for fear either of them would be suspected of casting the Evil Eye—and what Colley sees are two police officers, sure enough, both as big as life and twice as wide. They are neither of them wearing the blue, they are not uniformed cops, but then, who would expect uniformed cops to be sitting a liquor store? They look exactly like any detective Colley has ever seen in his life, and they are both holding guns in their fists, and Colley notices something else that is wrong, notices it at once, and has the feeling now that this goddamn movie he is in has suddenly turned into a negative print because the detectives are holding their guns wrong.

He realizes all at once that both of them are left-handed, they are both holding their pieces in their left hands as they come down a narrow aisle formed by two standing racks. The racks are made of metal, they are green, they are maybe eight or ten feet high, and they are neatly stacked with whiskey bottles. The detectives are each at least six feet tall, they come charging down the narrow aisle like bulls coming into an arena. At the far end of the aisle, Colley sees an open door. There's a room back there, he can see cartons piled on the floor. That's where the cops were staked out, in the room back there, waiting for somebody to hold up the joint. Probably a lot of liquor-store holdups in the neighborhood, cops decided to stake out one or two places, see if they'd get lucky. Either that, or some stoolie heard him and Jocko were going to hit the joint, in which case the cops weren't here waiting for just *anybody,* they were here specifically waiting for him and Jocko to come in and make their move. Colley wonders which it is. He will spend the rest of his life wondering about it. In the meantime, the cops are here. Whyever or however, they are here.

Cops have always scared him, and they scare him now. The one in the front position is ludicrously holding a shield in his right hand. The shield is a regular detective's shield, gold with blue enamel, maybe three inches long, two inches wide, pinned to a leather case. The flap of the case is hanging down toward his wrist, and he's got the shield cupped in the palm of his right hand. In his left hand he's got the piece. He holds the piece close to his hip, almost resting on the hipbone there; it's the same gun Colley is holding in his hand, a Colt Detective Special. The other cop keeps weaving from side to side as he comes down the aisle, as if he's trying to get a look around his partner at the bad guys who are holding up the store. When they reach the end of the aisle, they fan out in two directions, one of them coming toward Colley, the other going toward Jocko at the counter.

The one coming toward Colley is the man holding the shield. He holds it like a warrior's shield, never mind just a little badge. He holds it like one of King Arthur's knights. With that shield out in front of him, nothing's going to happen to him. He's Lancelot, with his fuckin shield there. For the first time in his life Colley wants to use the gun. Not because he's *that* scared (though he is very scared) and not because he's angry the job is going wrong (though he's angry, too) but only because he wants to show the cop how fuckin *dumb* he's being with that shield. What does he think it is, a magic shield or something? Hold it out in front of you, it protects you from the bad guys? Hell it does, Colley thinks, and pulls the trigger.

The cop is about to say "Police officers!" again. He gets only part of the word out. He says "Po" and then the bullet takes him right in the mouth. It's as if the bullet rams the

rest of the word back into his throat and breaks it up into
a thousand red and yellow and white globules that come
flying out the back of his head and splatter all over a Seagram's poster behind him. He does an almost comic skid, the
force of the bullet knocking him backward, his feet still
moving forward and flying out from under him. He goes into
the air backward, hangs there for an instant in an upside-
down swan dive, his arms thrown wide, the shield in one
hand, the gun in the other, his back arched, his head thrown
back and spurting blood. Then he crashes suddenly to the
white vinyl tile floor, knocking over a wine rack. There is the
sound of bottles crashing. Burgundy, Chianti and Bordeaux
are suddenly spilling deeper reds into and around the bright
screaming red that is still pouring from the back of the cop's
head. Colley watches all this in fascination. He does not yet
realize he's shot a man. He certainly does not realize the man
is already dead.

Jocko is now facing the aisle the cops came out of. The
second cop, the one who'd been weaving down the aisle like
a broken-field runner, stops cold in his tracks when he hears
the gun exploding and the bottles crashing. He doesn't turn
toward the noise. Instead he immediately levels his gun at
Jocko, as if Jocko is the one who fired the shot. Colley stands
just inside the door, looking at the man on the floor. In the
background, near the register, he sees Jocko and the second
cop squaring off, but he keeps his eyes on the man he just
shot. It is beginning to dawn on him that he shot a man. The
man lies there like a bundle of old clothes. *Move,* Colley
thinks. *Get up!* There are two shots in rapid succession now,
crack, and then *crack,* it never goes BANG like in the comic
strips. Two sharp *cracks,* differently pitched. Colley registers
the fact that the shots come from two different guns, but he
keeps watching the man on the floor, he does not take his
eyes off the man on the floor. There is another *crack,* the air
is hanging blue with smoke now, the store stinks of cordite,
the air conditioner is causing the smoke to swirl in patterns

that make the room go in and out of focus. For a moment Colley thinks he is going to faint.

There are two men on the floor now.

Jocko is coming toward him.

Colley's eyes go *one, two, three*: the man he shot, the other man lying on the floor some six feet from the cash register, and Jocko staggering toward him. He does not realize at first, he is very slow to *grasp* things in this fuckin movie, he does not realize that Jocko has been hit. Then he sees that Jocko has his left hand hooked like a claw, and he sees that blood is pouring from under the sleeve of the windbreaker and into Jocko's cupped hand, and spilling from the hand onto the floor as he comes toward Colley. Jocko's eyes are out of focus, it looks as if he is going to pass out. He has the gun in his right hand, and to steady himself he reaches out with the hand that's running blood and clamps the hand onto Colley's sleeve. The summer-weight fabric soaks up the blood, the blood spreads along the sleeve, Colley can feel it wetting his skin. He loops his arm around Jocko's waist. Jocko's gun clatters to the floor, and all at once he goes limp. Colley starts dragging him toward the door.

At the door, he stops and looks back at the man he shot.

The man is not moving.

There are suddenly too many things to think about. Where's the car?—that's the first thing; he can't remember where Teddy parked the car. He has one arm wrapped around Jocko, his left hand clutched in Jocko's belt, supporting him that way, Jocko's left arm dripping blood onto Colley's hand, he can feel the blood sticky and hot. In his right hand he's still got the gun, but he can't turn the doorknob without putting the gun away, and this suddenly becomes another problem that seems impossible to solve. He stands there supporting Jocko, and feeling the steady flow of Jocko's blood, and behind him the counterman is yelling obscenities at him, yelling them in a steady monotonous senseless stream, and he cannot for the life of him figure out how to put away the gun and turn the doorknob.

The door opens magically.

He expects it will be an entire police precinct coming in the store here, but it's only Teddy. Teddy's face is all squinched up and sweaty, he looks as if he's going to start bawling any second. But he loops Jocko's right arm over his shoulder, and together they drag him out on the sidewalk. The heat out there comes up into Colley's face like a puff of black smoke. He almost chokes on the heat. He begins to sweat profusely as they carry and drag and pull Jocko up the block—where's the car, does Teddy know where the car is? —the sweat coming through his clothes, or is that Jocko's blood? A lady stops in the middle of the sidewalk and looks at them. Colley yells at her, he doesn't even know what he yells, and she backs off a pace. He yells again, and she moves away even further, and he remembers one time at the Bronx Zoo when a tiger in his cage began roaring and everybody backed away; the lady is backing away like that now.

Teddy opens the front door of the car, and Colley throws Jocko in on the seat, but Jocko's front legs are hanging out on the sidewalk. This becomes another problem he doesn't know how to solve. He can't close the door with Jocko's legs hanging out like that, but Teddy is already running around the front of the car, Teddy is already in the car, Teddy is slamming the door on his side, Teddy is *starting* the fuckin car, he yells at Teddy to *hold* it a fuckin minute! He keeps staring at Jocko's legs hanging out of the car, trying to figure out how to get them inside. Teddy is hollering at him now *Get in, Colley, for Christ's sake, get in!* but he keeps staring at Jocko's legs until finally it occurs to him that all he has to do is swivel Jocko around on the seat, change the position of his body so that his legs are inside the car too. He puts both arms under the backs of Jocko's knees, and he swivels him in that way, and then he steps back as though he has all the time in the world to examine what he's just accomplished, even though Teddy is still yelling at him to get in the car.

He floats on sneakered feet to the back door of the car, and reaches out in slow motion for the handle, and opens the door and gets inside. He hears the solid thump of the door when it closes behind him, but he has no recollection of having pulled it closed. He is remembering instead the ridiculous gold and blue shield. He is remembering the red and white and yellow globules that exploded from the back of the man's head. What he finally tells Teddy is close to the truth, but it is not the exact truth. He is unconsciously editing the memory, the way in confession when he was a kid he edited his sins so Jesus Christ our Lord wouldn't have suffered in vain and so God Almighty wouldn't send down a lightning bolt to strike him dead right there in St. Augustine's.

"I shot a man," he says.

He does not say, "I killed a cop."

As Teddy runs the red light on the corner, Colley is thinking only that his grandmother wouldn't go to her own brother's funeral because it took place on the thirteenth day of the month.

TWO

They were worried that the lady in the basement had seen the blood.

They had parked the car behind Jocko's building, and then had come in through the back door, into the basement, carrying Jocko between them. There was a lady there near the washing machines, but she was busy putting in detergent and they went right by her, hoping she'd think it was some guys bringing home a drunken buddy. She hardly looked at them as they went past her to the elevator. But now they were worrying she had maybe seen the blood.

Jocko was still bleeding.

The blood had slowed to a steady seep, but it was still coming from under the sleeve of his windbreaker and dripping onto the floor of the elevator. There was no one in the elevator with them, they were grateful for that. They had driven past the front stoop of the building first, and had almost lost heart when they saw all those people sitting there on the steps talking; this was ten o'clock on a hot night in August, and nobody was eager to go upstairs to apartments like furnaces. It was Teddy who got the idea to drive around to the big open parking lot behind the building, then go in

the door to the basement. The sleeve of Jocko's poplin windbreaker was covered with blood, and his pants were covered
with blood, and there was almost as much blood on Teddy
and Colley from carrying him.

"You think she seen the blood?" Teddy asked again.

"No," Colley said, "she didn't see it, stop worrying about
it, will you?" But he was worried himself.

The elevator stopped on the fifth floor, and they eased
Jocko out into the hallway, and then belatedly looked around
to see if anybody was there. Without a word—they knew
where the apartment was, they had both been here before—
they turned to their right and started toward the end of the
hall. Behind them, the elevator doors closed, and the elevator
began whining down the shaft again. Outside apartment 5G,
Colley rang the doorbell.

"Just like Jeanine to have gone to a movie," Teddy said.

"No, she'll be home. Night of a job, she'll be home,"
Colley said, and rang the bell again. They could hear chimes
sounding inside the apartment. Colley thought he heard a
television set going, but that might have been in the apartment next door. He pressed the bell button again. The peephole flap suddenly went up, and then fell again an instant
later. They heard the door being unlocked—first the deadbolt, then the Fox lock, then the night chain. The door
opened wide.

Jeanine stood slightly to the side to let them past. She
didn't scream, she didn't say a word. She'd already seen them
through the peephole, so she knew something had gone
wrong. She just watched them silently now as they moved
past her into the living room, and then she closed and locked
the door behind them—first the deadbolt, then the Fox lock,
and then the chain. They were standing in the middle of the
living room waiting for her to tell them where to take her
husband, who was dripping blood all over the rug. She didn't
ask what happened, she didn't ask how bad it was, she didn't
say a word. She began walking toward the rear of the apartment instead, and they followed her without being told to

follow her. Jocko was beginning to weigh a ton. He was a big man to begin with, and now they were practically dragging him across the floor, his feet trailing, his two hundred and twenty pounds multiplying with each step they took.

"In the bathroom," Jeanine said.

They managed to squeeze him through the narrow bathroom door by going through it sideways, and then they sat him down on the toilet bowl, and Jeanine began undressing him. She was wearing white shorts cut high on the leg, an orange halter top, no shoes. Her long blond hair was hanging loose around her face as she took off his windbreaker and then began unbuttoning the white shirt under it. Both the shirt and the windbreaker were soaked with blood, and each time she brushed her hair away from her face, she got blood on her cheek and in the hair itself.

She had good features going a bit fleshy; Colley guessed she was in her late thirties, maybe closer to forty. Her eyes were dark green, not that pale jade you saw on most light-complexioned women, but a deeper green—like an emerald a burglar had once showed him. She had a good sensible nose with a tiny scar on the bridge that made it look like she'd lived with the nose a long time, had sniffed around with it a little, had maybe stuck it in places where it didn't belong, and had it broken or slashed. The nose and the eyes and the mouth, those were what gave her face definition. The mouth was full, the upper lip lifting gently away from her teeth, so that you always saw a flash of white and got the impression she was parting her lips about to say something. Her skin was very white; he imagined she turned lobster-red in the sun. Years ago she'd been a stripper down in Dallas, Jocko told him, and she still had a stripper's body, heavy breasts in the halter top, generous hips, good legs showing below the brief shorts, thighs a bit fleshy, like her face, but the calves firm, tapering to slender ankles. Her feet were big. Her feet were peasant's feet. They didn't seem to go with that face and that body.

DEC 1 1976

BAKER COUNTY
PUBLIC LIBRARY
BAKER, OREGON

She lowered Jocko's shirt off one shoulder and then gently tugged the sodden material away from the wound and slid the sleeve off his arm. Colley caught his breath when she exposed the wound. There was only a small hole where the bullet had gone in, but on the other side of Jocko's arm, just behind the biceps, the exit hole was enormous. Colley could see a bone inside the arm. He turned away.

"This is bad," Jeanine whispered.

He nodded. He did not look at the wound again. He had not expected the damage to be this bad, in spite of all the blood, in spite of the fact that the cops had been carrying .38-caliber pistols.

"Take off his shoes and socks," Jeanine said.

Colley stooped at Jocko's feet and began unlacing his shoes. There was blood even on the shoes—*Jesus,* what a mess! He got off the shoes and socks and then he helped Jeanine pull down Jocko's pants and take off his undershorts. Jocko had red crotch hair, same as the hair on his head. He had a very small pecker. Colley was surprised, big man like that. Massive head, red hair curling on it, eyelids closed over those pale-blue eyes, menacing eyes hidden now by the closed lids; his face looked almost cherubic except for the curl of his lip betraying the meanness even when he was unconscious. Power in the wide shoulders and huge chest. Must've lifted weights as a kid, blood on the bulging pectorals, tiny contradictory prick. He was still unconscious, but he twitched now, and grunted something.

"You going to need me?" Teddy said. "I want to get rid of the car. Hot car sitting out there with blood all over the front seat."

"Go ahead," Jeanine said.

"Okay to call my wife? She's gonna be wondering."

"Phone's in the bedroom," Jeanine said, and went to the sink, and put a stopper in it, and let the water run. Teddy went down the hall to the bedroom. Jeanine soaped a sponge, and then went to where Jocko was sitting on the toilet bowl, and began washing the wound. Down the hall, Teddy was dialing the phone. The apartment was silent except for the clicking of the phone dial and the tiny splashing sounds Jeanine made when she dipped the sponge into the sink and lifted it from the water. There was blood on her white shorts. Blood on her thigh, too. Down the hall, they could hear Teddy's muffled voice. Jeanine pulled the stopper from the sink, and then turned on the hot- and cold-water faucets and tested the stream of water with her hand. With a clean washcloth she began rinsing off Jocko.

Teddy came back up the hallway and leaned in the bathroom doorway. "I'm gonna split," he said. "Get rid of the car." He hesitated. "Were they both dead, Colley?"

"I don't know," Colley said. "Two cops sitting the store," he explained to Jeanine. "In the back room there."

"Him and Jocko walked into a stakeout," Teddy said.

"Minute Jocko threw down on the old man, the two of them came out the back yelling fuzz."

"You shot two cops?" Jeanine said.

"I only shot one of them. Jocko . . ."

"Never mind *who* shot them," Jeanine said. "I'm asking—"

"Yeah, two cops got shot."

"They both looked dead," Teddy said. "Colley, they really looked dead to me. That one laying closest to the door, his brains were all over the floor."

"Great," Jeanine said.

"They surprised us," Colley said.

"Great," she said again. "Two dead cops."

"I ain't so sure about them being dead," Colley said. "I ain't even sure about the one Teddy says had his brains . . ."

"It'll be on television later," Teddy said. "I'll bet it's on television. Two cops getting killed."

"Look, we don't know for sure . . ."

"They're dead all right," Teddy said. He looked very owlish and wise and sad behind his glasses. He also looked exhausted. He had been busy since early that morning, boosting the car in Brooklyn, and he still had to get rid of it. Before the holdup it had only been a stolen car. Now it was a car that had been used in a felony murder ... Well, Colley wasn't sure either *one* of them was dead. Man could *look* dead without *being* dead.

"I'll call you in the morning," Teddy said.

"You going outside like that?" Colley said.

"Huh?"

"All that blood on your clothes?"

"Shit," Teddy said. "You got something I can put on, Jeanine? Just something to ..."

"Jocko's clothes'd be too big for you," Colley said.

"There's some stuff from when Bobby was here," Jeanine said. "His brother."

"All I need's a raincoat or something," Teddy said.

Together they went out of the bathroom. Colley could hear them rummaging around in one of the closets. Jocko mumbled something, and then fell silent. Colley heard them in the hallway again, heard the front door opening and closing, heard Jeanine relocking it. Teddy had left without saying goodnight. He heard Jeanine padding barefooted toward the bathroom again. She came in and took a big white towel from the towel bar. Jocko was still unconscious; his head lolled to one side as Jeanine began drying him. Watching her, Colley was reminded of something—he couldn't place what. He was completely absorbed, watching her. Down the hallway, he could hear a clock ticking someplace. He kept watching her. The wound had stopped bleeding completely. She patted it dry carefully, and then took some stuff from the medicine cabinet over the sink, and squeezed something from a tube onto the wound, and then put a gauze pad over it, and wrapped it with bandage and adhesive tape.

"Help me get him in the bedroom," she said.

Colley took him from behind, and Jeanine lifted his legs, and they carried him down the hall to the bedroom. He got heavier each time they moved him; Colley was beginning to think this was what hell must be like—lifting and carrying Jocko through eternity.

In the bedroom, Jeanine let his legs go while she pulled back the spread and then the blanket. Colley stood there supporting Jocko, the weight of the man pulling on his arms and his shoulders and his back. His own legs were beginning to tremble.

"Come on," he said.

"Yes," she said, and nodded.

He had the feeling she wasn't even talking to him. She had pulled the blanket to the foot of the bed and was coming around to where Colley stood with Jocko collapsed against him. She seemed completely involved with her own thoughts. She picked up Jocko's legs as if she were picking up the handles of a wheelbarrow. Together they moved him onto the bed.

"You better cover him," Colley said.

She pulled the sheet up over his waist, and stood there looking down at him for a moment. He was breathing evenly and regularly. In the hallway outside, a light was burning; they turned it off before they went into the living room. There was a television set against one wall. Colley instantly looked at his watch. It was ten-thirty. If either of those cops was dead, the eleven o'clock news would surely carry the story.

"Place looks like a slaughterhouse," Jeanine said, and shook her head. "Do we have to worry about cleaning up right this minute?"

"What do you mean?"

"Are you expecting *company* is what I mean."

"Cops, you mean?"

"Cops, I mean."

"No, no."

"You sure?"

"Well, I'm not sure. But even if the old guy . . ."

"What old guy?"

"Behind the counter."

"Great, did you shoot *him*, too?"

"No, no. Come on, Jeanine, it couldn't be helped."

"What about him?"

"I'm saying even if he gives them a good description of us, well, it takes time, you know, to check files, you know, and come up with mug shots and fingerprints and like that. They might *never* get to us. I mean, even if the old guy remembers what we look like . . ."

"Colley," she said, "if those cops are dead, they'll get to you."

"Well," he said.

"Even if only *one* of those cops is dead . . ."

"Who said anybody's dead, huh? Teddy was only in the store there a minute, when he come in to help me with Jocko. Whyn't you ask *me*, huh? I was the one in there with Jocko when the shooting started. I'm the one ought to know what happened in there."

"All right," she said, "what *did* happen in there, Colley?"

"They surprised us, that's all. Jocko threw down on the guy behind the counter, and next thing you know there was fuzz."

"Who was the one started shooting?"

"The one coming at me," Colley said. "Holding out his badge. He was left-handed, Jeanine, both of them were left-handed. They had their pieces in their left hands, how you like that?" he said, and shook his head in amazement. "Listen," he said, "you got anything to drink around here? I could really use a drink."

"There's booze in the kitchen," she said.

"You want one?" he said.

"Mix me a light Scotch and water."

"I'm not moving in," he said, "I just want to see the news. I'll go right after the news, you don't have to worry."

"Who's worrying?" Jeanine said, and looked at him.

"Well, I didn't mean actually *worrying.*"

"What *did* you mean?" she said.

She was still watching him. He couldn't read the look on her face. He knew she was angry because of the shooting in the liquor store, and Jocko getting hurt. But there was something else mixed in with the anger.

"What I meant is I know you're upset right now," he said, and got up quickly and went out into the kitchen. On the counter near the refrigerator there was an almost full bottle of Scotch and an unopened bottle of bourbon. He pried an ice-cube tray loose from the freezer compartment and put a few cubes in each of two glasses. He was pouring Scotch liberally into both glasses when he remembered she'd asked for a light one, so he poured more heavily into his glass, which made hers light by comparison. "Did you say water in this?" he called to the living room, but she either didn't hear him or didn't care to answer him. He himself wanted soda, but there wasn't any in the refrigerator, so he put a little water in both glasses and then carried them out to the living room. The living room was empty. Down the hall, he heard the shower going. He looked at his watch again. It was a quarter to eleven, plenty of time before the news came on.

He turned on the set, and then sat on the sofa and took a good heavy gulp of his drink, and then another heavy gulp, and then just began sipping at it slowly. Down the hall, the shower was still going. The apartment was still except for the steady drumming of the water and the drone of the television set. A movie was on, he watched it only because he did not want to think about what had happened in the liquor store. He did not want to believe that either of those two cops were dead.

He could accept them being hurt bad, but he didn't want to believe they were dead because then he might just as well admit he himself was dead. You kill a fuckin cop in this city —*any* city, for that matter—that was it, Charlie. So he didn't want to believe he had killed that cop. Until he knew otherwise, why then, he chose to believe the man was only hurt bad. Stupid bastard running at him that way, holding out the badge as if it was a shield could protect him from harm. Like people hanging St. Christopher medals in their car. All those crazy bastards on the highway, you needed more than a St. Christopher medal to survive.

The sound of the water stopped. He kept watching the movie. He had no idea what the movie was about, no idea who the actors were. Down the hallway, he heard the bathroom door opening. Silence. The ticking of the clock. On the street outside, filtering up to the open windows, the distinctive laughter of a black woman. In the distance, the sound of an approaching train rattling along the elevated tracks on Westchester Avenue. Summertime. It was summertime in that apartment and beyond those open windows. Summertime. And he had shot a cop.

When she came back into the room, she was wearing faded blue jeans and a white cotton T-shirt. No bra, her breasts moved fluidly beneath the thin fabric as she came barefooted into the room. She looked clean and cool and she brought the scent of soap with her. She looked younger, too, possibly because the narrow jeans hid the fleshiness of her thighs and gave her a long, slender look. Stopping just inside the door to the room, she put her hands on her hips and stood there watching the television screen. The movie had just gone off. Another train went roaring past on the avenue a block away, smothering all sound. Jeanine looked for her drink, saw it on the coffee table and bent over to pick it up.

The anchorman came on just then to give a quick summary of the news. They both turned to watch the screen, Jeanine standing to Colley's left, the drink in one hand, the other hand still on her hip. The anchorman was saying something about a demonstration outside the U.N. Building. Jeanine sipped at the drink, her eyes on the screen. Now the anchorman was talking about a three-alarm fire in the Wall Street area. Colley was hoping there wouldn't be anything

about the robbery. If they didn't report it on television, that
would mean neither of the two cops had been hurt bad. But
then the anchorman said, "In the Bronx tonight one detective was killed and another seriously injured when a pair of
armed men attempted to hold up a liquor store on White
Plains Avenue. And in . . ."

"There it is," Jeanine said.

"Shhh," Colley said.

". . . the Brooklyn Battery Tunnel, a three-hour traffic jam
caused tempers to flare while temperatures soared. Details on
these in a moment."

"One of them's dead," Jeanine said.

"I heard."

"Great," she said.

"Shhh, I want to hear if they . . ."

"Just great."

She seemed about to say something more, but instead she
angrily plucked a cigarette from the box on the coffee table,
and struck a match with the same angry, impatient motion,
and then walked to the easy chair across from the sofa and
was about to sit in it when she saw she still had the burnt
match in her hand. She pulled a face and came back to the
coffee table and put the burnt match in the ashtray there.
Then, instead of going back to the easy chair, she sat cross-
legged on the floor in front of the couch, and silently and
sulkily watched the screen. The commercial was over, the
news team came back to elaborate on the events the anchorman had earlier summarized. Jeanine dragged on the cigarette and let out a stream of smoke. They were showing
footage of the Wall Street fire now; it was really fascinating,
fires fascinated Colley. They began interviewing a fireman, he
was telling all about the people they'd rescued from the top
floor of the office building. Then, suddenly, the liquor store
appeared on the screen.

There it was, all right, it was really funny seeing it there
on a television screen. Earlier tonight Colley had felt the job

itself was like a goddamn movie, and now it really *was* a movie, right there on television. Only thing missing was the actors. Camera was roving around outside the store, showing the lettering on the plate-glass window, *Carlisle Liquors,* and the bottles in the window, focusing on a sign that was advertising something for $3.99, and then moving away to the front door, the door was opening, the camera moving into the store itself, going in through the door, showing the blood-stains on the floor, and then continuing to move deeper into the store, toward the cash register, to show where the second cop had been shot.

It was just like all the newsreel movies Colley had ever seen on television, with bad lighting, most of the scene dark except for the area right near the lights, camera jogging and bouncing, reporter explaining what had happened earlier and hoping the audience would be able to reconstruct the action. This time Colley had no trouble at all reconstructing the action; Colley had been *part* of the action. The reporter finished by saying the second cop had been taken to Fordham Hospital. Then he smiled and said, "What's the weather for tomorrow, Frank?"

Colley got up and turned off the set just as the weatherman appeared in front of his map. He went back to the sofa then, picked up his drink, drained the glass, and set it down on the coffee table.

"Now what?" Jeanine said.

"I don't know what."

"He's dead, you killed a cop."

"I ain't so sure I'm the one who killed him," Colley said.

"You just heard ..."

"It could've been Jocko. It could've been the one *he* shot."

"What difference does it make?" Jeanine said. "You were in there together, you're accomplices ..."

"All right."

"... you killed a man!"

"All *right,* I said!"

"Great," Jeanine said.

"I want another drink," he said, and went out into the kitchen. As he mixed the drink he thought what a lousy break it was, the cop dying. He was beginning to convince himself the cop had really fired first, that if only the cop had played it cool, if only everybody had kept their heads inside the store there, the cop would still be alive. As he took ice cubes from where they were melting in the tray, he became aware of how hot the apartment was. He'd been so busy carrying Jocko in, and then watching the news, he hadn't had time to concentrate on anything else. But now he felt the heat, and felt the bloodstained clothing sticking to his flesh, and called from the kitchen, "What's the matter with the air conditioner?"

"Nothing," she said.

"Whyn't you turn it on?" he said.

"What for?"

"Cause it's hot as hell in here."

"I don't feel hot," she said, and he remembered Jocko telling him how much she liked the heat, how she'd been born in Florida someplace—where had he said? He went back into the living room and said, "Where you from in Florida?"

"Fort Myers."

"Yeah, Fort Myers, that's what Jocko said. You like it when it's suffocating like this, huh?"

"Right, let's talk about the weather," she said. "We just heard the cop is dead . . ."

"Yeah, that's a lousy break," Colley said.

"But let's talk about the weather, okay? You think it's going to rain tomorrow? Maybe if it rains the cops won't come looking for you."

"They probably won't come looking for us anyway," Colley said. "I doubt the old man will finger us." He drank from his glass, nodded thoughtfully, and then said, "He was scared, you know. When Jocko threw down on him. He might figure if he fingers us, we'll go back and hurt him."

"He might also figure you won't be *able* to go back and hurt him," Jeanine said.

"What do you mean?"

"He might figure you'll be in jail a long, long time."

"Well, you always get *out* of jail, you know."

"They bust Jocko for this one, it's his third offense. They'll throw away the key."

"Yeah. But, you see, the old man don't know that. The old man in the liquor store. He don't know us from a hole in the wall. So he'll be afraid to finger us, you see."

"You *hope,*" Jeanine said.

"Well, sure, I *hope.* I mean, who the hell can say for sure what anybody'll do nowadays? Who can figure that cop starting to shoot there in the liquor store? Comes running at me holding out his badge and shooting before he hardly has the words out of his mouth."

"What words?"

"He yells 'Police officers!' and starts shooting."

They were silent for several moments, drinking. Outside, another train roared past. The windows were wide open, but not a breeze came through into the apartment. Colley debated asking her again to turn on the air conditioner. Instead he finished his drink, sucked on one of the ice cubes for a moment, and then said, "You mind if I fix myself another one of these?"

"Go ahead," she said.

"You want another one?"

"Just freshen this a little," she said, and handed him her glass.

He carried both glasses out into the kitchen. The Scotch bottle was almost empty. He poured some of what was left into Jeanine's glass and the remainder in his, and then he added a little water to both glasses and carried them back into the living room.

"What it is," he said, handing Jeanine her glass, "you get lots of cops, they're trigger-happy. They'll shoot little kids carrying water pistols, you know that? Not that we were carrying water pistols," he said, and laughed, and then took a long swallow of the drink. The booze was beginning to reach him. This was his third, and he'd poured all of them with a heavy hand, just the way he'd have poured them if the job had gone off okay. Always drank after a job, man had to celebrate, didn't he? This one hadn't come off, but it was the first one that hadn't since they'd been working together, so what the hell, have a little drink anyway. He was beginning to feel a little hazy, and very comfortable and cozy here in the living room. Safe. He was beginning to feel safe.

"Thing I'm worried about . . ." she said.

"Yeah?"

"Is I hope we won't need a doctor for him."

"I don't think we'll need a doctor."

"You know anybody?"

"No."

"Who'd come, I mean. If we needed him."

"I don't know anybody."

"So what do we do if he starts bleeding again?"

"I don't know. I think he'll be okay, though. He's a strong guy."

"Oh, yeah, he's strong, all right," she said. "Take more'n bullet to kill old Jocko. Take a stake in his *heart,* you want to know," she said, and laughed, and then sobered immediately and glanced past Colley toward the hallway, as though afraid the laughter might have disturbed Jocko.

"How long you been married?" Colley asked.

"Three years."

"You were a stripper when you met him, huh?"

"No, who told you that?"

"Jocko said you used to be a stripper."

"Yeah, but that was before I met him. I haven't been stripping for seven, eight years now. This is August, ain't it?"

"Yeah, August."

"I quit stripping eight years ago November."

"I didn't realize that."

"Yeah, I've been out of it a long time."

"How come you quit?"

"Getting old, sonny," she said, and smiled.

"Yeah, sure," he said.

"How old do you think I am?"

"Thirty-two, thirty-three."

"Come on," she said.

"Okay, thirty-seven, okay?"

"I'm forty-four," she said. "I was thirty-six when I quit. Girl gets to be thirty-six, even if she takes good care of herself, she starts looking it, you know what I mean? Starts getting a little flabby."

"You don't look flabby to me," Colley said.

"Thanks. Guys coming to strip joints, they don't want to look at somebody who's over the hill, they want to see firm young bodies."

"You got a great body," Colley said.

"Thanks."

"I mean it."

"I said thanks. Also, I was getting static from my husband. Not Jocko, this was my first husband. He said it was wrong what I was doing, shaking my ass and getting guys all hot and bothered. *He* turned out to be a junkie with a habit long as Southern California, but he was always bugging *me* about being a stripper, can you imagine? Those were the days, all right," she said, and rolled her eyes and sighed.

"Did you like being a stripper?" he asked.

"It wasn't bad," she said. "Actually, it was exciting sometimes."

"How do you mean?"

"Turning guys on," she said. "I'd go out there, you know, and the drums'd be banging, and the lights'd be on me, and

I'd start throwing myself around, and it would reach me sometimes." She shrugged. "You know what I mean?"

"Sure," he said.

She shrugged again, tossed her head slightly, and then took another cigarette from the box on the table. He watched her while she lighted it. She shook out the match, and he watched her breasts moving under the T-shirt, and then she walked to the window and he watched the motion of her hips in the tight blue jeans, and he kept watching her as she stood by the window with one hand cradling her elbow, hip jutting, the other hand holding the cigarette and bringing it to her mouth. The sky outside was filled with stars. There wasn't a chance of it raining anytime soon, not with all those stars in the sky. Heat would probably last another day or two. He kept watching her.

"They're all the same, actually," she said. "I told Jocko I was thinking about taking a job in a massage parlor, they get good money those girls. He hit the ceiling, said that was nothing but whoring. I don't happen to think it's whoring. A massage ain't the same as whoring."

"Well, lots of massage parlors, it's more than just a massage," Colley said.

"You ever been in one of those massage parlors?"

"Oh, sure."

"What do they do in there?"

"Well, they do a lot more than just massage a man."

"What do they do?"

"Let's just say I can see why Jocko hit the ceiling. If you were my wife, I wouldn't like the idea of you working in a massage parlor."

"How about my being a stripper?"

"That might be different," Colley said. "I don't know how I'd feel about that."

"Uh-huh," Jeanine said, and nodded.

"You're thinking I'd hit the ceiling, right?"

"How'd you guess?" she said.

"Maybe I would. Good-looking woman like you," he said, and quickly picked up his glass, and discovered it was empty, booze sure went fast around here. He tried to remember whether the bottle in the kitchen was Scotch or bourbon, the bottle that hadn't been opened yet; he suspected it was bourbon, wasn't good to mix Scotch with bourbon. He was feeling exceedingly content now, sitting there in the living room watching Jeanine. The job had gone wrong, true enough, but there was something very pleasant about being here with Jeanine, something reassuring about her standing there at the window looking out, though he wondered just what the hell she found so fascinating out there.

He debated complimenting her on her body again, woman didn't tell you how old she was unless she wanted you to say she looked terrific. But just then another train went by outside, and she turned toward the sound of it, probably wanted to read all that terribly interesting graffiti sprayed on the sides of the cars, "Spider 107" or "Shadow 49" or "Spic 32," dumb bastards scribbling all over the city. If she ever turned away from that window, maybe he'd look her straight in the eye and tell her she had great knockers. You've got great knockers, Jeanine, did you realize that? No, of course she didn't realize it. She'd only been a stripper for Christ knew how long, only had guys yelling and hollering every time she took off her bra and twirled it in the air, but no, she didn't realize she had great knockers. I'm stoned, he thought. I killed a fuckin cop, this is my third drink, my fourth drink, who the hell's counting, I don't know what the fuck I'm doing, and don't give a shit besides.

"You've got great knockers," he said.

"Thanks," she said.

"What are you doing there by the window?"

"I was just thinking," she said.

"What about?"

"I was wishing something, actually."

"What were you wishing?"

"That Jocko would die."

He was not sure he had heard her correctly. He reasoned that she could not have said what she'd just said because he'd seen her a little while ago giving tender loving care to Jocko, even though Jocko had a very small pecker, very tender loving care indeed, washing out his wound and gentling him, yes. You did not wash away a man's wound and then wish he was . . . *wish* he was dead.

"You want to know something about your friend Jocko?" she asked.

He shook his head. No, he did not want to know something about his friend Jocko. Jocko was his fall partner and you did not go around looking at your fall partner's wife and thinking she had great knockers . . . had he said it out loud? No, he did not want to hear nothing more about Jocko, nor see him naked besides with his red crotch hair and his tiny little prick.

"Your friend Jocko beats me," she said.

"No, no," Colley said, and shook his head.

"Yes, yes," Jeanine said. "He hasn't missed a day since I came up to New York. How long've I been in New York now? When did I come up from Dallas?"

"I don't know," Colley said. "Two months ago? Five?"

"I came up on the twentieth of May. What's today?"

"Saturday."

"The date, I mean."

"I don't know," he said.

"August sixteenth, ain't it?"

"Yeah," he said.

"That's three months," she said.

"Yeah."

"Look at this," she said, and seized the bottom of the T-shirt in both hands and pulled it up over her breasts. Her rib cage, her chest, the slopes and undersides of her breasts were covered with angry black-and-blue marks. "*That's* your friend," she said, and lowered the shirt again.

"Listen," Colley said, "you shouldn't be saying such things about Jocko."

"Why not?"

"He's my fall partner, we work together. It's not right to say such things."

"You still think you've got a little gang going, don't you?" Jeanine said. "You killed a cop tonight . . ."

"No, no," he said, and shook his head.

"Yes, yes, and for all you know, the *other* cop might die, too. But you still think you've got a little holdup gang going. *Jesus!*" she said.

"I just don't want to hear nothing more about Jocko," he said.

"Are you afraid of him?"

"No."

"Sure you are."

"No, I am not afraid of Jocko," he said.

"Sure you are," she said again, and smiled.

"Fine," he said, "have it your way. Fine. You got something I can wear out of here? I think I better leave."

"Are you drunk?" she asked suddenly.

"No, sir, I am not drunk," he said.

"Jesus, how did you get so drunk?"

"I am not drunk," he said.

"You'd better get in the shower," she said.

"Wash off the blood," he said.

"Wash off the *booze*. How'd you get so drunk, man? Go get in the shower. You know where the shower is?"

"Know where the shower is," he said.

"Right down the hall there."

"Right down the hall."

"Go ahead now."

"Thanks," he said, and went down the hall to the bathroom. He was surprised to discover that he had a big pistol, big .38 Detective Special in his pocket. He pulled the gun out and placed it on top of the toilet tank and then was further surprised to learn that his pants, his jacket and his shirt were stained with blood, where'd he get all this blood on him? He took off his pants and saw that his undershorts were soaked with blood, too. There was dried and crusted blood on his left arm, and on both hands, and all over his face. He wondered if he should get in the shower with his clothes in his arms, and then dropped them in a bundle on the tile instead. He got into the shower, drew the curtain closed, opened it again to make sure his gun was still there on the toilet tank, and then closed the curtain and turned on the water and almost scalded himself. He backed away swearing, adjusted the water gingerly, and then looked around for the soap.

He soaped his crotch and the hair on his chest and under his arms and remembered that when he was in prison, first thing anybody soaped when they got in the shower was their crotch. Not that he looked. Guy in prison saw you looking, he figured you were ready to be turned out as his punk, next thing you knew he was making a heavy play for you. This was nice soap, it smelled, nice, he guessed it was Jeanine's. Big guy like Jocko wouldn't use sweet-smelling soap like this, pecker sure came as a surprise, though. He wondered if Jeanine had seen him looking at Jocko's pecker. He didn't want her to think he was, you know, *looking* at it. Nothing wrong with a little curiosity, though. Guy's sitting there, nothing wrong with checking him out, see how you shape up in the world. Nothing wrong with using Jeanine's soap, either. Besides, it was the only soap here in the bathroom, so what the hell. So he'd smell like a bed of roses, so what?

There was a guy in prison, his name was Kruger, he was as big as Jocko. They all called him the Kraut, he had a scar on his cheek, they said he'd been in the German army during World War II, before coming to New York, where he got busted. What he got busted for, he took a thirteen-year-old girl up to a hotel room, burned her with cigarettes, raped her, broke both arms and legs, dislocated her jaw, blackened her eyes, knocked out seven of her teeth. He left her for dead, she sure as hell *looked* dead. But the girl was still alive, and she identified him by name, the stupid bastard had given her his real name when he'd picked her up in Central Park. Why she'd gone up to that hotel with him was anybody's guess, guy old enough to be her father, take one look at him you *had* to know he was a mean bastard. First time Colley saw him in prison . . .

Listen, how'd we get on *this?* he thought. Listen, let's get off this, okay? You start thinking about that fuckin Kruger, you'll take the nice fine edge off this fuckin high, who the hell wants to think about *that* bastard? Standing in the yard there, smoking his cigarette. Standing there. Cool gray eyes, that scar on his face. He turned his eyes to Colley, and he grinned, and a chill went up Colley's spine. He came over then, and stuck out his hand, and Colley shrank away from him, terrified, and he grabbed Colley's hand in his own and squeezed it, squeezed it so hard it felt like he was going to break all the bones in it, and he kept grinning all the time, grinning.

In the shower now, Colley shivered. The water was hot, the water was pouring down on him in a steady sobering hot stream, but he shivered thinking of Kruger. He hadn't known what Kruger wanted from him then, and he still didn't know. It wasn't sex, Kruger had his steady punk, a slender blond kid who'd been busted for pushing dope and who Kruger had turned out two days after the kid drove up. So it wasn't sex, he didn't want sex from Colley, Colley didn't know *what* the hell he wanted. Followed him around all over the joint. Colley'd get in the shower, he'd check six ways from tomorrow to make sure the Kraut wasn't anywhere around. Then, minute he turned on the water and started soaping himself, the Kraut would suddenly appear, grinning, and he'd step behind Colley and grab his ass in both hands, and squeeze the cheeks so hard Colley thought he would faint from the pain. Rotten son of a bitch bastard! Three and a half years in prison, and the Kraut dogging him day and night, hurting him. Just hurting him for the sheer fuckin pleasure of it. Like Jocko, he supposed. Like Jocko putting those black-and-blue marks all over Jeanine, what the hell was wrong with a man like that? He thought of Jeanine. He thought of Jeanine lifting the T-shirt up over her breasts. He thought of her stripping for a roomful of men. He soaped himself and thought of her.

There was a knock on the bathroom door, he almost didn't hear it over the sound of the water. His hand stopped.

"Yeah?" he said.

"You okay in there?" Jeanine said.

"Yeah," he said.

"All right to come in? I've got some clothes for you."

"What?"

"You can't leave here in your own clothes, all that blood on them."

"Oh, sure. Come on in."

The door opened. The shower curtain billowed in toward him, the plastic sticking to his legs. The water was drumming against his groin, his prick was standing up stiff with the water drilling it and the soap running off him in long white streams.

"I'll put them here on the counter," she said.

"Thanks."

"I hope the pants fit you."

"Yeah," he said. He heard the door opening and closing again. The room was full of steam now, he was beginning to tremble from the steady pressure of the water. Abruptly, he turned off the shower, and then pushed the curtain back on the rod, and stepped out of the tub.

He looked down at himself. He looked around the room. He found a clean towel and dried himself, and then found the clothes she'd brought him, Jocko's brother's clothes, he guessed. There was no underwear or socks, only a pair of pants and what looked like an old sweater. Just the thing he needed on a hot August night, a ratty old sweater. He put on the pants without any underwear, and debated putting on the bloodstained shirt again, but decided in favor of the sweater, no matter *how* damn hot it was. He still had to go down in the street, and all he needed was some cop stopping to ask about the blood on his shirt. There was only a little blood on one of his socks, so he put on the socks and shoes, and then he combed his hair with a comb he found on the countertop, lots of long blond hair tangled in it, probably Jeanine's. He lifted the gun from the toilet tank and put it in his pocket. He pulled back his shoulders and opened the bathroom door.

Jeanine was standing in the doorway to the bedroom.

"He's still out," she said.

"Yeah," Colley said. "Listen, I'm gonna split now. I'll call you tomorrow, okay?"

She walked him to the front door. He could hear the clock ticking. "Be careful," she said, and unlocked the door for him.

"Goodnight," he said.

He stepped into the hallway. The door closed behind him. He heard her fastening all the locks again. He looked at his watch as he went down the hallway to the elevator. It was close to midnight, another day. He rang for the elevator and stood watching the indicator bar as the elevator crept up the shaft, these goddamn projects never put in quality merchandise.

When he reached the street he began walking toward the train station on Westchester Avenue. He thought about the job as he walked, thought about how wrong the job had gone, couldn't have gone wronger—he'd killed one cop, Jocko had shot another one. *Shit,* he thought. Times he wanted to quit this fuckin racket, get himself a nice girl, his mother was always telling him to get himself a nice Italian girl, settle down someplace. Times like tonight he was tempted to do it. Who the hell needed this kind of life?

He felt the gun in the pocket of the pants.

Its bulk felt good against his leg.

THREE

There was trouble in the street.

He got back to the old neighborhood at a little past midnight, but he was afraid to go into his mother's block because there were two police cruisers parked just outside the pizzeria. The heat hadn't let up a bit, the night was still sticky and moist. Men were milling around in their undershirts; women in flowered housedresses were standing with their hands on their hips, looking up the street toward the police cars. Most of them were black.

The neighborhood had been strictly Italian when Colley was growing up, and then it had turned Puerto Rican, and now it was black. His mother still lived here, you couldn't dynamite her out of that apartment. She'd been living upstairs from the pizzeria for twenty years, from when Colley was nine years old. Had black friends who came in for coffee every morning. Nice black ladies who'd moved uptown to the Bronx, same as Colley's mother had twenty years ago. Nice black ladies whose sons Colley had probably met when he was doing three-to-seven upstate for armed robbery.

He wanted to get rid of the gun.

He wanted to get out of these borrowed clothes and hide

the gun someplace; those police cars up the street were making him nervous. He stopped a white guy going by and asked him what the trouble was.

"Nigger cut somebody in the bar," the guy said.

"The pizzeria, you mean?"

"Yeah," the guy said, and walked off.

Colley looked up the block again, and then began walking in the opposite direction, around the corner and onto the avenue. This was Saturday night, he didn't expect to find Benny home, but he went up the three flights to Benny's apartment anyway, and knocked on the door and waited.

"Yeah?" a voice said.

"Benny? It's me. Colley."

"Colley? Hey, Colley!" Benny said through the door, and Colley heard him fumbling with the lock, good old Benny, and then he threw the door wide and looked out at Colley, beaming, his arms spread, his head tilted, his palms open; he looked like a jolly fat pope giving a blessing. *"Paisan,"* he said.

"Hey, *paisan,*" Colley said warmly, and stood there nodding foolishly, and grinning, and opening his hands the way Benny had his hands open, but suspecting he didn't look anywhere near as popelike as Benny did. "You gonna ask me in?" he said.

"No," Benny said, "I'm gonna let you stand in the hall. You hear this?" he said to someone in the apartment. "He wants to know if I'm gonna let him in."

"So let me in already," Colley said. He was chuckling now, Benny always made him chuckle. He hadn't seen Benny for maybe six or seven months, since just after he'd thrown in with Jocko. He had put on weight, Benny had. He'd been fat ever since Colley could remember, but now he was even fatter. He put his arm around Colley and led him into the apartment.

A girl was sitting at the kitchen table. There was an empty

glass in front of her, ice cubes melting in it. The girl was maybe nineteen years old. She was wearing a long flowing white robe with embroidery around the yoked neck, tooled sandals, a red-and-white-striped kerchief on her head. She had black hair and brown eyes and a very dark complexion. She was even darker than Benny, whose grandparents had come from Palermo around the turn of the century. Everybody on the block used to kid Benny about him being half-nigger. This was when they had the club. Benny used to say, "*I'll* give you half-nigger," and throw the arm salute. He really was very dark, but not as dark as the girl.

"This is Naomi Bernstein," Benny said. "Naomi, meet my best friend in the entire world—Colley Donato."

"How do you do, Colley?" she said, and extended her hand.

"Naomi's from Mosholu Parkway," Benny said. "I met her in Poe Park."

"Is Colley short for something?" she asked.

"Yeah," he said. "Nicholas."

"I'll bet a lot of people ask you that."

"Only everybody I meet," Colley said. "But it's better than Nick. Nick sounds like every wop you meet in the street."

"Don't get offended," Benny said.

"Who's offended?" Naomi said.

"Colley's Italian, it's okay for him to say it. Naomi belongs to— What's the name of it?"

"You know the name of it."

"I forget," Benny said, and shrugged. "It's an organization protects niggers, spics, wops and kikes," he said, and burst out laughing.

"I'm glad you think it's funny," Naomi said.

"You want a drink, Colley?" Benny said.

"You'd be surprised how much prejudice there is in this city," Naomi said.

"You Jewish?" Colley asked.

"How'd you guess? With a name like Bernstein, what'd you think I was?"

"I thought you were maybe an Arab."

"You mean *this*?" she said, indicating the robe. "My aunt sent it to me from Israel."

"It looks like what the Arabs wear."

"There are very close cultural ties between Jews and Arabs, believe it or not."

"I believe it."

"You want a drink, yes or no?" Benny said.

"You talking to me?" Colley said.

"No, I'm talking to the wall."

"I'll have another gin and tonic," Naomi said. "How about you, Colley?"

"No, nothing," Colley said.

"That's a nice sweater," Naomi said. "Very chic, those holes in the elbow. You're a very snappy dresser, Colley."

"Lay off," he said.

"Then don't give me any crap about what *I'm* wearing, okay?" she said.

"Hey, watch your mouth," Benny warned. "Maybe you didn't understand this is a friend of mine."

"I thought *I* was a friend of yours, too," Naomi said.

"Not like Colley. You got that?"

She glared at him sullenly.

"You got that?" Benny said again.

"I got it," she said.

"Then here's your drink," he said, and put the gin and tonic down in front of her.

"Thanks," she said.

"Take it in the bedroom," Benny said. "I want to talk to Colley."

She looked at him.

"Do what I tell you," Benny said.

"I think I'll go home instead," she said.

"You go down the street this time of night, you'll get raped," Benny said. "You want some boogie to jump out a doorway and rape you? Get in the bedroom there. You trying to embarrass me in front of my friend?"

"No, but . . ."

"Then get in there," Benny said. "And take off that thing your aunt sent you. You look like a goddamn Arab, Colley's right."

The girl hesitated.

"Go on," Benny said.

Her lip was trembling.

"Go on."

She sighed heavily, and then left the room. Colley could hear her sandals slapping on the floor as she walked through the apartment. He heard a door open and then close.

"What's the matter?" Benny said immediately.

"There's cops in front of my mother's building, some nigger stabbed a guy in the pizzeria. I don't want to go up there just yet."

"What *else,* Colley?"

Colley hesitated.

"Come on, this is *me,*" Benny said impatiently.

"I shot a man," he said. "Benny, I killed a cop."

Benny nodded.

"It was on television," Colley said.

Benny nodded again. "I seen it. A liquor store?"

"Yeah."

"I seen it," Benny said again. "That was you, huh?"

"Yeah."

"They looking for you yet?"

"I don't think so. I think it's too soon."

"Who saw you? Did anybody see you?"

"The guy behind the counter."

Benny nodded. "Maybe he won't finger you. Sometimes they're scared. Especially a cop dead, you know?"

"That's what I figure."

"He might think you'll come back for *him* he opens his mouth."

"That's just what I figure."

"You want to stay here tonight?"

"I don't know what I want to do," Colley said. "I think I'll go over my mother's. Once the cops leave, I think I'll go over there. They can't be too much longer, huh? It's only some nigger stabbed a guy."

"They'll just throw him in the car, is all," Benny said, and shrugged. "Look, you can stay here if you want. Don't let *her* bother you," he said, and gestured with his head toward the rear of the apartment. "She's mad at herself cause I got her shooting dope. I picked her up in Poe Park, this was last Friday night, she's coming on like a big hippie, you know, smoking pot like it's going out of style. I get her down here, I tell her listen, baby, you want something'll really blow the top of your skull, try some of this. She says what's *that*? I tell her it's scag. She says what's scag? And then she tips it's dope, it's heroin. No, thank you, she says. Thanks a lot, but no, thanks. That was last Friday. Sunday, she shot up for the first time. I got home from church, I went to eleven o'clock mass, you know me, Colley, I like to sleep late . . ."

"Yeah," Colley said.

"I got back to the house, it must've been a little after twelve, she asked me was there any pot left? I tell her we're all out of pot, why don't she try some of the real stuff? She shrugs and says why not? She's been shooting a nickel bag a day ever since. She's half hooked already. Few more days, I'll have her on the street peddling her ass. How you like that?" he said, and laughed.

Colley laughed too.

"Listen, you sure you don't want to spend the night?" Benny said.

"No, I got to get going," Colley said, and stood up.

"*Paisan,*" Benny said, and beamed like a pope again, his arms wide, his head tilted, his palms open in benediction.

. . .

The police cars were gone.

Colley went up the street and looked in the pizzeria, see if there were any guys there he knew. There was only a black guy sitting in one of the booths near the juke box, girl with him had an Afro looked like the bride of Frankenstein in blackface. Colley'd seen that picture on television, couldn't tell whether it was supposed to be a put-on or not. He guessed not. He guessed it was just such an old movie that it *seemed* funny, even when it was supposed to be scary. He nodded to the bartender, and the bartender nodded back, but Colley figured the guy didn't know him from a hole in the wall. He went outside into the hot August night again. Two black girls were standing in the doorway to his mother's building.

"Well, well," one of them said.

The other one pursed her lips and made a kissing sound.

Colley went right by them. Hookers in his mother's building, great. His brother Al kept saying it would be traumatic to move their mother out of the building. His brother Al was thirty-five years old. He was a Buick dealer in Larchmont; Albert L. Donato, it said on his brother's showroom window. The L stood for Lawrence, but Al never told anybody what his middle name was. Lawrence sounded faggoty to Al. Al had gone to college for two years, planning to become an accountant; he'd changed his mind when the opportunity to buy into the Buick dealership came along. An uncle in New Jersey had put up the money for the dealership. Uncle Nunzio. Dear old Uncle Nunzio. When Colley got busted the first time—this was when they had the club, and he shot Macho Albareda in the throat—Uncle Nunzio wouldn't go the bail for him. Set Al up in an automobile agency at the age of twenty-one but wouldn't go the five-hundred bail for his other nephew. Nice man, Uncle Nunzio. They finally had to ask Al for it, which Colley's mother hadn't wanted to do, which was why they'd gone to Uncle Nunzio in the first place. Al was always using words like "traumatic" or "personality disorder" or "acting-out neurotic." He especially used "personality disorder" when he was talking to Colley man-to-man.

"Nick," he would say—he was the only person on earth who called him Nick—"I want to talk serious to you. I understand, Nick, from what Mama tells me, that you didn't learn too much while you were in jail."

"I learned a lot while I was in jail, Al."

"Yes, I'm sure. But I'm not talking about what you might have learned from people who are acting-out neurotics," Al said. "Mom tells me you came home only to pick up your clothes, and then you moved right out again, that you're living someplace downtown . . ."

"Al, I'm twenty-eight years old, that's a little old for somebody to be living with his mother."

"Nick, I want to tell you something . . ."

"Yes, Al."

"Nick, when a man lives by the gun . . ."

"Yes, Al, I know."

"He dies by the gun."

"Yes, Al, you told me before."

"And a man who has to commit robberies . . ."

"Yes, Al."

"Is a man with a serious personality disorder."

That particular conversation had taken place just before Christmas. Colley had met Jocko a few days afterwards, and they had done their first job together on Christmas Eve. Colley supposed Jocko had a personality disorder, too. He knew one thing for sure. It had certainly been traumatic tonight in that liquor store. It had certainly been traumatic pulling the trigger of the .38 and watching the back of that cop's head come off and splatter onto the Seagram's poster. Yes, Al, that was traumatic. That was probably more traumatic than moving Mom out of this building full of hookers would be.

He began climbing the steps to the third floor. There were cooking smells contained in the building, and they blended with the heat of the day to create an overpowering stench that almost knocked him back down the stairwell. The cooking smells were alien. When he was a kid growing up in this building, the smells were always Italian, promising feasts at best, or at the very least, simple meals that were wholesome and familiar. He never felt at home in any apartment that wasn't Italian; the cooking always smelled of worlds he could never hope to fathom.

There was this kid he used to work with in the stockroom of a company downtown, this was before he joined the club, before he got busted that time. Colley was just fifteen, he remembered he had to get working papers in order to take the job. The kid was Jewish, he lived down on Hester Street, the Lower East Side. One time, after work, he asked Colley would he like to come home for supper with him. Colley went, and when he got in the house there was an old Jewish man reading his newspaper, and cooking smells in the house, those strange cooking smells. The food turned out to be pretty good, Colley couldn't figure out *how,* with all those funny cooking smells.

Later, him and the kid sat on the front stoop and talked. The kid said he wanted to be an opera singer. Told Colley he was studying Italian in high school because lots of operas were in Italian and he wanted to be able to sing every opera there was in the world. They tried talking a little Italian together, but Colley spoke only what he'd learned from his grandparents, which was the Neapolitan dialect, and the kid spoke what he'd been taught in school, the Florentine, so they had a difficult time of it. Colley couldn't remember the kid's name any more. He always wondered whether the kid had made it as an opera singer. That had been fourteen years ago; if the kid was going to make it, he'd have made it by now.

Colley knocked on the door to his mother's apartment.

He waited. He could hear sounds everywhere around him in the building, Johnny Carson's voice clearly identifiable in the apartment next door to his mother's, upstairs someone shouting, a toilet flushing someplace; he rang the bell again, and then looked at his watch. It was twenty minutes to one, but this was a Saturday night, and he didn't expect his mother to be asleep so early on a Saturday night. She'd either be watching television—he didn't hear anything inside there —or else out playing poker with her friends. He reached into his pocket for his key chain. He carried a key to the apartment only because his mother insisted on it.

"Suppose I'm away sometime, and you want to come in?" she said.

"Mom, you never go away," he said.

"I went away that time to Daytona Beach."

"Mom, that was six years ago."

"So? I could still go away. How do you know?"

"Mom, if you *did* go away, why would I come up to the Bronx?"

"You might want to use the apartment," she said. "Take the key, Colley, please. Suppose something happens to me? I'm not getting any younger, you know."

"That's right, Mom, you've got one foot in the grave."

"You'd at least have a key, you could open the door and see if I was dead."

"Mom, you're only fifty years old. Not *even* fifty."

"That's right, and how old was your father when he died, may he rest in peace?"

"Okay, Mom, let me have the key."

"God bless you," his mother said, and kissed him on the cheek.

Colley unlocked the door, opened it, and reached in for the light switch. His mother had a Mickey Mouse lock on the door, you think she'd know better, especially in a neighborhood getting blacker every day. He locked the door behind him, and then went through the apartment throwing on lights ahead of him. The apartment was a railroad flat, the rooms strung out one after the other so that you had to pass through one room to get to the next. The room he grew up in was at the end of the apartment, the single window in it overlooking the back yard. When he was a kid, he used to look out the window and see the waiters from the pizzeria out there having a smoke on a summer night. Once he looked down and saw one of the waiters dry-humping a girl against the brick wall of the building.

There was maple furniture in his room. A bed, a butterfly chair with paisley cushions, a low dresser, and a higher dresser that had one part of it looked like a wide drawer, but when you opened it the front fell down to become a desk. His mother kept that maple furniture waxed and polished as if she was expecting the queen of England to come there and use the room whenever she was in New York. Surprised his mother hadn't sent the queen a key. That maple furniture had been a big deal when they moved up from Harlem. His mother had hit the numbers for two thousand dollars, that was the biggest anybody had hit in a long time. When they moved to the Bronx, she'd bought the maple furniture for his bedroom, and also a new couch for the living room. That was a long time ago.

In Harlem, he'd shared a room with Al. When they got up here to the Bronx, Al was fifteen. There were three bedrooms in the apartment, it was really a pretty good apartment and a nice neighborhood in those days. Their mother took the biggest bedroom for herself, of course, the one with the windows overlooking the street. On hot summer nights like tonight, she would put a pillow on the window sill and look down at the street; it was the best entertainment value in New York. Al got the second biggest bedroom—but it was Colley who got the new maple furniture. The furniture still looked brand-new. There was a maple lamp on the dresser, made to resemble a candlestick with a shade on it. Colley snapped on the lamp and took the gun out of his pocket.

He'd never had this particular gun with him here in his mother's house. Only time he carried a gun nowadays was when he was going to a job or coming off it. Man didn't carry a gun and risk getting busted for no reason. He didn't know where to hide the gun now. He went out of the room and down the hall to the bathroom, passing what used to be Al's room, but what his mother now used for her sewing machine and her card table. That's where she probably was, out playing poker with her cronies. He thought he might take a towel from the bathroom, wrap the gun in it, and hide the gun and towel on the shelf in his closet, the back of the shelf there. But his mother would probably miss the towel, she probably knew exactly how many towels she had in the bathroom, she'd want to know what happened to the goddamn towel.

He went past the bathroom and into the kitchen—he was still holding the gun in his hand—and in the kitchen he put the gun on the enamel-topped table and looked in the cabinet under the sink to see if she had any of those plastic trash bags, but she didn't have any of those, either. He saw some brown paper bags from the A&P under there, though, folded neatly alongside the garbage pail. He took one of these, and shook it open, and then picked up the .38, and put it in the bag, and folded the bag around the gun. You couldn't tell there was a gun inside there. For all you knew, it could be a ham-and-cheese sandwich.

He smiled, went out of the kitchen, and walked down the hall again to what he still thought of as his room even though he'd moved out of the apartment eight months ago. He opened the closet door, pulled the light cord, and then shoved the gun way to the back of the shelf. His mother found it, he'd tell her he was holding the gun for somebody. She wouldn't find it, though; she wouldn't be searching for it, so how could she find it? He still kept a few clothes here in the apartment, and he took a pair of khakis from a hanger

now, and also a short-sleeved sports shirt. He didn't visit his
mother too often nowadays, but whenever he did come up
to the Bronx, he liked to make himself comfortable. He'd
come uptown wearing a suit and a tie, for example, like when
he came up last Easter on the subway, and then he wouldn't
feel like hanging around all day in a suit, so he'd change into
a pair of jeans and a sports shirt, like that. Clothes didn't
mean very much to him. You got some guys, they scored on
a job, they went crazy buying clothes. Colley spent the
money on booze and women and nightclubs. He loved going
to the Copa after a big score. Go in there with a blonde on
your arm, guys in there knew you were somebody. Throw a
few bills around, grease the skids, get a table up front, blonde
sitting there with you.

He took off his shoes and socks—he'd have to wash out
the socks before his mother got home, there was still some
of Jocko's blood on one of the socks—and then he took off
the borrowed sweater and pants. He found a pair of clean
underwear in one of the dresser drawers, and then he put on
the khaki pants and the sports shirt and a clean pair of socks
and the same shoes he'd been wearing on the job tonight—
Jesus, how had things managed to go so wrong?

He went down the hallway to the bathroom.

While he was washing his socks he heard a boom of thun-
der and saw lightning flash against the pebbled glass of the
bathroom window. Almost immediately, it began raining.

The club was called the Orioles, S.A.C.

The "S.A.C." stood for "Social and Athletic Club," but
everybody on the block knew the Orioles was a bopping
gang. There had been an Orioles down in Harlem long before
Colley was born, back in the forties. When he was still a little
kid, guys used to talk about the Orioles and what a great and
powerful club it had been, with thousands of members all
over Harlem and even in the Bronx. All the clubs died out
in the late forties, early fifties; dope killed the clubs. Guys

shooting heroin didn't want to be bothered rumbling in the streets with other clubs. Didn't want to be bothered about *anything,* in fact, except getting that glassine bag and ripping it open and cooking the shit in a spoon, man, and shooting it into a vein. Harlem didn't have any clubs when Colley was growing up there in the fifties.

Harlem—Colley's Harlem—was the area between First Avenue and Lexington Avenue, stretching from 125th Street on the north to 110th Street on the south. There were two other Harlems: Spanish Harlem, which was just west of the Harlem Colley knew; and Black Harlem, which was all the way over near Lenox Avenue, Colley guessed, somewhere all the way over on the other side of the city. There were Puerto Ricans coming into Colley's Harlem even then, crossing the imaginary boundary line that was Lexington Avenue, drifting over from Park and Madison, moving into apartment buildings that had been exclusively Italian during the war years, almost filling up the project on 120th Street, *bodegas* and Spanish restaurants popping up everywhere; the neighborhood was changing.

That's why Colley's mother decided to move up to the Bronx. His father had died from cancer two years before, and all of his mother's relatives had moved either to Jersey or Long Island, so there was nothing to keep her in Harlem any more. Then she hit the numbers for two thousand dollars, and one of the ladies in her poker game mentioned that an apartment was available on her block, so they'd packed up and made the move.

There were no clubs in the Bronx, either. Not at first. It really was a nice neighborhood. But when Colley got to be fourteen, fifteen, the clubs started up again. This was the sixties now. He began noticing guys wearing the Oriole jacket, black jacket with orange cuffs and a picture of a bird on the back, the bird colored orange, the lettering *Orioles, S.A.C.* in orange just below the bird; the bird was perching on the "O" in "Orioles." Colley noticed the guys in the jackets, and he asked about them, and learned that they called themselves a club, but he knew they were a gang. He steered clear of them. His brother Al knew all about street gangs because he was six years older than Colley and presumably remembered the gangs in Harlem dying of heroin pollution. He warned Colley to keep away from them. He was still in college at the time, and was learning a lot of new words. "Gangs are full of kids with personality disorders," he told Colley.

Anyway, Colley did manage to stay away from the Orioles or any of the other gangs until just before the summer he turned sixteen. That was almost a year after he'd had the stockroom job with the Jewish kid; he was in fact thinking of taking another summer job, going down to the employment agencies downtown, looking over the blackboards to see what jobs were chalked on them. He wasn't thinking of joining any damn street gang. But one day in school this fat kid Benny sat down across the table from him in the cafeteria. Up to that time, Colley had seen Benny around the neighborhood, wearing the orange-and-black jacket and strutting like a fuckin bigshot. He knew he was an Oriole, but he didn't know his name. Colley was working on a crossword puzzle in one of the books he used to buy; it was Benny who started the conversation.

"You like doing those things?" he said, and Colley looked up. Benny wasn't wearing the Oriole jacket. Colley learned only later that it wasn't cool to wear the jacket to school. Teachers got nervous seeing the Oriole jacket, or any *other* club jacket in school. That's because most of the teachers had grown up in the forties and knew all about street gangs and were afraid of street gangs starting up again.

"Yeah, I like crossword puzzles," Colley said.

"You must be a good speller."

"I'm not bad."

"I can't even spell my own name," Benny said. "Gallitelli.

Benny Gallitelli. No *wonder* I can't spell it," he said, and laughed. "Can you spell Gallitelli?"

"I don't know," Colley said.

"Try it. I'll give you a hint, it starts with a G."

Colley spelled the name on the first try. Benny seemed amazed.

"You got to meet my English teacher," he said. "She can't even pro*nounce* it, no less spell it. What's *your* name?"

"Colley Donato."

They went through the whole "what's-that-short-for" routine, Benny expressing surprise that anybody named Nicholas would be called Colley; his own brother was named Nicholas and he'd always been called Nick or Nickie. Colley explained that he had a cousin named Nicholas, and when they were little kids, all the aunts and uncles and goombahs used to call one of them Nickie and the other one Colley, to tell them apart. That's how he'd got the name Colley. Benny said he could understand this because he himself had a pair of cousins both named Salvatore, and the family called one of them Salvie and the other one Sally.

It seemed to Colley that Benny was sounding him about something, but he didn't know what. Finally, Benny started talking about the Orioles, and Colley figured he was trying to find out whether or not he'd be interested in joining the club. The club was just a bunch of guys who'd got together because they liked hanging around with each other, Benny explained. And also for protection.

"Against what?" Colley said.

"Against whoever wants to start up with you."

"Nobody ever starts up with me," Colley said. This was true. He was small in comparison to some guys his age, but he'd begun lifting weights when they moved to the Bronx and he was muscular and hard, and guys thought twice before they picked on him.

"You never know," Benny said.

"Well, nobody bothers me," Colley said. "Really."

"You still might need protection sometime."

"What for?"

"How do I know what for?" Benny said. He seemed irritated all at once. "Guys could jump you for no reason at all."

The next day, on his way home from school, half a dozen guys jumped Colley for no reason at all. They were all wearing Oriole jackets. They knocked out two of Colley's teeth and closed one of his eyes. That night he went looking for Benny in the street, and found him sitting on a stoop two blocks from the pizzeria. There was a wrought-iron railing to the right of the stoop, and steps leading down to the basement of the building. The basement windows were painted over with green paint, and you could see the brush strokes where the lights from inside were shining through. A record player was going, a rock group singing a doo-wah, doo-wah, doo-wah riff. A girl laughed.

Benny was smoking a joint. Sitting there all alone, wearing the black jacket with the orange cuffs, his name stitched in orange over the heart, *Benny*. Puffing, holding in the toke, letting it out at last. Joint down to a roach already. "Hey, man," he said, "how you doing?"

"Not so hot," Colley said. "Some of your friends knocked out two of my teeth."

"That right?" Benny said.

"Yeah," Colley said. "Also, they closed my right eye. See it here?"

"That's a shame," Benny said.

"You suppose they're downstairs in the basement?" Colley asked.

"Maybe. Why?"

"I don't like getting jumped for no reason," Colley said. "I'm limping. Did you notice I was limping? They hurt my ankle, too." He *was* limping, that part of it was true. But nobody had hurt his ankle. He was limping because he had a baseball bat inside his pants, running the length of his left leg. "Are they down there?"

"I guess they're down there," Benny said, "but I wouldn't go down there if I was you."

"Why not? I got a question I want to ask them."

"Like what?"

"Like who told them to beat me up."

"I did," Benny said.

"Why?" Colley said.

"To teach you respect."

"For what?"

"For the Orioles."

"So you had them knock out two of my teeth, huh?"

"That's right," Benny said.

"And close my eye, huh?"

"Yeah."

"Benny," Colley said, "there are going to be some cripples," and he pulled the baseball bat out of his pants.

Benny was slow getting off the stoop; the pot had reached him and his eyes were a little glazed and he was grinning from ear to ear because he was so fucking pleased with having taught Colley respect for the Orioles, S.A.C. Colley brought back the bat as if he were swinging at a ball coming in very low over the plate. Benny let out a yell when the bat connected, and four or five guys came running up out of the basement to see what was the matter. They were surprised to find Benny lying on the sidewalk with a bone splinter showing through his pants leg, and they were even more surprised to see Colley coming down the basement steps toward them, the bat in his hands.

You didn't have to tell anybody raised in the slums that a baseball bat was a deadly weapon. The guys saw the bat and recognized Colley as the kid they'd beat up that afternoon, and they saw Benny writhing in pain on the sidewalk, and they did an almost comic bunching-up in the doorway, some of them back-pedaling, some of them still running forward, all of them too late to do a goddamned thing about Colley or the bat. Colley started laying that bat into them, swinging that fuckin thing like a machete, doing just what he promised himself he'd do when he looked in the mirror and saw those two teeth missing in the front of his mouth and that big swollen purple sunset of an eye. All the while he was swinging the bat, the girls kept screaming inside, and some guys —he never did see *who* they were because they were afraid to come out of the basement—kept swearing and crying (it sounded like), and telling him they'd get him for good, he'd never be able to walk the street again.

It was *Benny* who didn't get to walk the street. Not for six weeks, anyway, because that's how long his leg was in a cast. And one of the guys in the club, a big musclebound jerk named Ernie, was wearing a bandage on his head for almost a month, and one guy had a broken wrist, and another guy had his forefinger and his middle finger together in a splint. Wherever Colley went, he carried the baseball bat with him. Even to school. Teacher in one of his classes told him he was going to report Colley to the principal if he continued bringing the bat to school with him. Colley said to the teacher, "Mr. Gersheimer, if I don't bring this bat to school with me, I'm going to get killed. Would you like my blood on your hands, Mr. Gersheimer?"

"Nobody's going to kill you, don't be silly," Mr. Gersheimer said. But his face went pale, and he never mentioned the bat again.

Just before school ended for the summer, the doctors took the cast off Benny's leg. That was when Colley bought the gun. He bought it from a black kid who was on the high school band. The kid was stealing instruments from the band room, and then trading them for handguns, which he sold to whoever could pay the price; apparently there was a bigger market for pistols than for trumpets or clarinets. The guns were cheap crap; Saturday-night specials. The one Colley

bought was a .25-caliber pistol. It was the first gun he ever
owned. To pay for it, he stole money from his mother's
pocketbook. She never even found out the money was missing, but if she'd asked him about it, asked him if he'd taken
it, he'd have told her yeah, it was a matter of life and death.
The day after he bought the gun, he went around to the
Oriole clubhouse again.

Two guys were on the front stoop, they went running
down the basement the minute they saw Colley. Benny came
out a minute later. No cast on his leg. Lost a little weight,
too, but still fat as a pig and black as a nigger.

"I have a gun in my pocket," Colley told him at once.

"Yeah?"

"That's right."

"What do you want here?"

"I want to tell you anybody starts up with me, I'll kill
him."

"There's already a warrant out on you," Benny said.

"Don't give me any of your bullshit gang talk," Colley
said. "Warrant, *shit!* I'm telling you I'm going to *use* this if
I have to," he said, and pulled the gun from his pocket and
stuck it right in Benny's face. "You the president of this
asshole gang?"

"No," Benny said, and looked at the gun.

"You told me you were the one . . ."

"Put up the gun, man," Benny said.

"Had me beat up."

"That's right, watch the piece, will you?"

"If you ain't the president . . ."

"*I'm* the president," a voice said. "What the fuck you
want around here?"

Colley turned. Ernie was coming up out of the basement
room. Ernie was the one whose head had been in bandages
for a month.

"Well, well," Colley said, and laughed. "You're the man
whose head I busted. Well, well." The gun made him feel

very cool and very tough. "I didn't know I was busting the
president's head," he said. The president made one funny
move, he was going to be the *ex*-president. The *former* president. The *late* president.

"If you're the president, how come it was Benny gave the
order to have me jumped?" Colley said.

"Benny's the war counselor," Ernie said.

"The war counselor, huh?" Colley said, and laughed
again. "Well, well."

"He told us you were putting down the club . . ."

"I didn't say nothin about your fuckin club," Colley said.

"You told Benny you was safe. You told him you didn't
need no insurance."

"Oh, are you insurance salesmen?" Colley said. "I didn't
realize that."

The gun was still pointing right at Benny's nose, and
everybody was getting nervous. Not as nervous as Benny,
who was expecting to get shot any minute now. But pretty
damn nervous. They had guns of their own in the gang
armory, but the armory was six blocks away, at Concetta's
house, and right *here* was a guy with a .25 under Benny's
nose. They kept looking up the block for fuzz, and then
looking back at the piece under Benny's nose. Benny kept his
eyes on Colley's face. He was figuring he would know when
Colley was about to squeeze the trigger; if only he kept
watching Colley's eyes, the eyes would telegraph, and then
Benny would duck away in time. Faster than a speeding
bullet, that was Benny Gallitelli.

"He came home and told us you thought you were hot
stuff," Ernie said. "So he's the war counselor, so I told him
to get up a raiding party . . ."

"You guys always talk like this?" Colley said. "Man, I
never *heard* such shit in my life. *War* counselor, raiding
party . . . what the hell *is* this? An Indian tribe?"

"That's the kind of talk got you in trouble the first time,"
Ernie said.

"Ernie, do you see this gun in your war counselor's left nostril?" Colley said.

"I see it, I ain't blind," Ernie said.

"Don't get him mad," Benny said.

"If I pull this trigger, your war counselor's going to be breathing from his nose up on the *roof* while he's still here down in the *street*. Now what I'm going to do, Mr. President, I'm going to ask you whether you want a war counselor without a nose, or whether you want to call off this fuckin warrant shit and make peace. Because if you *don't* want peace, then, man, you've got war with a crazy guinea, I'm telling you. The first thing I shoot off is fat Benny's nose, and the next thing I shoot off is *your* balls, Mr. President. So what do you say?"

"You're holding the cards," Ernie said. "Right now you're the one holding the cards. So okay."

"Ernie," Colley said, "what you say right *now* sticks forever, you dig? You don't say you want peace now, and then tomorrow I get jumped. No way, Ernie. I want your solemn word, or else lard-ass here will be chasing his nose over the rooftops. Swear on your fuckin mother, Ernie."

"I swear on my mother," Ernie said.

"*What* do you swear, you cocksucker?"

"I swear we won't try to hurt you."

"Never. Say never."

"Never. We won't try to hurt you never."

"You swore it on your mother," Colley said. "You heard him swear it on his mother."

He put the gun away, and turned his back on them, and went up the street. The next day Benny came to him and asked if he would like to become a member of the Orioles. Colley said he would think it over.

A week later he told them yes.

FOUR

It had stopped raining by the time he got down to the street again.

He had hung his socks up to dry in the bathroom, and had also left a note for his mother on the kitchen table so she wouldn't come in the house and drop dead of a heart attack when she saw a pair of men's socks in the bathroom. The rain had washed the streets clean, washed away the contained heat of the day as well; everything smelled fresh and clean and sweet. He could remember when he was a kid in Harlem, stomping around barefooted in the gutter rainwater. He could remember shooting immies after a summer storm, spanning the marbles in curbside puddles.

He could remember, too . . . Yeah, it had been raining that afternoon, yeah. This was in the Bronx, he was just sixteen, this was after he'd joined the Orioles, that first summer with the club. It was Benny who brought the girl around. She lived four or five blocks from the clubhouse, she was maybe fourteen. When Benny brought her down the basement that afternoon, she was wearing a miniskirt and a cotton blouse; there was a button missing on the blouse, he could still remember the blouse flaring open over a white brassiere underneath. She and Benny stood just inside the basement door. The record player was going. "This is Laurie," Benny said. "Laurie likes to fuck, don't you, Laurie?"

The girl was, well, like a little retarded. They took off her blouse and played with her tits, she had very big tits, and then they took off her panties and one after the other they fucked her on the sofa, her skirt bunched up around her waist, while the Beatles sang their little hearts out. There were six guys in the clubhouse that afternoon. Four of them were virgins, including Colley. It was raining when it got to be his turn. Colley was the third one with her. Ernie, the president, went first of course. Then the war counselor, Benny. Then Colley, who was sergeant at arms, in charge of breaking heads with baseball bats if guys didn't pay attention, or smoked dope, or chickened out when the shit was on with another club. The girl giggled all the while he was fucking her, and the rain beat against the painted basement windows. Colley felt embarrassed later on.

The girl's father came down the club the next day, big ginzo could hardly speak English, Colley didn't think there were still greaseballs like that around. Big wop kept yelling they'd taken advantage of his innocent daughter. "You take anvage my Laura," he screamed, goddamn sanitation man, still wearing the brownish-green uniform trousers and an underwear top, came there straight from work to protect his daughter's honor, stopping home first to take off his shirt and grab a quick glass of courage-bolstering wine, which the Orioles could smell on his breath as he stamped around the clubhouse making threatening noises. Ernie told him he should take better care of his daughter if he didn't want her to get fucked, and then he told the wop to get out of the clubhouse before somebody shot him. Colley was sitting on the sofa, tossing the small .25-caliber pistol on the palm of his hand. The wop looked at the gun and then yelled that he was going to do something about this, and off he went huffing and puffing. He never *did* do anything about it cause he was

afraid the Orioles would come after him, and also he didn't
want it known around the neighborhood that his moron
daughter had been gang-banged.

Colley walked through the rain.

He wasn't sure where he wanted to go or what he wanted
to do. It was close to two in the morning, the streets were
rain-slick and almost deserted, except for some black dudes
shuffling along with that sideways glide they thought was
cool, elevator shoes, big pimp hats even though none of them
were booking pussy. Thought it looked cool to resemble
pimps. Take a man like Benny, he *was* a pimp, but he looked
like your Uncle Dominick come to play the mandolin on
Sunday.

It was funny the way most of the guys in the club grew up
to be just what you expected. Benny was always bringing
girls around, and now Benny was a pimp. Ernie was always
looking for a fight—big hands on him, swollen knuckles—
and now Ernie was a heavyweight boxer, fought under the
name of Ernie Pass, which was short for Ernie Passaro. And
Duke, who they'd kicked off the club for shooting dope, he
turned into a full-time junkie, later kicked the habit cold
turkey and began pushing the stuff. He got busted just after
Rockefeller changed the laws in New York State; you ever
saw Duke again, he'd be eighty-five years old with a long
white beard. Duke's mother still went up to see him every
month in Sing Sing. Some fuckin trip up there, Colley's own
mother used to come up when he was doing his three-to-
seven for . . .

There.

There it was.

Exactly what he meant about guys turning out just the way
you expected—*including* himself. On the Orioles, he'd made
his rep with a gun. Reason they'd come around kissing his
ass was because he'd stuck that gun up Benny's nose and was
ready to pull the trigger. *Would* have done it, too, anybody'd
given him any shit that day. First time he got busted was

because of a gun. That was January, the winter after he'd joined the Orioles. The shit was on with another club named the Dragons, bunch of spics who could hardly speak English, they had these silk jackets made up with a dragon curling all over the back, you'd think it was a fuckin Chink gang instead. Kid on the club was named Macho. He gave himself the name, it was supposed to mean he had balls. Macho came around one day, said something to one of the girls. Sounded her. Petie was sitting right on the stoop, this was in front of the clubhouse. He heard what Macho said to the girl, he jumped up off the stoop. "Hey," he said to the spic, "watch your mouth, you hear me?"

Macho didn't say a word. Macho pulled a blade and stuck it in Petie clear up to the handle. They had to take Petie to the hospital, put seven stitches in his side. After that, the shit was on, and the one they were especially looking to get was Macho.

That January, Colley was still carrying the .25 he'd bought the summer before. It wasn't a bad piece. You got some of those Saturday-night specials, they fell apart in your hand first time you used them, or they blew up in your face, whatever the hell. That's because they were made so cheap. This one wasn't a bad pistol. It was called an Astra Firecat, and it was made in Spain and imported by Firearms International. It cost about thirty dollars brand-new; Colley had bought it secondhand from the black kid who was stealing band instruments, but it cost him thirty dollars anyway. On the grip, down near the bottom, the word FIRECAT was stamped into the metal. It wasn't a bad name, and it wasn't a bad gun, either. Or at least that's what Colley thought at the time, when he was still a kid and getting used to guns. It was the Firecat that Colley had shoved under Benny's nose. It was the Firecat that he'd tossed in the palm of his hand the day Laurie's greaseball father came down the club yelling. It was the Firecat he used to shoot Macho in the throat one January night.

Colley was sixteen years old; he had turned sixteen in July. July the fourteenth, that was his birthday. He told everybody he met that he was born on Bastille Day. Hardly anybody knew what the fuck he meant. Only one guy in prison, guy named Brenet, whose mother and father had come here from France, knew what Bastille Day was. They were in the laundry working, Colley had this job in the laundry at the time, he mentioned to Brenet that he was born on Bastille Day. Fuckin dope started singing the *Marseillaise* at the top of his lungs, pig comes over, says, "Hey, what's going on here?"

"It's a code," Brenet tells the pig. "We're planning a break, and we're singing about it in code."

"What are you, a wise guy?" the pig says, but his eyes are slitted and there's a suspicious look on his face. He doesn't know whether to believe Brenet or not. Brenet nudges Colley in the ribs and says, "Seven o'clock, pass it on." Colley takes a chance on the pig having a sense of humor. "Seven o'clock," he says to the pig, "pass it on," but he doesn't nudge him in the ribs. Nudge a pig, he's liable to nudge you back with his stick and throw you in the shitter for a month.

"Very funny," the pig says.

Sing Sing was always a barrel full of laughs.

Colley missed going to prison when he was sixteen only because a judge took pity on him. Peered down from behind his bench and his spectacles, saw clean-cut Nicholas Donato in his blue-serge Communion suit, looking up at him out of his baby browns, decided to suspend sentence instead of sending him away. The crime they'd charged Colley with, rightfully, was second-degree assault. If he'd been a bona-fide adult, the crime was punishable by five years in a state penitentiary, or a fine of a thousand dollars, or both. But Colley was a "young adult," defined in the Penal Law as someone who was more than sixteen but not yet twenty-one, and if he'd been convicted of second-degree assault, he would have been sentenced instead to a reformatory for "a period of unspecified duration, to commence and terminate as pro-

vided in PL 75.10." In such a case the court would not have
fixed a minimum or maximum sentence. That was good.
Even better than that, Colley's lawyer thought, would be for
him to plead guilty to the lesser charge of *third*-degree assault.

The assistant district attorney prosecuting the case was of
Hispanic heritage, just like his client Luis Josafat Albareda;
Colley learned Macho's real name only after he'd shot him.
The assistant D.A. told Colley's lawyer that whereas criminal law was most assuredly the bargain basement of the legal
profession, he would not allow Colley to cop a third-degree
assault plea, not when a weapon was involved, not when a
.25-caliber pistol had been used to shoot poor Luis Josafat in
the throat, causing him to lie bleeding in the snow for three
hours without proper medical attention—that was because
Colley had planned his ambush well, catching Macho in a
deserted alleyway that ran between two apartment houses.

"Hey! Macho!"

Macho turned and was already reaching for his blade
when Colley opened up. He fired twice. The first shot missed
him. The bullet hit the alleyway wall and sent a piece of brick
flying into the air, and then went ricocheting, *zing, zing, zing,*
and Colley pulled off the second shot and blood began spurting out of Macho's neck.

The assistant district attorney argued that poor Luis Josafat had lost part of his larynx because of the shooting, and
now spoke through a voice box—"this fine boy who is only
seventeen years of age will have to go the rest of his life in
this handicap position," the assistant district attorney said,
sounding very much like Pancho Villa, and actually getting
a laugh from Colley's attorney, who quickly covered his
mouth with his plump little hand. When it was pointed out
to the assistant D.A. that poor Luis Josafat was a kid who'd
himself been arrested many times for crimes ranging from
possession of narcotics to attempted rape to burglary to assault, the assistant D.A. decided to forsake Hispanic fealty

in favor of job security, and promptly agreed to the lesser charge.

The judge was Italian; that didn't hurt either.

"Colley? Is that you?" the voice said.

He stopped stock-still in the center of the sidewalk.

"Colley?" she said.

"Yes?"

"Colley?"

It was getting to be like one of his grandfather's operas. All right already, he thought. It's Colley. So who the fuck are *you*?

"Terry," she said.

He looked. Tires hissed against the rain-slick asphalt.

"Terry," she said again.

In the neon stillness, steam escaped from a curbside sewer. Jesus Christ, he thought. She looked . . . Jesus Christ. The last time he'd seen her was four years ago . . . was it five? The year before he got busted for armed robbery when the fuck was that? How could he forget the year, the month, the day, the exact hour and minute, the squad car pulling to the curb as he ran for his own car, "Hold it, motherfucker," nice language for a police officer. "*Hold it*!" and they threw him up against the wall, and tossed him, and one of them found the pistol where he'd thrown it in the gutter the minute he heard the cop yelling at him. Four years ago this September eleventh. And a year before that, Teresa Brufani had left for Vermont. She'd been twenty at the time, he'd been twenty-four. He looked at her now. He knew she was Terry, she had just told him as much. Otherwise, he would not have known her.

He remembered her hair as brown and soft; he would cradle her face in both hands, and she would lean over him and her hair would cascade over his own face, and she would bend her lips to his. The hair was blond now, clipped close to her head in a mannish cut. Huge gold earrings on her ears. Blue eyeshadow on her lids, lipstick gash on her mouth. She had never worn makeup when he'd known her years ago, not even lipstick.

She was wearing a black trenchcoat, the collar high on the back of her neck, the belt pulled tight at her waist. She had on platform shoes that easily added two inches to her height; he felt short in her presence when always before he had felt much taller. She was smoking a cigarette, and she dropped it to the sidewalk at once, and stepped on it even though it hissed out immediately against the wet pavement. He remembered that once, long ago, he had objected to her smoking, and she had given it up for him. He himself smoked two packs a day. But she had given it up for him. He remembered everything about her in that instant.

"Hello, Terry," he said.

They stood some four feet apart from each other, looking at each other, the steam from the sewer drifting across the sidewalk between them. They had been intimate for close to three years, and then she had gone to Vermont, and he had continued doing what she said she could not bear, and eventually he'd got busted for doing it. Seven years, the judge had said. Tough shit, next case. Now they stood four feet apart from each other on the sidewalk, five years apart, a century apart. They would not touch, they would not move toward each other, they stood looking at each other like strangers, which they were, looking at each other through the steam.

"Hey," she said.

"How you doing?" he said.

"Great," she said. "Great."

"I thought you were in Vermont."

"No."

"That's what I thought."

"I've been back since May."

"Well," he said.

"Boy," she said, "running into you like this."

"Yeah," he said.

"You want to buy me a drink, or . . ."

"Yeah, sure," he said, "sure."

"Or you want to just stand here all night?"

"No, yeah, I want to buy you a drink. Hey, how about this, huh?"

He took her by the elbow and they walked up the street to the Blue Moon. There were three black dudes on the sidewalk, they looked Terry up and down. This was the old days, Colley'd call the Orioles out, those fuckin niggers'd be in the hospital in a minute. He gave them a dirty look. One of the niggers laughed as though his buddy had cracked a joke. Colley gave him another dirty look, and he turned away. Inside, the juke box was going. A rock song, Colley didn't recognize the tune or the group. You grow up, you don't know who's playing what any more. There was a mixed crowd in the place—white, black, a few Puerto Ricans. Colley found a booth too near the kitchen and too near the juke.

"This okay?" he said.

"Yeah, sure," she said.

"It ain't too near the kitchen, is it?"

"No, no, it's fine."

"Cause I hate cooking smells," he said.

"Yeah, but I don't see anything else, do you?"

"No," he said.

"So fine," she said, and grinned, "What're we gonna do? It's the only game in town."

"Right," he said, and returned the grin, and helped her out of the coat. He was surprised at what she was wearing underneath. She was dressed like for a party. One of those clinging synthetic fabrics, cut very low in the front and high on the knee, scalloped edge to the skirt, long sleeves. Green.

"You been out?" he said.

"Huh?" she said.

"You're all dressed up."

"Oh. Yeah," she said.

He hung up the coat, and they sat opposite each other in the booth. Colley looked around for a waiter. A black guy was leaning against the juke box, looking over the selections. In the booth across the aisle, a black girl was sitting with two black dudes. She waggled her fingers at Terry, and Terry waggled her fingers back.

"Who's that?" Colley asked.

"Friend of mine," Terry said.

"You living around here now?"

"Yes," she said.

"How was it up there in Vermont?"

"It was pretty good."

"So why'd you come back?"

"I got tired of it."

"What were you doing up there, anyway?" he said, and tried to catch the waiter's eye.

"We had a shop," Terry said.

"Who's we?"

"Me, and two other girls, and three guys. We made things and sold them in the shop."

"What kind of things?"

"You know. Rings, enameled pins, and necklaces . . ."

"Oh, it was a jewelry store," Colley said.

"No, no, we sold other things, too. Place mats, you know, and silk-screened T-shirts, and sandals. We all made things and sold them in the shop."

"What'd *you* make?"

"Me? I made these— There was this boy came through with beads he'd bought in Iran. We bought the beads from him and I made necklaces out of them."

"Was there money in that?"

"Not a lot of money, but enough to live on."

"But you got tired of it, huh?"

"Yeah," Terry said, and nodded.

"Hey, over here," Colley said, and snapped his fingers at the waiter. The waiter came over to the table.

"How's it going?" he said to Terry.

"Not bad," she said.

"What do you want to drink?" Colley asked.

"The usual," she said.

Colley looked at her.

"How about you?" the waiter said.

"I'll have a Dewar's and water," he said. The waiter walked away. "You come here a lot?" Colley asked.

"Since I been back," Terry said, and nodded. "So what've you been doing?" she asked. "When did you get out of jail?"

"Just before Christmas."

"You on parole, or what?"

"Yeah, I'm supposed to be on parole."

"What does that mean, *supposed* to be?"

"Well, I don't go see the parole officer."

"Can't you get in trouble for that?"

"Sure," he said. "But you can get in trouble just crossing the street, am I right?"

"They could send you back to jail, though, couldn't they? For not going to the parole officer?"

"Yeah."

"So why don't you go?"

"I don't want to," he said.

"You really should go."

"This sounds like old times," he said. "When was it—four, five years ago? You were always bugging me to get out of it."

"You *should* have got out of it."

"Sure, sure," he said.

"You got busted, didn't you?"

"That was just a bad break."

The waiter brought their drinks. Terry's "usual" was a shot glass of whiskey with a tumbler of water on the side. She lifted the shot glass, winked at Colley over it, and then tossed back the shot.

"You drink it straight now, huh?" he said.

"Yeah," she said, and picked up the water tumbler.

They were silent for several moments. Colley was finding it difficult to think of anything to talk about. Last time he was with her, she'd told him she was going up to Vermont. He'd wanted to know why she was going all the way up there, and she'd told him she wanted to get away from him. If he quit what he was doing, she wouldn't go. But if he continued . . . Listen, he'd said, go, stay, do whatever the fuck you want, I ain't changing my life style for nobody. He looked at her now. She smiled at him over the water tumbler. Then she put down the glass, opened her bag, and took out a pack of cigarettes.

"I see you're back on the weed," he said.

"Yeah," she said, and struck a match and held it to the end of the cigarette. She blew the smoke up at the ceiling, and then leaned back in the booth, one arm resting on the leatherette top, the other bent, her elbow on the table, the cigarette trailing smoke. "How was prison?" she said.

"Lousy," he said. "How you *think* it was?"

"Where were you, anyway?"

"Sing Sing."

"That's supposed to be a good one," she said.

"There *ain't* no good ones," he said.

"That's where Di Santo got sent," she said. "He told me it was a good one."

"Di Santo got sent to Attica."

"No, Sing Sing."

"Attica, don't tell *me*. It was Attica."

"Where's that?"

"That's in New York, too."

"Well, wherever. Di Santo said it was a good one."

"It's worse than Sing Sing. That's where they had all the riots, few years back. Where a lot of guys got killed."

"That must've been while I was in Vermont," she said. "I hardly even read a newspaper while I was up there. We didn't even have a radio in the house."

"Who's *we*?"

"Me and the other kids. We all lived together in this old run-down house we were renting."

"What were you, like hippies or something?"

"No, no," Terry said, and shrugged. "We just lived together, is all."

"Three guys and three girls," Colley said.

"Yeah."

"What did they have, these guys? Long hair?"

"Yeah."

"Beards?"

"Yeah."

"So they were hippies, right?"

"Look, call them what you want, okay?"

"I'm calling them what they *were*. Hippies is what they were. What'd you do up there all the time? Smoke dope all the time?"

"Yeah, we smoked dope all the time," Terry said, and sighed. "And had orgies."

"What?" Colley said.

"On Tuesdays," she said.

"What?"

"We had orgies on Tuesdays," she said. "All day Tuesday. That was the orgy day."

"I'm trying to be serious, and you're kidding around," he said. "You left the Bronx, you were a nice girl, you didn't even know what the fuck a marijuana cigarette *was*. So you go up there to Vermont with those fuckin hippies, and all of a sudden you—"

"I went up there because you wouldn't stop what you were doing."

"You can't expect a man to change his way of—"

"You were a crook, Colley," she said.

"That's right. I was a crook," he said. "I still *am*, you want to know. Right."

"Right. And I didn't want to be around when they busted you. It was as simple as that. The way you were going, I knew it was just a matter of time before they busted you. So I went to Vermont. Because I loved you," she said, and the table went silent, the bar went silent, the street went silent, the entire world went silent.

"Well," he said.

"Yes," she said.

Their voices were softer now. She had reminded him that she had loved him, and perhaps it no longer meant anything to him, perhaps people do not want to hear that once they *were* loved, perhaps all they want to hear is that they *are* loved, here and now, in the present, never mind the fuckin past; but she had loved him, she had just told him she'd loved him once upon a time, long, long ago.

"I loved you, too," he said. The words sounded strange to him. The moment they left his mouth, he wished he hadn't said them. He felt suddenly in danger for having said them. He did not even *know* this blonde with the butch haircut and the dress cut so low you could almost see her nipples. Green eyeshadow on her eyes, lips a bright painted red, cigarette smoke trailing up past her face. "That was a long time ago," he added quickly.

"Yes," she said. "People change," she said. "But I can still remember."

"Sure," he said, and nodded. His glass was empty, he wanted another drink. He signaled to the waiter, and when he came to the table he ordered a double this time, and asked Terry if she wanted anything, and she said she wouldn't mind. They were silent until the waiter brought the drinks, as though neither of them was willing to explore the territory that had just been opened. The moment the waiter put the drinks down, they reached for the glasses. Terry again swallowed the shot in a single gulp and then picked up the tumbler and sipped at the water. Colley took a large swallow and then set his glass down.

"Do you remember the time we went to Coney Island," she said, "and the Ferris wheel got stuck, and we were up there for close to three hours? Do you remember that, Colley?"

"Yes, I remember that," he said. He sipped at his drink and listened to her as she described a sky full of stars, the lights of the amusement park below, the sound of music from the calliope, the breeze blowing in off the Atlantic. They had held hands and talked about the future. Trapped on the Ferris wheel, he had promised for perhaps the tenth time that he would quit doing robberies. The promise had moved her to tears, and they had sat there swinging in the chair at the top of the wheel, and had talked about when the wedding would take place, and what kind of straight job Colley might get, and where they would live—should they stay in the Bronx, or maybe move to Mt. Vernon or even further up? He was lying even then. He had planned and cased a job for the very next night, and he knew he would go through with it, whatever he promised her tonight on this wheel. He wanted to reach up and touch the stars.

He had stolen her from Ernie, she used to be Ernie's girl. Ernie was already boxing by then, this was two years after the club broke up, the Duke had already turned junkie, and had kicked the habit, and was pushing the stuff; everybody said he had Mafia connections, but Colley doubted it. Benny already had himself two girls by then, both experienced pros who were bringing in enough cash every week to keep him living pretty good. His ambition, he told Colley, was to have a string of twelve girls, be a gentleman of leisure. Colley told him it'd take a better man than Benny to control a dozen girls, and Benny threw him the arm salute. Colley himself had already done a dozen or more robberies and was beginning to make a good living at it. He sounded Benny about coming in with him, said he could use a good driver. Benny said he would rather stick to his girls. That was how the situation stood when Colley met Terry.

He met her when she was seventeen and he was twenty-one; she was engaged to Ernie Pass at the time. They were all calling him Ernie Pass by then because he was boxing professionally, was in fact on the road all the time, fighting in tank towns, which was how come Terry Brufani was alone so much of the time. Colley met her at a confirmation party, a big ginzo affair, ham sandwiches and beer in a hall on Westchester Avenue, one of his cousins three or four times removed. The Brufani family had been invited, too, and there she was—Terry Brufani, seventeen years old, ripe as a Sicilian olive. They danced together the whole night, but when he asked her if she'd like to go see a movie or something next Saturday, she told him she was engaged to Ernie Pass.

"Do you know him?" she said. "Ernie Pass, the prize fighter?"

"Yes, I know him," Colley said, "I once broke his head."

He checked with the guys the next day, and they all told him it was true; she *was* engaged to Ernie, they planned to get married in the spring. Colley said, "That's very interesting to know," and he went to the candy store and looked up her phone number and called her up. Her mother told him she was at work. He asked where she worked, and Mrs. Brufani said in the bank on Fordham Road and Jerome Avenue. Colley looked at his watch. It was two o'clock. When Terry came out of the bank at three, he was waiting for her on the sidewalk. That night he took her to bed with him in a motel on the Post Road, up past Parkchester. She wasn't a virgin, he didn't know anybody who *was* a virgin. She told him Ernie would kill them both if he found out.

He didn't wait for Ernie to find out. In Colley's experience, the guy who picked up the marbles was the guy who made the first move. You went into a grocery store to rob the place, you didn't wait for the guy behind the counter to pull out a shotgun. You stuck the pistol in his face, you told him shut up or he was dead. That was the way he'd done it the first time, and that was the way he was *still* doing it. The first place he'd held up was a pawnshop on Tremont Avenue. He went in there thinking he would get himself a good camera. This was when he was nineteen. He had got off with the suspended sentence on shooting the spic in the throat, and he had met all his obligations, and the record was clean. They still had the club, but there wasn't much bopping any more, and the younger kids were beginning to take over. By the time him and Benny and Duke and Ernie were nineteen, twenty, the younger kids were beginning to think of them as old men. Some of the guys—Jimmy Giglio and Petie Sanero —were already married. One guy, Angelo Di Santo, was doing time in Attica.

Colley decided he needed a camera, and he also decided he was going to go into a camera store and shove a gun in the man's face and steal the camera. Then he decided instead he would go in a pawnshop, and he picked the one on Tremont Avenue. When he got inside there, he told the man to shut up, this was a stickup, but for some reason he didn't ask for a camera, he instead asked the man to give him all the money in the cash register. He came away from the job with eight hundred dollars and some change. He never knew why he'd done that first robbery, or why he continued sticking up places.

When they had the club, they occasionally shook down kids for nickels and dimes, and of course they were always shoplifting in this or that store. But Di Santo was the only guy in the club who had really been into it, you know, into *real* crime. Not bullshit stuff like pushing dope or running a stable of hookers or taking numbers bets, like Jimmy was doing even though he was already married. Di Santo had been doing burglaries before he got busted and sent to Attica. What they got him for was burglary one, he was going to be up there in Attica a long, long time. Colley often tried to remember how he'd felt that day of the first robbery, what had gone through his head *before* he'd done it. His motivation, you know. All he could remember was that he really wanted a camera bad. And he'd decided to steal one. And he'd decided to use a gun. But then, why had he picked a pawnshop instead of a camera store? And why had he taken money instead of a camera? He couldn't figure it out. He never could figure it out.

The thing with Ernie Pass came to a head when Ernie got back from some town upstate where he was on a double bill with a black fighter named Tornado Jackson, who incidentally had belonged to a club named the Scorpions, which the Orioles had gone up against many times in the past. Colley didn't wait for Ernie to come to him. He knew Ernie would have heard about him and Terry by now, so he went straight up to Ernie's house. Mrs. Passaro was in the kitchen, standing at the stove, roasting peppers over the gas jets.

"Hey, hello, Colley," she said. "You never come around no more."

Mrs. Passaro said that to all the guys who used to be in the club. She took it as a personal insult that none of the guys stopped in to talk to her or have a glass of milk in her kitchen now that Ernie was a boxer and on the road all the time.

"Where's Ernie?" Colley said.

"In his room," Mrs. Passaro said, and gestured with her head toward the doorway leading out of the kitchen. Colley knew where Ernie's room was; when they were kids he'd go up there early in the morning, wake Ernie up, then both of them would go around getting all the other guys.

Ernie was awake now and listening to the radio. This was maybe ten o'clock in the morning, a shaft of sunlight was coming through the window next to Ernie's bed. There were pictures of him all over the wall, boxing pictures—Ernie with his gloved left hand tucked under his chin, right hand cocked to deliver the knockout punch, Ernie posing with the big bag, Ernie with his arm around the guy who was his manager, Jew named Oscar Holmes, who had changed it from Horowitz. There were also three-sheets on the wall, printed in red and blue, announcing the bill wherever Ernie happened to be fighting. The three-sheet in the center of all the others announced Ernie at the very bottom of the bill in St. Nicholas

Arena. That was probably the biggest fight he'd ever had. He'd lost it, incidentally.

Colley got straight to the point. "Ernie," he said, "I want to tell you this before you hear it from any—"

"I already heard it," Ernie said.

"About me and . . .?"

"You're doing me a favor," Ernie said. "You're welcome to her. I been racking my brain trying to figure how I could ditch her. I met this girl in Albany, I've been going with her for three months now."

"Well, okay then," Colley said.

He'd been expecting trouble, but everything was cool. He never did find out whether Ernie really did have a girl in Albany, or whether he was just shining it on, trying to avoid trouble himself. Either way, Terry was now officially his. It was just like taking money from some guy's cash register. Before you stole it, the money was his; after that, it became yours. Terry became his the morning he went up to Ernie's house; that made it official. On the way out, Mrs. Passaro said, "You want some chocolate pudding? I made some nice chocolate pudding."

He sat down at the kitchen table and had some chocolate pudding. From Ernie's room, he could hear the radio going. He had the feeling something was ending that day.

The black girl sitting in the booth across the way from them came over to the table, interrupting Terry's story about the night they were trapped on the Ferris wheel. She whispered a few words to Terry, and Terry nodded, and the black girl went back to sit with the two black dudes in the booth.

"I have to go now," Terry said, putting her cigarettes in her bag, and closing the bag, and sliding out of the booth. "It was nice seeing you again. Say hello to your mother for me, will you?"

"Hey, where you going?" Colley said.

"Thanks for the drinks," Terry said, and went over to the other booth.

"Hey!" Colley said.

The black dudes were standing now. One of them was looking Terry up and down, Colley felt like going over and punching the guy out. The black girl introduced them to Terry, and the dude who'd been looking her over put his arm around her, his fingers spread on her hip. Colley looked at the black girl, trying to place her. He suddenly realized she was the hooker who'd made the kissing sound in his mother's doorway earlier tonight.

He watched as Terry and the black girl went off with the two black dudes.

Jesus, he thought.

No, he was wrong.

Jesus.

He ordered another drink and sat there drinking alone in the booth, listening to tunes he couldn't remember, imagining things that probably weren't true—she probably just knew the girl to talk to, but the girl was a hooker, the girl had made kissing sounds in his mother's doorway. And the dress Terry was wearing, a party dress, this was Saturday night, true enough, but she'd been alone on the street at close to two in the morning, wearing a long-sleeved party dress— were the long sleeves covering tread marks on her arms, was she a junkie like almost every other hooker Colley knew in the world? No, he thought, hey, come on, she ain't a junkie, she ain't even a hooker, she probably just knows that girl, she'd told him up front the girl was a friend, hadn't she? When the girl waved to her? Sure, she had. Hell, his own mother had black ladies in for coffee, so why shouldn't Terry know a black girl, the whole fucking *neighborhood* was turning black, it was only natural to know black people if you lived around here. But the girl had made kissing sounds.

He suddenly had to take a piss. He got up from the table, surprised to find his legs unsteady under him—had he had *that* much to drink again? There were three black guys in the men's room. He always felt nervous when he went in a men's room and there were other guys in there leaning against the sinks smoking or talking—especially when they were black. He went into one of the booths and locked the door behind him, and unzipped his fly and took out his cock. Standing there with his cock in his hand, he began pissing into the bowl, and he began weeping because Terry was a whore, Terry was a junkie whore, and oh, Jesus, he stood there weeping and pissing, and he continued weeping long after the stream of urine stopped, stood there with his cock in his hand, looking down into the bowl and weeping.

At last he shook out his cock and put it back in his pants, and zipped up his fly, and wiped his eyes dry, and thought Jesus, Terry's a hooker, Jesus, she went off with those two guys, Jesus. He washed his hands and face at the sink, and he thought again of Terry back when they were kids—but no, we couldn't call ourselves kids, he thought. She was twenty and I was twenty-four, and that wasn't kids, but Jesus, how did I get so old so fast?

He went out of the men's room and over to the bar and climbed up on a leatherette stool alongside a black girl who was probably a whore just like Terry and her friend. He didn't say a word to her. He ordered another double, and when it came he sipped at it slowly. He didn't want to get too drunk. He suspected he was already too drunk, but he didn't want to get any drunker. The girl kept looking him over as if she was trying to decide whether he wanted a piece of ass or not, and then finally she said, "You got a match?"

He looked at her, and he said, "What *are* you, a hooker?"

"Yes," she said. "You got a match?"

"You want a match, or you looking for a john, which is it?"

"Right now, I want a match," she said.

"Here's a match," he said, and he took the book from his pocket and struck a match and held it to the tip of her cigarette.

"Thanks," she said.

"You know Terry Brufani?" he asked.

"No, I don't know Terry Brufani," she said. "Who's that?"

"A hooker," he said. "Like you."

"No, I don't know her."

"What the fuck *do* you know?" he said. "You don't know nothin. What *are* you?" he said. "A junkie?"

"What difference does it make?" she said.

"No difference. Whole fuckin *world's* full of junkies and hookers and fuckin armed robbers, what's the difference?"

"No difference," she said.

"None," he said. "Right."

"Right," she said.

"And burglars," he said.

"What?"

"In the world. Burglars."

"Right," she said.

It occurred to him that this was the second time he'd been drunk in four or five hours, six hours—who the fuck was counting? But that was because he'd killed a cop. Kill a cop, man's entitled to get drunk. Maybe he was entitled to change his luck, too, knock off a fuckin piece of black ass.

"What's your name?" she said.

"Colley," he said, "and for Christ's sake don't ask me what that's short for."

"What's it short for?"

"Nothing. What's your name?"

"Barbara," she said. "Don't ask me what that's short for."

"Listen," he said, "would you mind if I told you something?"

"What's that?"

"I have never been to bed with a black girl in my life."

"You're missing something," she said.

"It's good, huh?"

"Oh, my," she said.

"It is, huh?"

"Oh, my, my, my," she said.

"Well, maybe I'll give it a try," he said. "Listen," he said, "how much would it cost me?"

"Police officer," someone at his elbow said.

Colley automatically reached into his pocket for the gun, and then remembered the gun was up his mother's house, in the closet, the back of the closet. He turned, his fist clenched, ready to put up a fight, he had killed a cop tonight. But the cop here in the bar wasn't even looking at him; he was holding up his shield to the bartender. Another guy stood to his left, another fuckin plainclothes cop; *his* eyes were on the bartender, too.

"Yeah, what is it?" the bartender said.

He was a white bartender in a neighborhood going black, Colley figured he had cops in here every day of the week. Half of them were on the pad, probably bugging him about one bullshit violation or another—you didn't put out the garbage, your toilet's leaking, your napkins are dirty, your fuckin fly is open.

"Know anybody named Nicholas Donato?" the cop asked.

Colley froze.

"Nicholas *who*?" the bartender asked.

"Donato. He lives up the street, his mother does, anyway. Upstairs from the pizzeria. You know him?"

"Why do you want him?" the bartender said.

"You know him or not?" the cop said.

"You want some prices, huh?" the girl said.

"Yes," Colley said, and turned on the stool, and looked the girl straight in the face. She was the ugliest fuckin woman he'd ever seen in his life, blackheads all over her face, the kind of complexion only niggers had, wearing a blond wig that was lopsided on her head, pair of gold teeth in the front of her mouth, no bra under her dress, tits sagging to her navel.

"Yes, sweetheart," he said, "let's talk price."

"You saw the shield, or *didn't* you see the shield?" the cop asked the bartender.

"I saw it."

"Okay. Do you know a person named Nicholas Donato, and don't give me any bullshit about why we want him. Okay?"

"Why do you want him?" the bartender said.

The cop looked at his partner. "Wise guy," he said.

"Yeah," the partner said.

"All right, wise guy, he *killed* somebody, all right?"

"You want to spend the night with just me alone?" the girl whispered.

"What do you mean?" Colley said.

"You could also spend the night with me and my girl friend together."

"So you know where we can find him?" the cop said.

"Who'd he kill?" the bartender asked.

"A detective," the cop said.

"That's a shame," the bartender said. His tone made it clear that it wouldn't bother him if every detective in the city got killed tomorrow, together with the entire uniformed force. "That really is a shame."

"Did you say somebody killed a detective?" the hooker asked, leaning over Colley to address the cop.

"Yeah," the cop said, turning to her. "Liquor-store holdup on White Plains Avenue. We got a positive make from the other officer who was in there. So what do you say?" he asked the bartender. "You know him, or not?"

"No, I don't know him," the bartender said.

The cop turned to the hooker. "I hope you're not soliciting in here, sister," he said.

"Brother," she said, "I don't know what you mean by the word soliciting."

"Yeah, okay," the cop said, and he and his partner turned and started for the door. Over his shoulder, to no one in particular, the partner said, "Keep your nose clean."

"So what'll it be?" the hooker asked Colley. "Me and Cynthia for the night?"

"What?" Colley said. "Who's Cynthia?" In the mirror over the bar, he was watching the cops cross the room.

"Cynthia. My girl friend."

"Right, right," Colley said. His forehead was covered with sweat. He took out his handkerchief and wiped it. The cops were opening the door, the cops were going out onto the sidewalk. He got off the stool, hastily patted the hooker's hand, said, "Some other time, honey," and was walking away from the bar when the bartender said, "Hey, there's a *check,* you don't mind."

"Right," Colley said. "Sorry." He took out his wallet. The hooker was scowling at him. "How much is that?" Colley asked the bartender.

"Frank, what'd he have at the table?" the bartender yelled to the waiter.

"What do you mean, some other time?" the hooker said. She sounded like Flip Wilson doing Geraldine. "Whutchoo *mean,* some other time?"

"Some other time," Colley said. "Really, I'm busy tonight. How much is that, huh?" he said impatiently.

"Hold your horses," the bartender said. The waiter was standing at the service bar now, looking through his checks. He finally found Colley's and handed it to the bartender. "And you had a double here at the bar," the bartender said.

"Right," Colley said. "And take out for whatever the lady's been drinking, okay?"

"Thanks," the hooker said. It sounded like "Drop dead."

The bartender made change for a twenty. Colley pushed a two-dollar tip across the bar.

"Big spender," the hooker said.

Half a dozen police cars were in the street outside, and uniformed cops were all over the sidewalks, walkie-talkies in their hands, stopping people and asking them questions. He had never seen so many cops in his life except that time when he was still a kid living in Harlem, and a spic was holed up in an apartment in Spanish Harlem, somewhere between Park and Madison. He'd walked over with a friend of his and there was a regular siege going on, the cops with bullhorns and tear gas and shotguns, all of them wearing bulletproof vests, the spic in the apartment up there shooting down into the street. They finally got him out. The crowd in the street seemed disappointed. Here was a guy holding off what seemed like the whole damn police department, and these people in the street weren't too fond of cops to begin with, and they wanted the spic to stay up there forever, show the cops who was boss. But of course the cops killed him, and that was that, the party was over; the crowd began to disperse even before the ambulance attendants came out with his body on a stretcher, rubber sheet thrown over it.

Colley was beginning to understand the enormity of what he had done.

Rape an old lady, cut out her heart, hang her from a lamppost by her thumbs, police department got officially outraged. "Heinous crime," the Chief of Detectives said. "We are putting on it not only our Homicide Division, but we are pressing into service detectives and patrolmen from all over the city, including Staten Island, not to mention off-duty and vacationing policemen, be they plainclothes or uniformed." Next day, if they didn't catch the guy, the whole thing began to cool. By the third day the cops were yawning and asking each other how the Yankees were doing. But kill a cop? Kill one of their own? If you had a race riot here on this street, you'd get a handful of cops telling everybody to calm down while bricks were flying from the rooftops. But kill a cop? *Look* at the bastards. Had to be at least fifty of them going up to people and asking . . .

He stopped in the middle of the sidewalk.

The cops in the street here had something the detectives in the bar didn't have a few minutes ago. Colley saw now that a man in plainclothes was leaning against the fender of a '74

Chevy, handing out flyers, and he didn't have to guess what
was on those flyers, he goddamn well *knew*. One of them had
got away either from the detective who was handing them
out or from one of the patrolmen who'd been given it. The
escaped flyer was sticking to the wet sidewalk not three feet
from where Colley stood, and staring up at him was a picture
of himself as he'd looked four years ago, when he'd got
busted for holding up that tailor shop. They'd taken him first
to the Forty-sixth Precinct, where he'd been booked, and
then downtown to a cell in the Criminal Courts Building,
where they'd snapped his picture the next morning. In the
pictures, there were numbers across his chest. His hair was
longer then, and he had sported a mustache in those days;
he had begun growing the mustache right after Terry left for
Vermont. But the face was unmistakably his, a little fuller
perhaps, he'd lost a lot of weight in prison. All a cop had to
do was subtract the mustache and a few pounds, trim the hair
a bit, and there was Nicholas Donato himself in person—
right here in an armed camp of policemen who'd love nothing better than to shoot him dead on the spot.

A cop was approaching him, possibly because he was
standing there in the middle of the sidewalk looking down
at his own picture plastered to the cement. The cop had a
walkie-talkie in his right hand, and in his left hand the flyer.
They were keeping in close touch on this operation because
they were dealing with a mad cop killer here. They wanted
to make sure this fiend didn't shoot all of them in the back
while they were asking people in the street if they had seen
Nicholas Donato, this man here in this mug shot taken four
years ago.

"Excuse me, sir," the cop said.

Colley looked up. He did not have his gun with him; his
gun was in his mother's apartment. If he'd had the gun, he
would have opened fire at once, and then run—take his
chances, what the hell.

"Yes?" he said.

Another cop was coming up to where Colley and the first cop were standing on the sidewalk. "You get one of these flyers, Mike?" the second cop said.

"Yeah," the first cop said.

"Ugly son of a bitch, ain't he?" the second cop said, and laughed.

"Sir," the first cop said, "we're looking for a man named Nicholas Donato, he lives on this street with his mother. Would that name mean anything to you?"

"No," Colley said. "It don't mean nothin to me." He took out his handkerchief and blew his nose, and then he kept wiping the nose, cleaning it, practically polishing it, just so he could keep the handkerchief covering the lower part of his face.

"This is a picture of the man," the cop said. "It was taken four years ago, he might not have the mustache now. Would you recognize him?"

"No," Colley said, and blew his nose again. "I don't know him."

The second cop was staring at him.

"That it?" Colley said.

"Hold it just a minute," the second cop said, and looked at the flyer in his hand.

"Mike," he said, and was reaching for the gun holstered at his side when Colley broke.

He was used to running from cops in these streets. Years ago, when they had the club, he ran from trouble on the average of twice a week. The cops knew him by sight in those days. They knew Ernie, who was the president, and Benny, who was the war counselor, and Colley, who was the sergeant at arms. The big three. The ones who ran the Orioles. More than a hundred members in those days. Two dozen here on the block, another seventy-some spread for a radius of half a mile. One time, when the shit was on between the Scorpions and another Italian gang near the parkway approach, the leader of the Italian gang asked Ernie could he lend some help for a rumble supposed to take place in the park Saturday morning. Ernie said he could put a hundred guys in that park just by snapping his fingers. That Saturday they wiped up the street with those Scorpions.

There were shots behind him; they cracked with brittle precision on the cool early-morning air. The night people were out, they sat on stoops and congregated on street corners, they moved apart to let Colley through. The shots sounded unreal. After those shots fired in the liquor store, after those shots that had killed one cop and wounded another, none of these shots splintering the air sounded genuine. They served to alert the other cops, though. Cops hear shots, they see a man running, they don't have to ask if he's the victim or the perpetrator, they know automatically the guy running is the guy who done something wrong. Colley was running, and people on the sidewalk were stepping aside to let him through, *ducking* away, actually, because they could hear guns cracking, and they knew that meant bullets were flying, and bullets didn't always hit who they were intended for. There were cops behind him firing, and cops ahead of him beginning to get the drift of what was happening; they were only here looking for a man who'd killed a cop, they were only here with flyers and walkie-talkies and half a dozen police cars and half a hundred uniformed cops, and Christ alone knew how many plainclothes bulls, and they were confronted now with two cops firing at a fleeing man, but they were still looking puzzled. A pair of cops, in fact, parted to let him go by, and then shouted, "Hey! Hey, you!" after he'd passed them and gone around the corner.

He knew these streets, he knew running these streets.

There were more cops ahead of him, they didn't know what had happened around the corner, but they had heard shooting and enough time had elapsed now for them to have drawn their guns. They were in fact running toward the corner as he made the turn, and he wheeled sharply to his left, his leather-soled shoes skidding out from under him, he wished he was wearing sneakers like in the old days. But he didn't fall, he caught his balance at once and began running for the vacant lot alongside the grocery store.

There were no cops ahead of him, now they were all behind him, and they were all shooting. A bunch of black kids wearing gang jackets were standing under the lamppost, their eyes opening wide as they heard the shots and doped out something big was happening, not your penny-ante street-gang bullshit, man, but something tremendous, some thief running here in the night, some desperado, some crazed and demented killer. The jackets they wore nowadays looked seedy and faded and cheap, nothing like what the Orioles used to have when the club was riding high, nothing like what even the Scorpions had. And the Dragons—you had to admit those spics had some fancy jackets, the blood spurting from the throat of Luis Josafat Albareda, onto the front of the yellow silk, the name *Macho* in green thread over his heart.

Colley was in the lot now. There were rats in the lot, they scampered over the garbage, scaring him half to death, squealing, scurrying away noisily as he ran for the fence. The cops behind him were yelling different directions and orders and swearing and stumbling and generally behaving like the dumb bastards they were. "This way," or "Hold your fire, there's civilians," or "In the lot, he's in the lot," or "Get a car, we need lights," a babble of sound behind Colley as he ran over the familiar terrain toward a fence he'd scaled a hundred times or more in his youth.

He was smiling when he reached the fence. He knew that once he scaled this fence, the cops behind him were out of luck. He knew that beyond this fence was a maze of back yards and alleyways, basements in abandoned buildings, stairways to roofs that joined other roofs, shaftways to leap, roof leading to roof leading to roof, until he would emerge a block away and cross a street to enter yet another labyrinth of alleyways and back yards. In ten minutes he would be in a different neighborhood entirely, in what used to be Scorpion turf. The cops would be up the creek once he scaled that fence.

He jumped for it. He skittered up its wooden face like a cat with a thousand claws. He straddled its top as bullets whined around him, ricocheting off the brick wall of the abandoned building on the other side, and then he deliberately turned his head and looked back at the cops. He was giving them the edge, daring them to knock him off the fence with their popguns, knock off the cop killer, you bastards, and win yourselves a Kewpie doll on a cane—that night at Coney Island on the Ferris wheel, the promises he'd made, Terry turning out to be a hooker. Coming home had been a bust, all of it had been a fuckin bust except for this moment, this exhilarating moment with the cops running toward him over the garbage in the empty lot, the rats scrambling away, the guns popping against the night, tiny flashes of yellow, the bullets humming past his head: he was Superman, he was able to leap tall buildings, he was able to outrace speeding locomotives, he was invincible, he was indestructible.

He burst out laughing.

The laughter froze the policemen in their tracks.

The firing stopped.

In an instant Colley was over the fence and safe.

FIVE

Jeanine was still wearing the blue jeans and the T-shirt, she was still barefooted.

She let him into the apartment, and then she locked the door behind him and listened quietly while he told her what had happened. He was still feeling high after his run from the cops, not the kind of high he experienced when he was smoking dope, nor even the kind of jazzed-up, slowed-down high that was there each and every time he went into a store with a gun in his pocket. This was a combination of nervous energy and fear and excitement—the detective who was still alive had identified him from a mug shot and flyers had been run off, and now every cop in the city had a picture of him and was looking for him. On the way over here, his heart had nearly stopped every time he saw a squad car or even a lone patrolman standing on the corner under a lamppost.

He had read a story in one of those magazines that published true adventure articles, where it showed a bare-chested guy wrestling an alligator on the cover, and where inside it had ads for body-building and condoms and books on how to pick up girls. This particular story was about a guy who'd got lost in the jungle someplace, and it told about how he was in a state of intense excitement the whole time he was in there, listening for every snapping twig and searching the dark for glowing eyes and even learning how to interpret silences. Colley had felt that way coming crosstown to the apartment, and he still felt as though he was on some kind of dangerous mission that would end with him walking out of the jungle into civilization, big shining city in the distance there, music and booze and beautiful women.

He told Jeanine about how he'd been identified, and he thanked her again—even though he'd already thanked her on the phone—for letting him come over here when she knew the cops were on to him. She said that was okay, she hadn't been asleep anyway. She told him she'd spent some time cleaning up the place after he'd left and then she'd tried to sleep in here on the sofa, but all she did was toss and turn. Colley looked at the rug. She hadn't been able to get the bloodstains out.

"You should have used cold water," he said.

"I did."

"Wouldn't take them out, huh?"

"No. I washed your clothes, too, by the way. The pants said Dry Clean Only, but I figured it was better to take a chance ruining them than leave blood on them."

"Yeah, good," he said. "Did the blood come out?"

"Most of it."

"They were old pants anyway," he said.

"Jocko's still bleeding," Jeanine said, gesturing with her head toward the corridor and the bedroom. "Soaked through the bandage four times since you left."

"Looks like we're all in fine shape, don't it?" Colley said. "Next thing I expect to hear is Teddy got hit by a bus on the way home."

Jeanine smiled. "You want a drink?" she said. "There's only bourbon left, but if that's okay . . ."

"Yeah, with a little water," he said.

"You seem calm," she said.

"I'm pretty jazzed up, you really want to know."

"You look calm."

He shook his head.

"I'll get the drinks," she said, and went out into the kitchen.

He sat on the sofa listening to the ticking of the clock. He would have to ask her where the clock was. Could *hear* the thing all over the apartment, but couldn't *see* it anyplace. In the kitchen, he heard her opening the refrigerator. He thought of earlier tonight, of the way she'd showed him her breasts. Well, she was used to that, an ex-stripper. Still, it had been only the two of them in the apartment, Jocko unconscious down the hall. That was different from doing a strip in some joint. He got up off the sofa, started for the kitchen, and stopped. He listened down the hall, could hear nothing.

He went into the kitchen. "Need some help," he said.

"No," she said, "I'm doing fine."

Her back was to him, he studied her figure. He had telephoned her forty minutes ago from a black bar in Scorpion territory, after leaping rooftops and crossing back yards and racing through alleyways. He had called because he'd told himself he would need a gun now that the cops had identified him, and the only place he could get a gun was in Jocko's apartment. Jocko had guns. But Jocko also had a wife named Jeanine who'd pulled her T-shirt up over her breasts and showed them to him and then asked him if he was afraid of Jocko. Yes, he'd been afraid of Jocko then, and he knew that once he came down from this fantastic high, he would become afraid of Jocko all over again. He knew that if he did not make his move soon, if he did not go over to where she stood at the sink in those tight blue jeans, he would never do it.

She turned from the sink, moved to the counter alongside it, and put ice cubes into two glasses. The seal on the bourbon bottle was broken; she'd been drinking since he left the apartment. She poured whiskey into both glasses, added some water to his, and held it out to him. He went to her, and took the glass from her hand and they stood not three feet apart in the narrow kitchen, Colley against the refrigerator, Jeanine leaning against the counter. Her hands were wet, she wiped them on the thighs of the faded blue jeans, and then left them on her thighs, the fingers widespread. She looked up into his face, and suddenly there were no secrets, his eyes had told her everything she needed to know.

She kept looking into his face as he moved toward her, standing against the counter, her hands resting on her thighs. He could no longer hear the ticking of the clock. He put his glass down on the counter beside her, and then, slowly, lifted the front of the T-shirt the way she had lifted it in the living room earlier tonight, took the bottom of it in both hands and pulled the shirt up over her naked breasts.

She did not move.

She kept her hands on her thighs, the fingers spread. He noticed that she had long, slender hands, that the fingernails were painted a red as bright as the blood that had spurted from the dead cop's head, he did not want to think about that stupid bastard, he reached up for her breasts. The T-shirt was bunched above them, she stood with her shoulders back, the breasts jutting, a faint smile on her face now, her eyes slitted, a lazy languid look in them. The water tap was dripping. He could hear the water tap, and also the ticking of the clock again as he brought his open hands up to her breasts.

She leaned into his hands.

He touched her breasts lightly, he did not want to hurt her the way Jocko had, he was afraid of causing fresh bruises. There was a sheen to her skin, the flesh was taut, the globes shimmered with secret pinks and lavenders, mother-of-pearl breasts, he touched them gently, his fingers exploring. The skin around the nipples came as a course reminder of sex, blatant and rude, the circles of darker flesh erupting in pin-point nubs. The hardening nipples were a declaration, he responded to them wildly, tightening his hands on her breasts, cupping them to his mouth, kissing the freckled sloping tops and rounded sides, and then bringing his mouth up to hers, waiting wet and wide, and covering her lips with his.

She threw herself into him, she ground her hips against him, he visualized her on a small stage in a smoke-filled room, *I'd go out there, you know, and the drums'd be banging, and the lights'd be on me, and I'd start throwing myself around,* and he reached for the front of the blue jeans and found first the button and then the zipper. She was naked under the jeans, her nakedness there came as a surprise, the smooth shock of her belly, the sudden deep navel, the crisp tangled hair. He spread his fingers into her crotch and she pulled her mouth from his and whispered directly into his ear, a cannon shot in his ear, "He'll kill you." She was referring to Jocko, he knew she was referring to Jocko, but he could visualize only Kruger the Kraut grabbing him in the shower, Kruger squeezing his cheeks in both hands, squeezing, squeezing, and then stopping just before he fainted, and grinning and walking out, the other cons pretending nothing had happened.

"He'll kill you," she said again, but she was stepping out of the blue jeans, she was kicking them away across the kitchen floor, and reaching for him again, opening his fly, pulling him free with one swift tug and then leaning back against the counter, hands coming up behind his neck, mouth open, grinding again even before their bodies touched. He reached behind her and grabbed her naked buttocks in both hands and lifted her up onto the counter. He was spreading her wide when they heard the voice. He was opening her like a melon when they heard it. The first thing he thought was *It's the police;* he didn't know why he thought that.

"Jeanine," the voice said.

The voice was hoarse, Colley could not recognize it at first. But Jeanine knew the voice immediately and reacted to it at once. She put both hands against Colley's chest and shoved him away from her, closed her legs and slid off the counter and onto the floor. She was reaching for her blue jeans even before the voice said again, slightly louder this time, "Jeanine." There was no question mark at the end of that voice, this was not someone used to calling her and not having her come. This was someone who beat her often and brutally, who left her bruised and aching, this was *her* Kruger, and his name was Jocko.

To Colley, watching her, it seemed as though she came off the counter and moved swiftly to where the jeans were crumpled on the floor and stooped to them and reached for them with one hand and with the other hand tugged at the T-shirt bunched above her breasts, all in a single graceful motion instead of several separate, panicky moves. He saw the swollen breasts for just an instant longer before she pulled the shirt down over them again. The nipples were still erect, they poked through the thin cotton fabric, the nipples were the same but everything else was changing, everything else was on the edge of becoming a nightmare.

She was just beginning to come up out of her crouch, the blue jeans in her left hand. She raised her head, tossed her hair back over her shoulder, and then her lips parted just a trifle, and Colley saw terror come into her eyes as she stood erect and backed a pace deeper into the kitchen. She was naked from the waist down, the T-shirt reaching to just an inch above the tufted blond triangle of her crotch, and she was looking past Colley to a spot somewhere behind his left shoulder. He turned swiftly, and immediately caught his breath. Jocko was in the doorway to the kitchen. He was huge and he was naked and the bandage covering his shoulder was soaked through with blood, and blood was running down his arm the way it had in the liquor store just after he'd been shot, dribbling onto the floor, the clock syncopating its tick-tick-tick against the steady patter of Jocko's blood.

"What the fuck?" he said, and took a quick step into the kitchen, and what happened next happened so quickly that

Colley wasn't sure it was happening at all. With his good right arm, Jocko flicked Colley aside as though he were a eunuch caught in the sultan's harem. The motion was only a backward swipe of his arm as he moved past Colley toward where Jeanine stood cowering near the sink. But Jocko's strength was such that even though he'd been bleeding since shortly after nine o'clock, and was *still* bleeding, this casual motion of his arm could send Colley smashing violently against the wall, his head banging back against the plaster. Jeanine screamed. Colley, dazed, slid down the wall to the floor. Jocko brought back his right arm, the palm of the hand open, and then uncurled the arm like a pitcher throwing a curve ball. Jeanine's head snapped to the side with the force of the blow.

Jocko was upon her now. He seized the T-shirt in his big fist, twisted the thin fabric, and holding on to the fabric, his fist literally wrapped in it, he punched out at her, sending her flailing back against the refrigerator. He did not let go of the shirt. He pulled her off the front of the refrigerator, and then punched out at her again and again, still holding the shirt, bouncing her repeatedly against the refrigerator, Jeanine grunting each time his huge fist struck her chest or her breasts or her rib cage. The shirt was tearing. He pulled her off the refrigerator a final time, and swung her around against the counter. Letting go of the shirt, he brought his arm back and pistoned a short hard punch to her shoulder, and then punched her in the left arm, a blow so hard it caused the arm to fall limply to her side.

She was collapsed against the countertop now, her right arm across it, her hand flapping, grasping, the fingers opening and closing spasmodically, reaching, searching for something, anything. Each time Jocko threw a punch, the force of it rumbled through her body, and each blow sent blood specks flying from his wounded arm onto the white T-shirt. Colley was moving toward them to help her now, afraid to help her, feeling it would be useless to try, but knowing he would anyway. He saw Jeanine's hand blindly strike the handle of a bread knife in the drying rack on the counter. Her hand recognized the knife, her fingers closed on it. The knife blade clinked against a dish that was drying on the rack, and then the knife came around in an arc, high into the air above Jeanine's head, clenched in her fist just as Jocko drew back his arm to punch her again. Colley saw her eyes and knew she would kill him, and he thought *Yes, kill him, kill him!* but he shouted, "No, Jeanine," and then more sharply, "No, don't!" but he was too late.

The blade came down with tremendous force.

She was a big woman, and she was terrified, and she was angry, and she sank the fourteen-inch blade into his chest clear to the handle, plunging it in just below the right wing of his collarbone, and then pulling it free and plunging it in again in fury. "Jesus," Jocko said, and she pulled the knife free again, and her hand came up again, and Colley stood unable to move, watching as though paralyzed, and Jocko said "Jesus," breathing it this time, and Jeanine said "Yes," and plunged the knife again, and said "Yes," her voice rising, and "Yes" again and "Yes" and "Yes," each uttered affirmative coinciding with a plunge of the knife, "Yes" and "Yes" and "Yes," till Jocko fell, gushing blood, to the kitchen floor, and then she straddled him as though she were fucking him, and she kept plunging the knife into his chest and his throat and his face until finally the blade broke on the hard bone of his forehead, and even then she brought the handle and the broken blade down twice more before she realized the knife was broken, and then she stopped.

"Yes," she said.

She was breathing heavily. Straddling Jocko, she looked into his face and nodded. Then she got up slowly, and backed away from him a pace, and nodded again. She heard Colley behind her, and she whirled at once, her eyes wide, surprised to see him, surprised that she was not alone in the kitchen with the man she had just killed. She was still holding the broken knife in her hand, and for a moment Colley thought she would strike out at him blindly and in terror. But the surprise left her eyes almost at once, and he realized that she was not frightened, she had only been startled. Neither of them said anything. She took a quick step to the counter and put the broken knife down on its wooden top. She looked down at Jocko again, and then walked around him, and went to where Colley was standing. The broken knife blade had fallen onto Jocko's chest. It lay half hidden in the red hairs curling there. His tiny cock seemed to have shriveled in death. Only the rounded head peeked from the red pubic hair like a mushroom cap. His blue eyes were open wide and staring up at the ceiling.

"Close his eyes, for Christ's sake," Colley said, and moved past her and knelt beside the body, and made one abortive attempt to close the eyes himself, pulling back his hand before he touched the lids. Behind him, he could hear Jeanine's heavy breathing. He reached out again, and closed one lid with his thumb, the other with his forefinger. Jocko's face was crisscrossed with cuts. His throat had been opened with one deep slash of the knife, and Colley looked into the wound and saw exposed raw tissue there. He turned away immediately and brought his hand to his mouth, certain he would vomit.

Behind him, Jeanine laughed.

The laughter was dark and chilling, it seemed to rumble up from somewhere deep inside her, rising in her throat to find voice behind tightly compressed lips. Her eyes were mirthless. Looking into her face, he saw something that warned him to get out of this place now, before it was too late. Leave here, go, get away, run.

She held out her hand to him.

It was her right hand, the hand that had wielded the knife. The fingers and the palm were covered with blood. There was blood on the torn T-shirt and on the breast that showed where the fabric was ripped. There were flecks of blood on

her thighs. He was not sure why she was extending her hand.
He hesitated. When he did not move to her, she came to him,
and put her arms around his neck and moved her mouth
toward his and he saw—in the instant before they kissed—
that there was blood on her lips as well.

They made love on the sofa.

Through the open doorless jamb between kitchen and living room, Colley could see a thin line of blood trickling
across the kitchen floor. He was on top of Jeanine, she was
spread beneath him when he discovered the thin trickle of
Jocko's blood creeping inexorably across the kitchen floor.
And then he noticed for the first time that the springs were
jutting through the fabric on the easy chair opposite the sofa,
and he saw that the cabinet of the television set was scarred
with cigarette burns, and the ceiling plaster was chipped and
peeling, and there was a rust mark on the wall from a leaking
pipe, and the rug Jeanine could not get the bloodstains out
of was worn and faded—the place was a dump. Jocko'd been
in this business for more than fifteen years, and his place was
a dump. And he was dead on the kitchen floor, his blood
trickling toward the doorjamb while a stranger fucked his
wife.

Colley watched the blood. He did not know whether the
blood was *really* moving quite that slowly, or whether this
was the same phenomenon that took place in the liquor store
at nine tonight, or nine yesterday night, whichever. He always thought of the empty hours of the morning as part of
the night before; to him, it was still Saturday till the sun came
up and then it would be Sunday. On Sundays, *every* Sunday
when he was a boy growing up in Harlem, and later when
they'd moved to the Bronx, he'd gone to ten o'clock mass,
stopped going when he joined the Orioles and began doing
bad things. This was technically Sunday already, though he
was still thinking of it as Saturday night, and he was indeed
going to church, but the church was wet and dark and the

devil was the preacher. He'd seen the devil behind Jeanine's mirthless eyes, heard the devil's laughter echoing up out of her bowels, forcing itself onto her mouth, laughter exuberantly evil, reveling in the dark and brutal act that had just been committed. Slowly the stream of blood oozed its way toward the open doorjamb.

You live by the gun, you die by the gun.

That was Albert L. Donato speaking, noted Buick salesman and criminal psychologist. Jocko lived by the gun, yes, but tonight he died by the *knife,* and now he was on that kitchen floor dribbling out the last few drops of his blood while a stranger entered the cloister, gun in hand. Not a stranger, though. His good buddy, his fall partner, the man who went in with him on each and every job, sharing the danger and the fun, the man who was now sharing the wet and secret places of his wife, who, incidentally, happened to be the person who tore his flesh to dangling ribbons ... *Christ,* those tubes in his throat—was that the jugular, was that the trachea? Was that what the throat of Luis Josafat Albareda looked like after Colley shot him that time so long ago? His first gun. An Astra Firecat, a fucking peashooter, how could it have caused so much damage? Luis Josafat Albareda speaking through a voice box now, his Spanish accent sounding absurdly like the voice of Señor Wences: *You want to go back in the box?*

From behind countless footlights over the years, strutting in high-heeled, ankle-strapped shoes across hollow noisy stages, blue smoke rising, eyes on the tasseled G-string as she twirled it, blond tangled hair behind it, Jeanine promised sex unequaled, she promised skill and passion, hours and hours of unending excitment—she would take you where you'd never been, you would spend a steamy night with her in the devil's own chamber. Now she was going to deliver. Now she was going to honor all those markers she'd been handing out since she was sixteen years old, all those I.O.U.'s that were still unpaid. She was going to make them good now on this couch in this apartment where five minutes ago she'd committed bloody murder.

Colley thought of guns. His brother once told him that the pistol was of course a fixed psychological symbol, that whenever a man dreamt of a gun or even *thought* of a gun he was actually dreaming of or thinking of a penis. Colley wondered if his brother called his *own* cock a penis, or did he only use that word when he was discussing guns as fixed psychological symbols?

Colley loved guns, there was no question about that. He remembered his various guns now as Jeanine whispered in his ear, urging him to explode inside her. She'd killed one man in the kitchen by stabbing him to death with a fourteen-inch blade, and now he suspected she wanted to kill *another* one here in the living room by fucking him to death. He sensed it would be dangerous to leave this woman unsatisfied; sooner or later she would remind him of it in ways that might be unpleasant. What had been unconscious ten seconds before she whispered in his ear, commanding him to come—*Give it to me, baby, let me have it*—now became entirely conscious. Willfully, he thought of guns. Lovingly, he thought of their parts.

He thought of them as engines.

He thought of them as death machines.

He'd disassembled enough of them to know that their design was basically simple. He thought of that design now, concentrating on what caused the explosion in the barrel of a pistol, refusing to obey her whispered urgings, knowing he could not himself explode inside her or he would one day pay for it. She herself was paying all her markers, and perhaps that's all she wanted or needed to do—please him, satisfy him, leave him basking in the afterglow of her methodical assault. But he felt certain she was testing him somehow, having utterly destroyed a man bigger and stronger than himself and wanting now to reduce him similarly, coaxing and teasing and tormenting from him an orgasm he refused to release. He was afraid of leaking his juices into her vault. He was afraid that would be the same somehow as Jocko leaking his blood onto the kitchen floor. She suddenly rolled him off of her. She sat up.

Her mouth descended.

In the simplest of pistols, like the Colt .22 Derringer, there were only seventeen parts, and you could assemble the gun from scratch for about twenty-five dollars. In a more complicated gun, like the German Luger, there were fifty or more parts. Colley knew the names of the parts, he'd seen them spread on a clean white cloth in front of him, pieces of a deadly jigsaw puzzle. Front sight and breech block, toggle joint and firing pin, trigger bar spring stud . . .

He was frightened now. His mind frantically grasped for other names, breechblock catch link rivet, he was responding to something as primitive as his grandmother's fear of the number thirteen, believing that if he allowed himself to succumb to her mouth, she would destroy him more completely than she'd destroyed Jocko. She would devour his parts, she would drain him of his vital juices, she would suck from his cock the manhood he'd protected and preserved for twenty-nine years. There was nothing subtle about her attack now. She no longer wished to tantalize with slow bumps and grinds learned on rickety stages in smoky saloons. Her breathing was labored as she worked him liquidly, he was melting into her mouth, he was losing himself to her, he twisted his head violently . . .

In any gun, the cartridge sat in a narrow metal shaft. It was composed of case, primer, powder and bullet. When the trigger was squeezed, the spring action caused the firing pin to strike the back of the cartridge case, denting it and simultaneously causing an explosion of fulminate . . .

She lifted her mouth for just an instant.

"Come, you son of a bitch," she whispered.

. . . igniting the powder and propelling the bullet from the shaft.

SIX

She was cutting his hair.

He was sitting on a chair they had pulled in from the kitchen, and a dishtowel was draped over his shoulders while Jeanine worked on him. He was facing the open doorway. The trickle of blood had stopped. He could hear the ticking of the clock, he still did not know where the clock was. His hair kept falling onto the rug as she snipped away with the scissors. They had not bothered to put newspapers on the floor around the chair; they were going to leave the apartment soon and nothing could be any messier than the corpse they were leaving in the kitchen.

As she cut Colley's hair, she rambled on about what it was like growing up the daughter of a career soldier. They had showered together fifteen minutes earlier, and now he sat in the chair wearing Jocko's robe, the sleeves rolled up to accommodate the length of his arms, and she stood behind him wearing a blue smock. Listening to her, hearing the gentle reminiscent tone of her voice over the clicking of the scissors, seeing the steadiness of her hands, you would never guess she had killed a man less than an hour ago.

"I was born in what was supposed to be the worst year of

the Depression. Fact is, my father *joined* the Army *because* of the Depression, figured he'd get himself three squares a day. Did I tell you how old I am?"

"Fourty-four, you said."

"Right." She grinned suddenly. "How does it feel, being involved with an older woman?"

"It feels good," he said. He was lying. He was afraid of her. He was afraid of the pointed scissors in her hand. He was remembering the way she had butchered Jocko in the kitchen.

"I was still a kid while the Depression was on," she said. "It wouldn't have meant anything to me, anyway. We always had plenty to eat, the Army took good care of us. My father was a quartermaster. This was before World War II. We went all over the country, he kept getting transferred from post to post. Wherever there's an Army post, I've lived in the nearest town to it. Fort Benning, Georgia? I lived in Columbus when I was three years old. Fort Dix? I lived in Trenton. Fort Huachuca, I—"

"Fort what?" Colley said.

"Huachuca. That's in Arizona, outside of Tucson. I've been to every Army post there ever was, some of them don't even exist any more. When the war broke out, World War II, we were living in Louisiana, town named Leesville, have you ever been there?"

"No," Colley said.

"Fort Polk is down there," Jeanine said. "My father got shipped overseas in 1942. Instead of staying in Leesville, which is not exactly the biggest city in the world, my mother and I moved to New Orleans for a while, and then down to Florida—Fort Myers. That's not an Army post, that's just the name of the town. Fort Myers. That was in 1943, I was eleven years old. I grew up in Fort Myers. I love it down there. Do you know Sanibel Island?"

"No," Colley said. "I've never been down South."

The scissors stopped just beside his right ear. The silence was complete except for the ticking of the clock. He almost caught his breath. He turned to look up into her face. There was a distant look on it, she was remembering something private and cherished. She sighed then, and without saying another word about Sanibel Island, began cutting his hair again.

"My father got killed in 1944," she said. "During the Italian campaign. July. We got the telegram near the end of the month. He was killed in Sicily. I was twelve years old at the time. I cried for weeks, I couldn't seem to stop crying. I still miss him. I loved him a lot." She sighed again and fell silent. The scissors clicked into the clockwork stillness. Locks of his hair kept falling to the floor.

He had thought maybe they should bleach it, but Jeanine had said she'd never seen a homemade job that looked professional. When she was fifteen or sixteen she'd tried to touch up her own hair, make it look a little blonder and shinier than it naturally was, and all it did was come out cheap and brassy. And she was blond to begin with, don't forget. Colley had brown hair, and a dark brown at that. For his hair, they'd have to use twenty-volume peroxide and either a powder or a liquid bleach and proteinators, and they'd have had to bleach out the roots first, and then the ends—the whole job would have taken hours and would have come out looking shitty besides; anybody taking even a quick look at him would realize in a minute he'd bleached his hair because he was trying to change his appearance.

A crew cut, on the other hand, really *did* change a man's appearance, and looked natural besides. Your average person wouldn't know you'd cut your hair only this morning, he'd think you'd worn it that way forever. Cutting your hair short or shaving off your mustache didn't work with friends or relatives, they'd take one look at you and say, "Hi there, Joe, I see you cut your hair short and shaved off your mustache."

But with people who were working from a photograph of you, just a simple crew cut would be enough to throw them off the track.

"Come look in the mirror," she said.

He got up. His hair was all over the floor. He rubbed his hand across the top of his head and felt the bristles, and then he followed her down the hall to the bedroom. Jocko's blood was still on the sheets, Jocko's blood was all over this fuckin apartment, the sooner they got out, the better. There was a mirror over the dresser. He looked into the mirror. He was wearing Jocko's robe, which was too big for him, the sleeves rolled up, the shoulders far too wide. He would have looked scrawny in the robe even with a full head of hair, but with the crew cut he looked emaciated.

"It's awful," he said.

"I think it looks good," Jeanine said.

"It's terrible," he said, turning his head to the side to see what he looked like in profile. "Jesus, it's really awful."

"You want to look beautiful, or you want to get where we're going?"

"I don't even know where we're going," he said.

"We're going to Fort Myers," she told him.

It was still dark, he was beginning to think it would stay dark forever; they had done some bad things tonight, and the sun would never come up again, the sun would stay hidden in shame for the things they had done. Killing the cop—but that was self-defense really, the cop had a gun in his hand, he was yelling "Police officer"; you don't announce yourself as a cop unless you mean business, unless you intend to use the gun. He wondered again if somebody had snitched to the cops about the job. He did not know why it was so important that he know whether the cop had been tipped or not. If he could only call the police department and ask them whether the stakeout had been for just anybody, or did the cops know he and Jocko were going to hit the place. He really wanted to know. Because if they'd been waiting there for just *any-body,* why then, it made the killing of the cop seem, well, senseless. Because that meant the cop would have come run-ning out of the back room yelling at whoever walked in there with a gun. That meant the cop was yelling not at *Colley* but at the *gun* in Colley's hand.

He wished he could call the police department and find out. Maybe he'd ask Jeanine to call for him. Just to see if the stakeout was planned for him and Jocko. Because if it was *planned* for them, if the cops were specifically waiting for them, then killing the cop was very definitely self-defense, the way Jeanine killing Jocko in the kitchen had been self-defense. The way, when you came to think of it—though he wouldn't mention this to Jeanine—the way the German or the Italian who had killed her father in Sicily was also acting in self-defense and trying to save his own skin. The way Colley'd been trying to save *his* skin in the liquor store. Dumb fuckin cop had nothing to lose, Colley had fifteen years staring him in the face. Police officer, my *ass,* Colley thought. If my own *brother* tried to send me back to Sing Sing with that fuckin Kruger grabbing my ass, I'd put a bullet in *his* head, too, brother or not. Fuck him.

He needed a gun.

She'd cut off all his hair like Samson and Delilah, he'd seen that picture on television with Victor Mature and Hedy La-marr, she'd robbed him of his fuckin strength. He needed a gun now. He'd come to this apartment to get a gun, and he wasn't going to leave here without one.

"Where's the gun he had on the job?" he asked her. "Did he have it when we carried him in here tonight?"

"I don't think so," Jeanine said.

"You think he dropped it in the store?" Colley said. "That's bad if he did. Cause his prints'll be on it. Do they have this address for him?"

"I don't know," Jeanine said. "Let's just get out of here, okay?"

There was an edge to her voice, but she was packing unhurriedly, folding slips and panties and sweaters and putting them neatly into her suitcase. He thought of what had happened just a little while ago, Jocko caught in the threshing machine that had been Jeanine wielding a bread knife. Why hadn't she fallen apart immediately afterwards? Why were they still in this apartment, for Christ's sake, Jeanine moving to the dresser now to take out a stack of blouses, placing them squarely on the slips she had just folded and put into the suitcase. The clock ticking. When he found that clock, he would step on it, he would crush it beneath the heel of his foot.

"Maybe they don't have this address," he said. "Jocko moved around a lot, didn't he?"

"Yes," she said. She was at the closet now, stooping to pick up several pairs of shoes from the floor.

"Also, his parole was from Texas, isn't that right?"

"That's right, yes."

"So the cops here wouldn't have a sheet on him, except maybe he's wanted for extradition. What I'm saying is, even if they did get some good prints from the gun, they could only get a make from the F.B.I. files, and even then it wouldn't give them this address. So we got time."

"Okay," she said. "Fine."

"I know he had some spare guns, he told me he had some spares. A Walther, I think, was one of them. Do you know where he kept them."

"No, I don't," Jeanine said.

"You been here since April, and you don't know where he kept his guns?"

"Why don't you go ask *him,* " Jeanine said.

"You must have seen him take out the gun he used tonight, didn't you? Where'd he take it from?"

"I don't know," Jeanine said.

"Well, I ain't leaving this apartment without a gun in my belt."

He went to the dresser and opened the top drawer, and began rummaging through Jocko's underwear and socks and handkerchiefs. In the back of the drawer he found a box of 9mm Parabellum cartridges, which told him his memory had been right about the Walther. He also found a box of .38 Specials, which were the cartridges that fit the Colt Cobra that Jocko had used on the job tonight. And there was a third box of .32 Long cartridges. He was lifting the lid on this box to see how many cartridges were in it when the telephone rang, startling him. The box tilted in his hand, spilling cartridges onto the dresser top. The telephone shrilled into the apartment. Cartridges rolled off the dresser top and onto the floor. He saw his own startled image in the mirror and did not recognize himself for an instant, and again the phone rang. He looked swiftly at his watch. It was four-thirty in the morning, and the phone was ringing, ringing . . .

"Get it," he said.

"Suppose it's the police?"

"It won't be the police, they don't have an address . . ."

"You don't know that for sure."

"*Answer* the fuckin thing!"

Jeanine picked up the receiver on the bedside table. "Hello?" she said. She listened. "Hello, Teddy," she said.

Colley let out his breath.

"Yes, Teddy," she said. "When was that? Um-huh. Um-huh. Um-huh. Well, he's here, do you want to tell him yourself?" She handed the phone to Colley, and then walked over to the closet.

"Hello," Colley said into the phone.

"Hey, how you doin?" Teddy said.

"Not so hot," Colley said.

"They got a positive on you, huh?"

"How'd you know that?"

"I heard your name on the radio. I couldn't sleep, I got up and went to make myself a sandwich. I turned on the radio low while I was eating, I didn't want to wake the wife.

The announcer gave your name, said the police were con-
ducting a citywide search for you."

"Yeah," Colley said.

"How'd they get on to you?" Teddy asked.

"Son of a bitch recognized me."

"Who do you mean?"

"The other cop in the store. From when I got busted four
years ago."

"You're kidding me."

"I wish I was."

"Boy," Teddy said.

Both men were silent.

"How's Jocko doing?" Teddy asked.

For a moment Colley did not know what to answer.

"Colley?"

"Yeah."

"I thought we were cut off."

"No, no, I'm here."

"How's Jocko doing?"

"He's dead," Colley said. Jeanine was taking a skirt from
the closet; she turned to him sharply and looked directly into
his face. Colley nodded assurance. "Jeanine couldn't stop the
blood," he said into the phone. "I called here to see how
everything was, she told me to get over here in a hurry."

"Boy," Teddy said.

"Teddy, I'm going to make a run for it."

"Colley, am I in this yet?" Teddy asked.

"I don't see how."

"I keep trying to remember if Jocko had his gun with him
when he came out of that store. Because if he didn't, then
maybe they'll get prints from it and find out who he is and
start asking around. There's lots of people in this city seen
me and Jocko together."

"No, don't worry about it," Colley said.

"He had the gun then, huh? When he came out of the
store?"

"No, Teddy."

"He left it in there?"

"I think so."

"Well," Teddy said, "that don't sound too good. Guy who took a couple of falls already, they'll have a sheet on him in the F.B.I. files, next thing you know they'll be knocking on my door."

"How you figure that, Teddy?"

"Because when they ask around, they'll find out him and Teddy Stein were pals, so next thing you know Good morning, Mr. Stein, we'd like a few words with you if you've got a minute."

"No, I don't think—"

"And also, Colley, what were them cops doing inside there? Were they waiting for us to show? Did somebody snitch that we were going to hit that store?"

"I don't know about that. I been wondering that myself."

"Cause if that's the case, they know the whole fuckin gang, never mind just you."

"What do you mean?"

"If somebody set us up, then he must've also told the cops who we were, don't you think?"

"Maybe not. Look, Teddy, I'm in a hurry. Jocko's dead in the fuckin kitchen, and the cops know—"

"Where?"

"What?"

"*Where'd* you say Jocko was?"

Colley did not immediately answer. Teddy was wondering how a man who was supposed to have bled to death had managed to do it in the kitchen. He knew the layout of the apartment, and he was wondering. The clock was ticking. The clock was a constant unseen reminder of itself, like Death.

"In the kitchen," Colley said at last. "He's in the kitchen."

"How'd he get in the kitchen? You just told me—"

"Jeanine was in the kitchen. He yelled for her, and she didn't hear him, so he went out after her."

That was the truth. He had told Teddy the absolute truth. Now it was time to start lying.

"And that's where he died, huh?" Teddy said.

"Yes," Colley answered. It was still the truth. No need to lie, after all.

"Mm," Teddy said.

There was another silence.

"Colley?" he said.

"Yeah?"

"When you split, is Jeanine going with you?"

"Yeah."

"Where you going?"

"We thought Canada," he said immediately and intuitively. Teddy was worried and Teddy was suspicious, and he did not want Teddy to know they were headed in the opposite direction, toward Florida. Teddy might dope it out for himself, but Colley wasn't going to help him. He suddenly did not trust Teddy at all.

"So far, I'm the only one the cops ain't on to," Teddy said. "You they already made, and Jocko they'll make from whatever shit he left on the Cobra. Me, there's a chance they'll ask around and people will say 'Oh, yeah, yeah, the Jew with the glasses, yeah a good friend of Jocko's, I seen them around a lot together.' Or maybe the guy who set us up . . ."

"We don't know for sure we were set up."

"Well, *if* we were, okay? Before now he didn't tell the cops who was going to do the job, he only told them it was coming off. But now a cop's been killed, so he suddenly gets religion. He knows by now they already made you, so he figures he'll score a couple of points with the law. Bango, he nails Jocko and me in the same breath. I'm saying maybe, Colley."

"I follow you," Colley said. "But I don't think we were set up. I ain't sure, buf if that was the case . . ."

"I'm only saying maybe. On the other hand, let's say it was

a complete and total coincidence, okay? The bulls were in there waiting for *anybody* to hit, and we walked in out of the blue. Which means I'm clean. They know you, and they're gonna know Jocko very soon, but they don't know *me*, Colley."

"That's right."

"So, Colley, do I have to worry?"

"About what?"

"About somebody dragging me in this thing where so far I'm clean?"

"Who's gonna do that, Teddy?"

"You tell me."

"Why would I drag you in it?"

"Make things easier for yourself," Teddy said. "They pick you up, you might want to cop a plea."

"You're giving me ideas," Colley said, and tried a laugh. Teddy did not laugh with him.

"Colley, I don't want to have to worry about you."

"You don't have to worry."

"Colley, I never done time in my life, and I don't want to have to start worrying about it now. I got a wife and two kids, I don't want to get fucked up this late in my life."

"What do you want from me, Teddy?"

"I want your word, Colley. That if they pick you up, you don't know who was driving the car, you never saw the driver in your life."

"Yeah, okay, fine," Colley said.

"You promise?"

"I promise, yeah. Relax, willya?"

"Because, Colley ... I find out you snitched on me, I'll make sure you don't ever snitch on anybody else ever again. They send you to jail, Colley, they send me to jail, we could be in different jails a thousand miles apart, you'll *still* be sorry you snitched. I got friends in every fuckin jail in this country, they'll kill a man for a package of Bull Durham. I mean it, Colley."

"That's a good way to keep my friendship," Colley said. "Threaten me, that's a very good way."

"It ain't my fault this went wrong," Teddy said. "I wasn't in the store. It was you guys who fucked up. I coulda drove off, remember, but I came back to help you."

"Thanks," Colley said.

"Just remember," Teddy said.

"The Three Musketeers," Colley said.

"Yeah, *bull*shit," Teddy said, and hung up.

Colley slammed down the receiver. From across the room, Jeanine was watching him.

"He's worried, huh?" she said.

"Yeah. Fuck him," Colley said, and went back to the dresser and began looking through the drawers again.

In the bottom drawer he found two guns: a Smith & Wesson .32 and a Walther P-38. He loved that German gun. He'd loved it even when he was seven or eight years old, and his mother took him to the movies with her and he saw pictures about World War II, with all those Nazis carrying this very sleek and deadly handgun. He knew the gun as a Luger in those days. He used to do a German imitation, hold his right hand out with the index finger extended, "You zee vot I am holdink here in mein handt? Dot's a Luger, mein Herr, und I know how to use it."

Stamped onto the metal just below the breech of the gun were the words *Carl Walther Waffenfabrik Ulm/Do.* He didn't know what *Waffenfabrik* meant but he loved the look of the word, those fuckin Germans had style. Under that was stamped *P-38 Cal. 9mm.* The official name of the gun was the Walther P-38 Automatic, and the caliber was 9mm Luger, which is why there was a box of 9mm cartridges in the top drawer of the dresser. He hefted the gun in his hand, smiling. It was a beautiful piece, and Jocko had kept it in fine condition. Colley slipped the magazine out of the butt and loaded it with eight cartridges he took from the box in the drawer. He put another cartridge into the breechblock, and then tucked the gun into the left-hand side of his belt.

The .32 was not one of his favorites. The Model 30 was a six-shooter that came with either a two-, three- or four-inch barrel. This particular gun had a two-inch barrel, and Colley was grateful for that because it made it small enough to carry in the right-hand pocket of his pants. He had pulled his sports shirt out of his pants to cover the Walther, unbuttoning the two shirt buttons just above his belt so he could reach inside for a quick cross-draw. But the .32, even with the two-inch barrel, was a tough gun to carry tucked in your pants; you really needed a holster for it. There was no question of the sight snagging on anything in his pocket; it tapered back smoothly from the open end of the gun to a point midway between the muzzle and the cylinder. He rolled out the cylinder now, took six cartridges from the box in the drawer, loaded the gun, and then put it in his pants pocket.

He felt good again.

"Look," Jeanine said, and turned toward the window. "The sun's coming up."

Jeanine was wearing a pleated white skirt and a lime-colored blouse that picked up the color of her eyes. A white scarf was wrapped low on her forehead, blond hair falling loose on either side of her face. She wore no stockings, and she drove the small red car with her handbag on the seat beside her, white leather to match her sandals. Her right hand rested on the handbag, just over the clasp. There was forty-seven dollars in that bag; Colley had watched her count it out earlier, when they were taking stock. The car was Jocko's, a 1971 Pinto with New York plates. It had been parked in the lot behind the building, in the space allotted to apartment 5G. Jeanine was driving because Colley was a convicted felon on parole and the state wouldn't grant him a license. Jeanine's own license had been issued to her in Dallas, and was valid through September of that year.

Into a small valise Jeanine had brought up from Dallas, Colley had packed some of Jocko's sweaters and shirts, a dozen handkerchiefs and six pairs of socks. Aside from the clothes he had on his back, that was it. In the right-hand side pocket of his trousers, he was carrying the Smith & Wesson. In the waistband of his trousers, on the left-hand side, he was carrying the Walther. The boxes of cartridges for both pistols were in the glove compartment, together with the registration for the car. Colley's wallet was in his left-hand side pocket—the *hip* pocket was the sucker pocket, easily slashed with a razor blade; the best place to carry your stash was close to your balls, where you could feel anybody trying to lift it. Inside that wallet, there was sixteen dollars in cash— a ten, a five and a single. Together with what Jeanine had in the handbag, that gave them a total of sixty-three dollars. From the minute they counted up the cash this morning, Colley knew he would have to do another robbery. The only question was how soon. He thought about this all the way crosstown, and he thought about it on the way over the bridge into New Jersey. He did not want to do the robbery too early in the morning cause there'd be nothing in the till. But he wanted to do it while they were still in Jersey; he had relatives in Jersey, he'd been to Jersey before, it felt familiar to him. He was afraid of what lay beyond. He had studied the Mobil Guide map only briefly when they climbed into the car, and the names of those Southern states made him nervous.

You got those fuckin redneck cops down there, they beat the shit out of you in their crummy local jails and then sent you to work on the road gang forever. Forget about appeals, forget about paroles, you worked paving roads or cutting down forests all day long in the blazing sun and then you went back to the stockade where you ate chitlins and hog shit and ·got buggered by a big black nigger. That was what Colley thought the South was like. Southern cops and Southern jails, anyway. He'd had no real experience with either, but that was what he imagined it would mean, getting busted down there. So he wanted to do the robbery while they were still in Jersey, and before they crossed over into any of the Southern states. On the road map, it looked as if they had to cross into Pennsylvania before heading South, and he supposed Pennsylvania was okay, though he preferred Jersey. One thing for sure, Virginia sounded Southern as hell, and he didn't want no redneck Virginia sheriff shooting him in the leg with a Magnum. So it would have to be either Jersey or Pennsylvania, and of the two he preferred Jersey.

What he decided to hold up was a diner. This was Sunday, and there wasn't much choice. Unless you wanted to go in a church someplace and steal either from the poor box or the basket while it was being passed, why then, you were limited to either a place serving food or else a gas station. The gas stations nowadays, they had these safes stuck in concrete and the attendant stashed the money down inside them except for chicken feed he needed to make change, and a big sign said ATTENDANT DOES NOT KNOW COMBINATION TO SAFE, so that let out a gas station. It had to be an eating place of some kind, and Colley figured if he found himself an all-night diner, then the receipts from Saturday night might still be in the register, and maybe he could get himself a pretty good score instead of like, say, he hit a restaurant that had just opened for lunch, there'd be nothing in there but checks that had got paid at lunchtime. Anyway, it was still too early for lunch, and they'd probably be out of Jersey before lunchtime, so he kept his eye open for a diner that had a sign out front saying it was open all day and all night. He was in no hurry, long as they found one before they got out of Jersey. Never mind Pennsylvania, he had definitely decided now that it would be Jersey.

The day was bright and clear and cool after last night's rain. Great day for a robbery, you came out running, there was no danger of the car skidding off a wet pavement onto the sidewalk or into a lamppost; your driver hit the gas pedal and off you went. Jeanine was a good driver, he was grateful for that. Before he got busted and sent to Sing Sing that time, he had once used a girl driver on a job. She was a girl he was shacking up with, she seemed like a pretty level-headed broad and the times he'd been with her in a car she seemed to handle the wheel pretty good. Day of the job it was like a Keystone Kops comedy; this wasn't the job he finally got busted on, but it was a miracle it didn't turn out to be the biggest bust in the history of New York State. He had to smile, thinking of it now, though it certainly wasn't funny at the time.

He was working alone at the time; he had always worked alone before he threw in with Jocko. When he first started he even used to do his own driving, but then later he began cutting a man in for ten percent and that way had a car waiting at the curb for him. He had lost a very good driver just four weeks before he'd started shacking up with this girl; guy moved to California. The girl's name was Carter, that was her first name. She was a Wasp from New Canaan, Connecticut, she'd gone to prep school and college; she was looking for thrills, Colley guessed. Carter Hewlitt. She told Colley she'd been named after a mystery writer, Carter Dickson. She said her mother was a big mystery buff and loved reading Carter Dickson. She asked Colley if he'd ever heard of a mystery writer named Carter Dickson. Colley told her he didn't read mysteries and they got into a big argument about it. That was the night he told her he was an armed robber and that he was involved in real-life crime and didn't have time for reading any bullshit mysteries. She said, "These happen to be very *good* mysteries. These are locked-room mysteries."

He didn't know what a locked-room mystery was, and he didn't bother asking her. They started talking about going in places with a gun then, and she didn't seem shocked at all by what he did for a living, and she didn't seem scared either that maybe he'd pull a gun on her, blow her New Canaan brains out now that she knew he was a thief. In fact, she seemed very excited by all of it. He had the feeling she couldn't wait to go home and tell her mother all about the dashing crook she'd met. Be even better than Carter Dickson. Anyway, two weeks later she drove for him on this job. Everything inside the place went like clockwork. This was a place sold office supplies, copying machines, typewriters, expensive items like that. Colley figured there'd be at least a couple of grand in the register, and whereas it turned out there was only six fifty, that wasn't bad either for an hour's work, counting commuting time. It was the commuting time that nearly blew the job.

He came running out of the store with the money in a dispatch case, and he could see Carter sitting at the wheel of the rented car, her head craned over her shoulder, blond hair cut short, blue eyes alert. He heard the car starting. Great, she was on her toes, it was going like clockwork. He threw open the curbside door and climbed in, and grinned, and Carter grinned back and tossed her short blond hair and rammed the car into gear and instead of going forward, where there was a clear space, backed up into a laundry truck instead. Bam, they hit the truck, it had one of those very high bumpers, it smashed in the trunk of the car. Carter mumbled "*Shit!*" under her breath in a very refined New Canaan Wasp way, and then fiddled with the stick, and threw it out of reverse and into neutral and then into gear again, and looking straight ahead of her through the windshield, let out the clutch and stepped on the gas and the car backed up into the laundry truck again, right into the high bumper again.

By this time people were beginning to gather on the sidewalk to watch this cute button of a girl trying to park the car —they thought she was trying to *park* the fuckin thing instead of drive it away from a holdup! Colley had his gun in his hand below the window on his side, he was just waiting for the owner of the store to come out and start yelling cop. He had just beat the guy for more than six hundred bucks, the guy was either on the phone yelling cop or else he'd come out on the sidewalk and start yelling it in person to whoever'd listen. Carter tried again. She said to the gear shift, "Come on, motherfucker," in *not* such refined New Canaan Wasp tones, and then rammed the stick into what she hoped was first, and let out the clutch and stepped on the gas, and lo and behold, they were off and running at last.

"What's so funny?"

"Huh?"

"There's a smile on your face," Jeanine said.

"I was thinking of something happened a long time ago," he said.

SEVEN

The diner is here and now.

It is high noon in New Jersey and the sun is directly overhead when Jeanine pulls the red Pinto into the parking lot. There is a huge trailer truck parked over on the right, some distance away from the diagonal slashes painted onto the black asphalt in front of the diner. A smaller truck occupies two of the front-side spaces, and there are a handful of pleasure cars parked at angles on either side of it. A hand-lettered sign reads OPEN 24 HOURS. The sign is three feet high by six feet long and it is supported by a pair of high aluminum poles in front of the diner. It is the sign that caught Colley's eye when they were still a block away from the place.

On the right of the diner is a store selling automobile appliances, but it is closed; this is Sunday. On the left of the diner is an empty lot. There are a lot of used tires in the lot. Aside from the tires, the lot is scrupuluously clean. No tin cans, no trash, just the tires lying alone on their sides or piled on top of each other. It is almost as if the tires are out to pasture. The sky beyond the empty lot is clear and blue, there is not a cloud anywhere in sight. As Colley comes out of the car, he smells cooking grease. He has not had anything but a glass of orange juice and a cup of coffee early this morning. The smell of the grease almost makes him ill now. He considers going back to the car, hell with it, find a restaurant doesn't smell like this one. But the sign is huge above him, and it says OPEN 24 HOURS and that means the cash register inside there will probably be brimming full, and he wants enough money from this one job to last them all the way to Florida. He does not want to have to do a while string of jobs, especially not in the goddamn South.

He has no plan as yet. He does not know this place, he has not cased it. His normal M.O., even before he began working with Jocko, was to case a joint thoroughly before he hit, maybe even do two or three dry runs before the day of the job. That way, there were no surprises. Except for last night, when there were *two* surprises, both of them left-handed, both of them running out of the back room of the liquor store with guns in their fists. But normally, you case a joint, you learn the layout by heart, you plan your escape route, nothing's going to happen unless somebody gets dumb while you're inside and you're forced to use the gun. The way he'd been forced to use the gun last night because that bastard cop opened fire first.

The diner is all aluminum and glass, there are steps on either side of a small entrance cubicle. He chooses the steps on the right, closest to where Jeanine is waiting in the red Pinto. He opens the entrance door and sees first a telephone on the wall opposite and then the cigarette machine, and then another glass door leading into the main body of the diner. The place is air-conditioned, a wave of cool air rushes out at him as he opens the door and steps from the entrance cubicle into the diner, as though he is moving from some sort of decompression chamber. Inside the diner, directly to the right of the entrance door, is the cash register. He walks past it without seeming to give it a second glance.

There are booths on the front wall of the diner, on either

side of the entrance door. Red leatherette. Directly opposite the entrance door, running along the rear of the diner, is the counter, red leatherette stools ranged in front of it, mirror behind it. Pair of burly truck drivers at one end of the counter, both of them trying to make time with a skinny brunette waitress in a white uniform. Other end of the counter, guy in blue pants and shirt, probably the driver of the smaller truck outside. In the booths, four couples, two of them with children. Colley takes a seat at the counter. The cash register is directly behind him, he can see it in the mirror and he can hear the cashier talking into the telephone that rests on one end of the counter enclosing her space. She is talking to someone who is probably her husband. She is telling him how to work the oven so that it will clean itself. She is instructing him as to which knobs to turn and which buttons to push and which switches to activate. She speaks in a high whiny nasal voice and her instructions are impatient, as though she is talking to someone with either a very low I.Q. or very poor finger dexterity. Colley dislikes her at once. It will be a pleasure to shove the Walther P-38 in her face.

The brunette waitress knows Colley has taken a stool at the counter, but she is in the middle of a story to the two horny truck drivers, and she is not about to let a customer intrude on her private life. She finishes the story and both truck drivers burst out laughing and she stands there grinning at them, basking in the accolade of their laughter. Then she nods, having just played the Palladium to thunderous applause, and still grinning, walks to where Colley is sitting midway down the counter, his back to the cash register. On the telephone, the cashier is asking the dummy on the other end whether he understood the part about *locking* the oven, he has to make sure the oven is *locked*.

"Good afternoon, sir," the waitress says.

"Good afternoon," Colley says.

"Care to see a menu?"

"Please," he says.

He has no intention of doing the job while there are three truck drivers in the place, especially when two of them have been coming on with the scrawny brunette. All he needs is a pair of guys trying to show off for a girl, maybe making a grab for the gun when he shoves it in the cashier's face. He's not worried about the couples sitting in the booths. The two couples with children are just going to sit there and hope nobody in the family gets hurt, and the other two couples are an old man and his wife sitting in the booth closest to the register, and further down the aisle a teenage kid and his girl. Colley is only worried about the truck drivers. Not so much about the one sitting alone at the counter; he'll probably mind his own business once the gun comes out. But those other two still laughing at the joke the waitress told.

The waitress puts a menu on the counter in front of Colley, and then sets down a glass of water and a paper napkin and utensils, and then hurries on down the counter to where her enthralled audience is waiting. She leans close to the one sitting at the very end of the counter, big guy wearing a hat with some kind of button on it, and she whispers something to him, and the guy bursts out laughing, and the other guy says, "What? What'd she say?" and she whispers it all over again to him, and he starts laughing too. Then he stands up and stretches and Colley thinks he's about to leave, but instead he heads for the men's room. The minute he's gone, the one with the button on his hat engages the waitress in some serious whispered conversation.

Another waitress comes out of the kitchen. She's a country girl, plain face, straight brown hair, thick figure. She comes through the break in the counter on Colley's left and carries a loaded tray to where the old man and his wife are sitting in the booth closest to the cashier. She takes eggs off the tray, and a plate of toast, and two cups of coffee, and she asks the old man if there will be anything else. The old man looks at the food and then asks if she has any jam or marmalade. The waitress says she'll get some, and comes back through the break in the counter again and gets the marmalade and the jam from a shelf under the counter, and comes past Colley again and says to the old man, chirpily, "There you are, sir." The old man thanks her. He's a big guy, must have been a powerhouse when he was young, broad shoulders, thick chest, huge hands. His hair is white now, and he's wearing eyeglasses, and his hands shake a little when he picks up his food. Down the counter, the third truck driver calls for his check, and the country-girl waitress brings it to him. Good, Colley thinks. Now let's get rid of the other two.

The brunette is back.

"Have you decided yet, sir?" she asks.

"I'll have a pair of eggs over lightly," Colley says. "Cup of coffee and a toasted English."

"Bacon or sausage with the eggs?"

"Does it come with them?"

"Yes, sir."

"I'll have the sausage," he says, and then immediately says, "No, make it the bacon." Every time he orders sausage with his eggs, he expects them to bring Italian sausage, and then when they come out with those small skinny links, he's disappointed. This has happened to him maybe fifty times in his life, he orders sausage and then is disappointed. This time he remembers and catches himself. Trouble is, he doesn't much care for bacon. Maybe he should have told her no sausage, no bacon. But the girl is already on her way into the kitchen, pushing open the swinging door. He sees the short-order cook, guy with a beer-barrel belly, wearing a white T-shirt, sweat stains around the armpits and across his chest. Got on a little white hat, not a chef's hat, thing looks like a soldier's overseas cap, only in white. Tilted on his forehead. The door swings shut.

"You being taken care of?" the other waitress asks.

"Yeah, thanks," Colley says. Behind him, the truck driver who'd been sitting alone at the counter is paying his check. The cashier asks him, "Was everything all right, sir?" and the guy nods and takes a toothpick from a glass container on the counter. The cashier rings up the check, money comes tumbling down the cash register chute into the small metal receiving dish. Colley wishes he could see into the open drawer of the register, but the mirror isn't angled that way. "Have a nice day now," the cashier says. "You too," the truck driver says, and goes out.

In the mirror, Colley can see him buying cigarettes at the cigarette machine in the entrance cubicle. The door to the kitchen swings open again. The short-order cook is laughing and the brunette waitress has a grin on her face; she missed her calling, she should have been a stand-up comic. Down at the other end of the diner, the truck driver is coming out of the men's room, fiddling with his zipper. Colley is willing to bet eight-to-five that the guy did not wash his hands afterwards. Colley *always* washes his hands afterwards, even if he's only taken a leak. But he has noticed over the years that most guys don't bother washing their hands afterwards. He has also noticed that most guys don't even bother flushing the goddamn toilet afterwards.

In Sing Sing the cops would get mad as hell you didn't flush the toilet afterwards. Prison movies, all the prison security officers are called screws by the cons. Colley gets up to Sing Sing, he discovers the cops are called cops or pigs, just like outside. Fuckin pig is a fuckin pig no matter where he works. One cop up there, they called him the Shadow, he'd sneak up on a man before you knew what was happening. "The Shadow knows," he'd say, and give you a shot with his fuckin stick, the end of it, poke you with it hard. If he found a guy walking away from a toilet without flushing it, he was on that man in a minute, sneaked up on him like a whisper. "The Shadow knows," he'd say, and ram that fuckin stick in your arm, leave it black-and-blue for a month. Even so, guys up there didn't flush the toilets. Same as outside here.

The truck driver who came out of the toilet says, "Well, you ready to roll, Frank?"

"I was asking Jill here she maybe felt like dancing to-night," Frank says; he's the one with the button on his hat.

"What makes you think we'll be back tonight?" the other guy says.

"We're only going far as Washington, ain't we?"

"I thought we'd maybe stay over."

"I rather come back here, go dancing with Jill," Frank says.

"He's a good dancer, he tells me," Jill says. "Is that true, Eddie?"

"I never danced with him," Eddie says, and the jerks start laughing again.

Eddie and Frank, Colley thinks. Get the fuck out of here, Eddie and Frank. Get the rig rolling, lots of miles to cover before you get to Washington.

"So what's it going to be?" Jill asks. "Are we on for tonight or what?"

"What time you quit?" Frank says.

"Five o'clock."

"I'll call you before then. Soon's I see what kind of time we're making."

"You made some pretty good time right here in the diner," Jill says, and they all laugh again. She is writing out the check as she says this, the girl really missed her calling. She doesn't even look up at them, she just keeps writing, and they're practically rolling on the floor laughing at her re-mark. "Here you go, boys," she says. "Who's taking it this time?"

"I think it's my turn," Eddie says, and takes the check from her hand.

Frank gets off the stool like he is disembarking from a rodeo horse. He stretches his arms over his head, showing his belly when his shirt rides up. "I'll call you before five," he says.

"I'll be waiting," Jill says.

They laugh again, for no reason this time, and the two men

come down the aisle and stop at the cash register behind Colley. He sees them in the mirror as they pay the check. "Was everything all right, gentlemen?" the cashier says, and Eddie says, "Just dandy," and Frank says, "Best food in all Jersey," and the cashier rings up the check and chirps, "Well, thank you, I'm glad you enjoyed it. Have a nice day now."

Jeanine is sitting outside in the red Pinto. Colley is afraid the truck drivers will see her sitting there and wonder what the hell she's doing sitting there while her husband or whoever is inside the diner. He realizes he should have ordered sandwiches to go. Not something to eat inside here. So if anybody got suspicious of Jeanine, they'd think he was in here buying something for her to eat in the car. In the mirror behind the counter, he sees the truck drivers opening the door and stepping out into the entrance cubicle. Frank, the one with the button on his hat, stops at the pay telephone on the wall, and automatically feels in the coin-return chute to see if there is any change in it, cheap bastard. They both go outside. Colley waits until he hears their truck starting, hears the grinding of gears, the hiss of air brakes, the truck gearing up again as it enters the highway, and then the sound of its engine fading into the distance.

It is time to make his move.

"Eggs over lightly," Jill says, and puts the plate down in front of him, together with a second plate on which there's the toasted English. "You *did* say bacon, didn't you?" she asks.

"Yeah, bacon."

"Coffee's coming," she says, and turns to the big urn on the wall to the left of the swinging door to the kitchen, and draws a cup, and puts it on the counter next to the plate of eggs. "Cream and sugar?" she asks.

"Please," Colley says.

Behind him there is nobody at the cashier's counter; he wants to make his move immediately before a traffic jam starts. Jill picks up the sugar container from where it's sitting two stools down and carries it to Colley and sets it down on the counter in front of him. To the left of the coffee urn there's a small tray of creamers and she reaches for two of these now, her back to Colley. He is about to turn on the stool, and get to his feet, and throw the gun in the cashier's face. He is almost starting into motion when the swinging door to the kitchen flies open and the short-order cook comes out. He looks Colley directly in the face, and smiles.

"Hot back there," he says, and wipes his forearm across his upper lip. "Eggs okay?" he asks.

"Yeah, fine," Colley says, and picks up his fork. He does not want to throw down on the cashier while the short-order cook is out front. He does not know who the guy is, but sometimes in these small diners the cook is also the owner, and he doesn't want to have to shoot a man trying to protect what's in the till.

Jill is back now, she puts the two creamers in front of Colley. He rips the foil top off one of them and pours the contents into his coffee. Jill reaches into the pocket of her uniform, takes out a package of cigarettes, discovers it's empty, crumples it, and puts it in an ashtray. Then she comes through the break in the counter and goes outside to the cigarette machine. In the mirror, Colley sees her looking out at the parking lot as she rips the red cellophane strip off the top of the package. When she comes inside again, she says to the short-order cook, "Blonde sitting outside there in a red Pinto."

"Yeah?" the cook says.

"That's my wife," Colley says immediately. "She wasn't hungry."

"She should come in, cool off," Jill says.

"It's cool in the car," Colley says.

"Cool in here, too," the cook says. "Except back there by the stove."

"We didn't know it was air-conditioned," Colley says.

"Sign right on the door," the cook says.

"We didn't see it."

He's getting into an argument with the fuckin cook. What business is it of his whether Jeanine comes in or stays out or climbs up the OPEN 24 HOURS sign and throws a moon at the highway?

"You working half a day, or what?" the country-girl waitress says to the cook. She has just taken an order from one of the families at the other end of the diner, and she's back with her pad now. The cook takes the order slip from her, and looks at it, and goes back into the kitchen. Behind the counter, Jill is smoking her cigarette with obvious pleasure. The other waitress goes over to her and says, "Let me have a drag, huh?"

As Jill hands her the cigarette, Colley swings around on the stool, facing the cashier, and steps out with his right foot, and with his right hand he reaches into the shirt where the two buttons above the belt are unbuttoned. He feels the stock of the Walther, it is familiar to his hand, he knows the Walther, he has owned many of them in his lifetime. He pulls the gun out of his waistband and thumb-cocks the hammer even though he knows it can be operated by pulling the trigger. The cashier is dialing the telephone, he figures she's calling her dummy husband again to make sure he locked the oven. "Put that down," he says, and she immediately puts the receiver back on the cradle. Her eyes are wide, her lip is trembling, he figures she is about to scream. He uses Jocko's words. "See this?" he says, thrusting the gun toward her. "I'll shoot your face off you don't open the register fast. Now do it!"

The cashier is opening the register as he takes a step to the right, figuring to reach in over the counter and clean out the drawer. He catches her eye, he sees that her eye is looking past his left shoulder, and he whirls immediately and throws the gun on the country-girl waitress who already has the palm of her hand on the swinging door and is ready to push it open.

"Hold it right there!" Colley says, and the girl freezes, and now the place is deathly still because everyone in it knows there's a gunman at the cashier's counter. He reaches in over the counter and pulls stacks of bills from the cash drawer, one compartment at a time. Twenties, a good hefty stack, and then tens, and fives, and singles. He is reaching for the rolls of coins at the front of the cash drawer when the trouble comes. It comes from the least expected place; this weekend is just full of surprises. It comes from the old man.

He is standing, he is six feet four inches tall, the old fart, and he has the shoulders of a lumberjack and the chest of a wrestler and hands that could pull apart the jaws of an alligator, like that guy on the cover of the men's magazine where Colley read about being lost in the jungle. The old man's fists are already bunched, he is going to be a hero. He is seventy-five if he's a day, but he's still a big man who remembers when his enormous body surged with strength and power. His hands are shaking as he approaches, there are tears streaming down his face from behind the eyeglasses. He is crying for his lost youth and his lost power, he is crying because he's lived honestly all his life and cannot now condone this criminal act, he is crying because he suspects his foolhardy intervention may well result in his death. He is maybe crying for any one of these reasons or for all of these reasons—Colley only knows the man constitutes a threat.

Colley has killed a cop.

This old fart coming at him with his fists clenched and tears running down his face, closing the gap between them, coming closer and closer as Colley stuffs three rolls of quarters into his hip pocket, this old fart means nothing at all to him, he will waste him without remorse if the man tries to stop him.

He says, "Hold it, mister!" and just then the country-girl

waitress lets out a scream could wake the dead in every cemetery on Long Island, and Colley looks away for just an instant, and that's enough time for the old man to clamp his fingers on Colley's left wrist. "Let go," he says to the old man, and the swinging door to the back of the place opens and out comes the sweating short-order cook, and he's got a cleaver in his hand, he's going to protect his turf, he comes out of the kitchen like a fuckin Chinaman waving a cleaver in a movie about gold-rush camps.

Colley does not want to shoot the old man.

But the old man is clinging tightly to his wrist and the cook is coming through the break in the counter now, the cleaver in his hand, and there are a lot of people making noise now—the old man's wife in the booth next to the cashier's counter yelling "Harry, no, please, Harry," and down the aisle the girl with the teenage kid screaming like she's at a Stones concert. Colley can see past the old man and down the aisle to where one of the families is sitting in a booth and he sees a little boy with brown eyes and blond hair and he remembers his mother telling him that when he was small he used to have blond hair, didn't start changing to brown till he was five or six.

"Harry, let go of my fuckin hand," he says to the old man.

The old man is surprised to hear his name. He lets go of Colley's wrist and peers at him as though he's possibly made a mistake—is this someone he knows? If not, why has the man used his name so familiarly? Colley swings away from him and toward the cook, who handles the cleaver like it's a fly swatter, doesn't the son of a bitch know it's a deadly weapon? He's bringing it up over his head to swat Colley dead, what he doesn't know is that Colley's killed a cop, Colley has nothing to lose. "Mister," Colley says, and he is about to say "you are making a big mistake," but the cook is upon him, and Colley fires the gun instinctively and reflexively.

The slug takes the cook in the shoulder, he spins around

from the force of it, and slams against the counter. The old
man's mouth opens wide when he hears the explosion. He
seems about to take a step toward Colley again, but he thinks
it over and quickly changes his mind. Nobody's moving. The
cleaver is on the floor. The cook is bent over one of the stools
now, and blood is streaming down his arm the way it was
Jocko's last night.

"Okay now," Colley says.

He backs toward the door.

"Okay," he says again.

He opens the door and runs outside. Jeanine has already
started the car. He knows that what he should do is run for
the car, get into the car. But the car is headed for Florida in
the month of August and Colley doesn't want that kind of
heat, and he doesn't want the kind of heat that will come the
minute Jill tells the cops they're driving a red Pinto, probably
at the window right this minute copying down the license-
plate number, he is tempted to turn and take a look. He does
not want to be in a car that's halfway or maybe *all* the way
identified, and he does not want to be going to Florida in the
month of August, but most of all, he does not want to be with
Jeanine any more. Jeanine scares the hell out of him. Jeanine
drives with her legs wide-spread, the pleated white skirt high
on her thighs, and he can smell brimstone rising from her
cunt, and the whiff reminds him of the devil's laughter in the
kitchen, Jocko bleeding out his life—no, he does not want to
go with Jeanine to Florida or anyplace else on earth.

He begins running in the opposite direction.

He does not even hesitate to see what kind of look is on
her face. He is running northward, and he knows she cannot
turn the car anything but southward once she pulls out of
that parking lot, there's a divider separating the highway
lanes, that's it, my dear. He runs across the southbound lane
now, the traffic is light, this is Sunday, and he leaps the
divider and then crosses the northbound lane and runs into
a patch of woods on the other side of the highway. He does

not know where he is in New Jersey but he suspects he is not close to any sprawling metropolis like New York or even Newark, where his Aunt Tessa lives. As he enters the woods, he is reminded again of that story in the men's magazine, the guy lost in the jungle, and he wonders if civilization will be his Aunt Tessa's house in Newark, New Jersey. He knows one thing for certain. He is not going to any fuckin Fort Myers, Florida, he is going to New York City, man, the big apple, the *only* fuckin town in the entire universe. He is going to cut through these woods parallel with the road, and he is going to come out of them maybe a mile north of where he went in, and he is going to stick out his thumb and head for New York. He suddenly bursts out laughing, thinking of Jeanine starting up the Pinto and waiting for him to get in but instead he runs off in the opposite direction. He wonders if they'll tie Jeanine in with the robbery, throw her in the local hoosegow. Jersey cop comes over to her, "Well, well, miss, so you was an accomplice in a holdup, huh, miss?"

Laughing, Colley runs through the woods.

He is happier than he has been since straddling that fence in the Bronx and thumbing his nose at the cops chasing him. Not *really* thumbing it, of course, but letting them know just what he thought of them by hanging there against the sky and daring them. He is telling Jeanine what he thinks of her now. Big fuckin Amazon scaring him to death with that laugh boiling up from her gut, where'd she get that fuckin laugh? Probably had a hoodoo inside her, made her stab Jocko that way in a million places, broke the fuckin knife on his head, Jesus! Leaves are slapping his face as he runs. There are insects in the woods, and they are biting him, he is not used to this shit. He is a city boy, yessir, born and raised in that city across the river there, and that is where he's going, back to the city, back to where he will be safe again, never mind Fort Myers. She loves Fort Myers so much, let *her* go to Fort Myers, this kid's going to New York, yessir, going to make his fame and fortune there. Maybe go in the pimping trade with Benny, sign on as an apprentice, his job'd be breaking in the new girls.

He laughs again.

He is having a gay old time in these fuckin woods even though the leaves are slapping him and the insects are biting him. He is free of her, he has shaken that blond hoodoo off his back, he has turned her loose in the world where she can stab anybody comes near her, just so long as it's not *him*. Stab them all, sister, give it to them. Just stay far away from yours truly, Joe College with the crew cut. He laughs at the idea of wearing a crew cut. He is already planning on dropping in on old Benny, knocking on the door, maybe the Jewgirl opens it, this time she doesn't recognize him. She's still wearing the Arab thing, she looks out at him, doesn't recognize him with the crew cut. Wouldn't recognize him anyway cause Benny's got her stoned to the gills, Benny comes to the door, looks out, Colley says, "How you do, sir, I'm working my way through college selling heroin." Benny busts out laughing cause till that minute he don't realize the guy with the crew cut is Colley.

He has probably run about three or four blocks through the woods now, he can't be sure. If back there at the diner they have latched on to Jeanine, they are probably asking her questions about who she is and who the man is held up the place and shot the cook, fuckin dope with his cleaver over his head, and that will give Colley time. Time is what he needs. Time to run the mile or so in these woods and come out someplace further north and then thumb a ride to the city. He keeps running until he is exhausted, and then he drops to the ground and lies there breathing hard. In a little while he sits up and begins pulling bills from his pockets, the money he stole from the diner. There is three hundred and twelve dollars, including the three rolls of quarters. He figures that is not too bad. Counting the sixteen he already had, that makes three twenty-eight.

The woods are very still.

He notices all at once that the woods are very still, and he remembers again the story he read in the men's magazine. His heart is thudding heavily in his chest, he can hear each separate beat, can feel his own pulse in his ears, and is fearful for a moment that everything will remain forever in this hyped-up, slowed-down state. Everything will be a robbery forever, nothing will ever return to normal, they even will bury him in excruciating detail, a rose will fall into his open grave in twisting slow motion, hanging on the air, hanging, hanging, and finally dropping onto the black coffin top. He can hear his watch ticking noisily in the stillness of the woods, and then he hears the snapping of twigs and sees the leaves parting ahead an instant before the beast comes into the clearing.

The beast is a German shepherd, jowls pulled back over his fangs, growl rumbling up from his gut and into his throat. He runs three feet into the clearing, there is a second and a half of heart-stopping terror during which Colley scrambles to his feet, and then the beast is airborne. He hurls himself at Colley with jaws wide, saliva dripping from his fangs; he is all head and teeth. Colley throws his right arm up, bent at the elbow, the forearm across his chin and throat. The jaws close on his arm. He does not feel pain at first, he is too frightened. He sees only the beast's black nose dripping snot, and he sees the black-edged jowls and the teeth closing on his arm, joining on his arm, and he sees the sudden gush of blood, but he feels no pain for an instant.

And then the pain strikes.

It is excruciating, dozens of sharp needles penetrating his flesh, each a separate bleeding wound, each blinding in its intensity, he is certain he will faint. He wants to reach for the Walther in his belt, reach into the open two buttons and pull the gun free in a cross-draw, but the beast is fastened onto his right arm, he is going to faint, the fuckin beast will eat him alive in the jungle. He knows he is toppling backward and falling to the ground, and he knows this is the wrong thing to do, knows the beast will go for his throat, bite into his jugular, send his blood spurting up onto the floor of the forest. But he is helpless to stop his backward fall, the beast must weigh at least two hundred pounds, he is the biggest dog Colley has ever seen in his life, and he will not let go of Colley's arm, he is chewing on it like a fuckin soup bone, and blood is flying in the air as Colley falls to the bright-green ground, flailing his arm, trying to shake the dog loose.

He cannot reach the gun in his right-hand pocket, he cannot reach the .32 Smith & Wesson, which gun he doesn't like anyway. He fumbles with the bottom of the sports shirt hanging out of his trousers, trying to lift it up over the butt of the Walther, but the dog is kicking at him with his back legs, Colley is going to faint, he feels his life gushing out of him between the beast's jaws. The butt of the gun is facing in the wrong direction, he grasps nothing but air at first. He has managed to get the shirt up over the butt, and now he tries to twist his left hand so that he can pull the fuckin gun out of his belt, turn it, twist it somehow into firing position before the dog kills him. He knows the dog will kill him. The only thing that can save his life is the gun.

The dog lets go of his arm for a moment, and the pain is instantly eased, and then the dog is snapping at his face and biting at his shoulder, climbing all over him as he rolls over the green floor of the forest, staining the grass and the weeds with blood. The butt of the Walther is in his hand now, his left hand, he says under his breath, "*Here,* you son of a bitch!" and shoves his hand and the gun into the dog's open mouth as the dog comes at him again. The dog smells of horror and of death, the dog smells of hair and shit. He squeezes the trigger inside the dog's mouth just as the jaws clamp shut on his wrist. The explosion takes off the back of the dog's head, fur and bone and blood flying into the air, sunlight glistening on them. It is like the back of the cop's head. He watches in fascination. He is afraid the dog will bite his left hand off at the wrist, but there is almost no head left to the dog now, the nine-millimeter slug has taken away half of that fuckin triangular head and the jaws have gone lax and Colley pulls back his hand as the dog slides in slow motion to the forest floor. Colley fires at him again, and then again. He keeps firing. Something warns him that he is wasting ammunition, the cartridges for the Walther *and* the .32 are still back there in the glove compartment of the Pinto. But he keeps firing into the lifeless body of the beast nonetheless, watching patches of fur and gristle and blood fly into the air. The gun clicks empty. He throws the gun at the dog. He has never even been able to throw a ball straight with his right hand, and this is his left hand and he is throwing a gun, not a ball, and of course he misses. He kicks out at the dog, his foot colliding with the snot-running black snout, the back of the dog's head gone, he wants to kick out all the dog's fuckin teeth. He keeps kicking at the head.

Then he collapses to the ground, and rolls over onto his back and tries to catch his breath. He is afraid he will choke to death if he does not start breathing normally soon. His left wrist isn't bleeding at all, the dog barely had his teeth on it before the Walther went off inside his mouth. But his right arm is bleeding very badly. His right arm looks like a piece of meat in a butcher shop, his right arm looks as raw as Jocko's throat did when Colley looked into it earlier tonight. The dog's teeth were easily as sharp as the knife Jeanine used, and Colley is certain he will die the way Jocko died, leaking blood from the hundreds of teeth slashes on his arm. He knows he has to stop the blood, and he decides he should take off his shirt and wrap it around his arm. But he is trembling so hard and fighting so painfully to catch his breath that all he can do is lie on his back on the trampled weeds, his eyes closed, the sunlight flickering on his lids.

The sun goes out.

He thinks he is dead.

He thinks his heart has stopped beating, his heart actually *does* stop beating in that instant when the blackness closes on his lids. He opens his eyes at once. The man standing there against the sun, blocking the sun, is wearing dirt-stained bib overalls, no shirt under them. His arms are long and thin and covered with hair. He is holding a shotgun in his hands, the barrel cradled on the palm of his left hand, the stock in the crook of his right arm, his right index finger inside the trigger guard and curled around the trigger. Colley looks first at the shotgun and then up at the man's face.

It is thin and gaunt, the cheeks are sunken, there is a four-day beard bristle on the man's jaw, the man looks like the fuckin rednecks Colley has seen in the movies—but this is New Jersey, what is a redneck doing this far north? The man's eyes are a pale blue. Looking up into his eyes, Colley can hardly see any whites at all, the blue seems to consume the eyeballs, Colley is sure it is a trick of the light in the forest. But as the man continues to stare down at him, his mouth unmoving, his eyes unflickering, Colley begins to think this is not a man at all but is instead Death, the same Death ticking in the unseen clock in Jocko's apartment, the same Death that's been hounding him since nine o'clock last night when he shot and killed a fuckin police officer in a liquor store in the Bronx.

He does not know what Death wants of him, except his life.

The man suddenly reverses the shotgun, grasping the barrel in both hands. "You son of a bitch," he says softly, and swings the stock at Colley's head.

There is a clock ticking.

The side of Colley's face is throbbing where the shotgun stock collided with his cheekbone. The Smith & Wesson has been taken from his side pocket, he is aware at once of the absence of its bulk. The other gun, the Walther, is probably still in the woods. He feels suddenly naked. He is lying on the floor in one corner of a wooden shack. His arm is crusted with dried and drying blood. No one has cleaned it, no one has dressed it. A woman is sitting beside him and above him in a straight-backed wooden chair. She is in her late fifties, her eyes are blue, her hair is gray. She is wearing only a soiled slip. She smiles when he opens his eyes. The clock is on a shelf behind her head. The time is ten minutes past three. He knows it is P.M. and not A.M. because there is sunshine outside the window to the left of the shelf.

"He's out burying the dog," the woman says. She is still smiling. There is a gold tooth in the lower left-hand corner of her mouth. She has long thin arms like the man's and her knuckles are raw and red. The shotgun is leaning against the seat of the chair, the barrel not six inches from her right hand. "Shouldn'ta killed that dog," she says. "He loved that dog like his own son. Why'd you kill the dog?"

"He attacked me," Colley says.

"You had no right in them woods," the woman says.

Colley's arm aches. The bleeding has stopped, but he is worried about gangrene or blood poisoning or whatever— things he has only heard about and has no real knowledge of, except that he knows they can result from gunshot wounds and probably from dog bites as well—Jesus, does he have to worry about *rabies,* too?

"What were you doin in the woods?" the woman says.

"Taking a walk."

"That's posted property. Didn't you see the posted signs?"

"No. Listen, have you got something I can put on my arm here? I'm afraid it might get infected."

The woman shakes her head. "Shouldn'ta killed that dog," she says, ignoring his request. "You're gonna be in for it, he gets back."

He wonders if he should make a play for the shotgun now, before the man gets back. He does not think the man will kill him, because if he was going to do that, he'd have done it in the woods. But he can feel the throbbing bruise on the side of his face where the stock connected with his cheekbone, and he does not want to suffer a beating when the man returns. It has been his experience that bad situations only get worse. If you do not make your move when something is just starting, then everything gets out of hand later on and it is impossible to make a move that will change the picture. The woman is sitting there smiling, she seems frail enough, he decides he will make his move now, try for the gun, blow her brains out if she gives him any trouble. The woman anticipates him. She has seen something in his eyes, she has looked into his head and seen the wheels turning. She lifts the shotgun and points it at him and says only, "Don't."

"Relax," he says.

"Oh, I'm relaxed," she says, and smiles. "It's *you* better relax, mister."

He looks at her face. She looks like a hillbilly, what are hillbillies doing here in Jersey, he thought this was a civilized state? Her hair looks like rats are nesting in it, there is something crusted on her right check, pus or whatever, her lips are thin and cracked, the eyes are blue and cold and hard over the thin long nose and the smiling mouth, gold tooth in the corner. Behind her the clock ticks away minutes, throws minutes into the room onto the dirty floor; there are minutes twisting and turning on the floor.

"What do you want with me?" he says.

"Me? I don't want nothin with you."

"Then put up the piece and let me go."

"Sam told me to keep you here."

"I've got money," Colley says. "I've got more than three hundred dollars," he says, and reaches into his pocket and discovers the money is gone. "Where's my money?" he asks the woman.

"Sam took it. That was a valuable dog," she says.

"That was a *killer* dog," Colley says.

"Even so," the woman says, and shrugs and smiles. "He was a valuable dog."

"Okay if I get up?"

"No, you better stay right where you are."

"I'm cramped, I want to get up."

"That's too bad," she says. "Stay put."

"Fuck you, lady," he says, and is about to stand up when the smile drops from her mouth, the gold tooth winks out. He thinks for a moment she will squeeze the trigger and end it all right then and there. He is immediately sorry for what he said, but he is also too late. She comes up out of the chair, and before he can turn away, before he even realizes what her intention might be, she kicks out at his wounded arm. She is wearing worn and faded, laceless white sneakers, and her kick does not hurt as much as it might if she were wearing Army boots, but it sends immediate pain shooting into his skull nonetheless. He tries to roll away from her, but she lifts her foot and stamps on his arm, and then stamps on it again as if she is trying to squash a persistent bug, until finally he manages to turn the arm away from her so she cannot reach it. Her legs are unshaven, her slip is soiled, there is pus on her face, she lives in a filthy shack in the woods—but she objects to his language. She is a censor, this fuckin hag, and she has stamped her opinion onto his arm, causing it to bleed again, making her point much more emphatically than if she had, for example, merely washed out his mouth with soap. Satisfied, she sits again. Against the wall, Colley whimpers in pain.

The door opens.

He cannot see the door from where he is lying in the corner, but he hears it opening, and then he feels the floor-boards moving with the weight of the man who comes into the room.

"Over there," a voice says, and he recognizes it as the voice of the man who hit him with the shotgun, and he realizes there are two men, or maybe more, coming into the room—their combined weight is what causes the floorboards to tremble beneath him.

"He's got a dirty mouth," the woman says.

"He get funny with you, Myra?"

"No, but he's got an awful dirty mouth," she says, and laughs.

Colley keeps his hurt arm pressed to the wall, fearful she will try to step on it again. He wonders what he is doing in this shack with these hillbillies. Before the hound came leaping out of the woods Colley'd been counting his money, which was a civilized enterprise, and before that he was running and laughing. Now there are three hillbillies standing around him—the woman Myra with her hairy legs and her soiled slip, and the man Sam in his dirt-encrusted bib overalls, and another man wearing glasses and a pair of khaki pants and a sports shirt patterned with big red flowers. Fat man. Fat legs bunched in khaki pants, fat arms hanging from the short sleeves of the shirt, fat face. Cigar in his mouth. He takes the cigar out now and looks down at Colley.

"What's your name?" he says.

"What's yours?" Colley answers, and sits up.

"Will Hollip," the man answers, surprising Colley.

"I'm Jack Wyatt," Colley says, giving them Jocko's name; what the hell, Jocko is dead.

"Mr. Wyatt," Will says, "you shot Sam's dog here for no good reason . . ."

"The dog attacked me," Colley says.

"You were on posted land," Will says.

"That don't give anybody the right to turn a killer dog loose on me."

"That's the gentlest dog ever did live," Sam says.

"He sure is," Colley said. "You see what he did to my arm?" he says, and stands up and shoves the arm at Will. "How you like that, Mr. Hollip? Does that look like I killed him for no good reason?"

"Sam says—"

"Sam wasn't there, Sam didn't get there till it was all over. And while we're on Sam, look what he did to my face here."

"You do that, Sam?" Will says.

"He killed my dog," Sam says.

"And also Sam took three hundred and twenty-eight dollars from my pocket . . ."

"That's a lie, Will."

"And two pistols for which I have licenses. Carry licenses. They're restricted to hunting, but they're carry licenses, anyway." He is lying, but he doesn't think Will Hollip will realize it. He doesn't know who Will Hollip is, but he is pleading to him now as he would to a higher authority, as though he's been busted for the offense of killing a vicious dog, and has been brought to trial for it, and is now brilliantly pleading his own case to a benign fat judge who only needs a camera around his neck to be a tourist in Hawaii.

"You take two guns from this man?" Will asks.

"I did, Will. They'll help pay for the dog."

"If that mutt cost more than five dollars . . ." Colley says.

"Just watch it, mister," Sam says.

"Well, Mr. Wyatt," Will says, "I can understand how maybe the dog scared you, he's a big dog. But—"

"*Scared* me? He came flying out of the woods . . ."

"But I got to agree with my brother here that what you did was illegal. Sam, we better take him over to the trooper station."

Colley looks at fat little pot-bellied Will Hollip in his tight-fitting khakis and his flowered shirt, and he sees the resemblance now, the same blue eyes, the same shaggy brows —Will is simply a short, stout version of his big brother Sam. The three of them are watching him now, maybe waiting for him to make the move he should have made before it got too late, the way it is beginning to look too late now. Sam Hollip has taken the shotgun from Myra, who is either his wife or his sister, Colley can't tell which. There seems to be no family resemblance except for maybe the hairy legs. He has hung the shotgun casually over his arm, but his finger is inside the trigger guard and Colley suspects he will not hesitate to shoot him if he makes a break for it. Or, if Sam doesn't care to waste ammunition, he might simply hit Colley with the stock of the gun again, this time maybe *breaking* the cheek-bone, whereas last time he merely bruised it. Colley does not want to get shot, nor does he want his cheek broken or even bruised. He only wants to get out of here.

If these dopes take him to the troopers with a complaint that he killed their hound, it'll take the troopers ten seconds flat to realize that Colley is the man who held up the diner a mile and a half down the road, and then it'll take them another ten seconds to find the teletype the New York fuzz undoubtedly sent out, and here we have Nicholas Donato, folks, bona-fide cop killer—is there maybe a reward? old Sam Hollip will ask. Colley cannot allow them to take him in. He cannot allow these country hicks to be the cause of his going back to jail forever. Because this time it *will* be forever. He has killed a cop, and for that you get either forever in jail or else you get the death penalty. That is one of the crimes you can still be executed for in the glorious, glamorous State of New York—cop-killing. Yes, the sentence for murdering a "peace officer," as he is described in the criminal law, can be death, provided "there are no substantial mitigating circum-stances which render the sentence of death unwarranted." Kill a cop, and you are in trouble. Colley was in trouble even before he met these dopes. Now he is in even *more* trouble because these dimwits are going to lead him at gunpoint into the arms of the law and there goes the ball game.

He decides to make his move. His right arm is dangling uselessly, and dripping blood onto the wooden floor of the shack. As soon as he gets out of here, he will have to do something about the arm. But meanwhile, he has to get out of here. He has already tangled with old Sam Hollip, blue-eyed Death himself, and with the wiry, hairy woman who is either his sister or his wife—Colley would not be at all sur-prised if she's his sister, and he's humping her nightly here in the middle of the woods; ladies who can't stand the word "fuck" are sometimes ladies who are not too terribly shocked by incest. Either way, husband and wife or brother and sister, they are tough customers and he is not eager to come up against either one of them ever again. Which leaves fat Will Hollip, brother to Sam, perhaps brother or at least brother-in-law to Myra, fat Will Hollip of the tight khakis and flowered shirt. How do I get to you, Will? How do I use you to get out of this dumb situation that can cost me my life?

He does not know.

The shotgun is looking him in the eye, but he has got to make his move because the next thing that will happen is he'll be taken out to a car or a truck and driven to the state-trooper station. Or else he'll be marched through the woods to the highway and then to the trooper station, but either way he is going to be in the hands of the cops, and this time it will be forever. There is no way he can possibly explain to a judge and jury that he was returning fire in self-defense in that liquor store. They will say that's very nice to hear, Mr. Donato, but you shouldn't have been inside that liquor store committing a felony in the first place, next case.

He decides to faint. All he wants to do is get his hands on that shotgun. He's got only one good arm, and that's enough to hold a shotgun and fire it, provided it's been cocked—he suddenly wonders if the shotgun has been cocked. He is not as familiar with shotguns or rifles as he is with handguns, but this one looks like a slide-action repeater, and he wonders if the slide has been pulled back, cocking the gun. With only one good arm he will not be able to fiddle around with the slide and then get the gun in position again after he has it in his possession. He hopes it is cocked. He is about to give an Academy Award-winning performance, and the Oscar is the shotgun and he doesn't want it to turn out to be brass instead of gold.

"Look, Mr. Hollip," he says to Will, "that dog really did try to . . ." and he stops talking and puts his hand to his forehead, and then sways slightly, and then says "Uh, uh, uh," like that, and leans in against Will and collapses against him. Will doesn't know whether to grab him or what, he doesn't want to get blood on his nice Hawaiian shirt. He keeps backing away and flapping his hands until it's obvious he either has to catch Colley or let him fall flat on his face to the floor. He decides that's what he wants to do, let Colley fall flat on his face, so he opens his arms wide and takes a very quick step backward, and Colley tumbles forward as realistically as he can without getting splinters in his face. Sam still has the shotgun. Twenty-gauge. Put a nice hole in a man if it's fired up close.

"He's out like a light," Sam says.

"What you want to do with him?" Will asks.

"Give me a hand, we'll drag him over in the corner again."

Colley listens. He is listening for the sound of the shotgun being placed against the wall, the wooden stock hitting the wooden floor, or else being put on the table, the sound of metal scraping against wood or enamel. He is listening but he does not hear anything he hopes to hear. He wonders if he has made the wrong move, and then he begins to think Sam has simply handed the shotgun to his sister or his wife or whoever she is, the way he did earlier when he went out to bury the dog and fetch old brother Will. They are dragging Colley into the corner of the room. They are hurting him the way they are holding him, but he cannot scream or even wince, he is supposed to be unconscious. He has pulled this big fainting routine because he wants to get his hands—his *hand* actually, his one good hand, his left hand—on that shotgun, and now he doesn't know where it is or who has it and he hears Sam telling Will they'll need some rope, they'll have to tie this sumbitch up.

It is getting worse, it is only getting worse. He did not make his move when he was supposed to make it, whenever *that* might have been, and now it is about to get worse, they are going to tie him up and leave him to bleed to death in the corner. Their voices retreat just a little way from him, they are going to look for rope to tie up the city slicker. He opens his eyes. He can see Myra's hairy legs across the room

level with his line of vision, laceless white sneakers, and he
can see just a little past them to where Sam is standing, can
see the blue overall bottoms rolled up over the high tops of
his brown workshoes, but he cannot see Will Hollip nor can
he see the shotgun.

"Let me get a stool for you," Myra says, and suddenly the
stock of the shotgun appears magically beside one sneakered
foot. She is resting the shotgun on the floor, leaning it against
something, a cupboard or a table or a chair, he doesn't care
what—it is there on the floor some fifteen feet from where he
is lying in the corner. Myra leaves his frame of vision. He sees
only Sam's big shoes pointed in his direction now. Sam is
waiting for Myra to get a stool. Rope has to be on a shelf
someplace Sam can't reach, loving wife or sister is making
it easy for him. Sneakered feet again coming back into the
frame, Myra puts down the stool. Sam climbs up on the stool,
Colley sees only the backs of his high-topped shoes now.
That means Sam's back is to him, Will is Christ only knows
where, and the shotgun is still leaning against something, its
stock on the floor.

Colley makes his move all at once. No slow and steady
crawling across the floor, no sneaky tactics, he gets to his feet
in a crouch, like a track star about to break from the starting
line, and he's off in the same instant, sprinting across the
wooden floor toward the shotgun. The gun is leaning against
a square table, he can see the table now, and he can see the
gun, and he only hopes the thing has been cocked, because
otherwise he is dead. Myra has turned from watching Sam,
who is fishing in a cabinet high up on the wall. She sees
Colley crossing the room, and she knows just what he's
heading for, and she grabs the shotgun by the barrel just
below the sight, and is bringing it up with her left hand, her
right hand reaching for the stock when Colley gets to her. He
doesn't bother making a grab for the gun. Instead he punches
her in the stomach, as hard as he can with his left hand, and
she lets out a grunt and drops the gun, and staggers back

against the counter. Sam has turned at the sound of the running and the scuffling, and he's about to step down off the stool when he sees that Colley has picked up the shotgun and is holding it in just one hand, forward of the stock, his left index finger inside the trigger guard and on the trigger.

"Hold it," Colley says.

Fat Will is at the sink on Colley's left. He has been watching all this with some interest and much trepidation. He has probably never liked his brother's vicious dog, nor his brother's hairy wife or sister as the case may be, and he likes even less the notion of having a big shotgun hole put in him by a man who is bleeding and probably desperate. He just stays there at the sink, watching. His eyes tell Colley he hardly knows these two people, even though he is certainly related by blood to one of them and probably to both. On the stool, Sam says, "Easy now, boy."

"Easy, *shit,*" Colley says.

"Easy now."

"Get over here, Will!" Colley says.

"I didn't do nothin," Will says.

Sam has a coil of clothesline in his hands. He stands on the stool like a man who's supposed to be making a speech in Union Square, probably a speech about how inhuman it is to hang people. There he is with the rope, ready to demonstrate his propostion, but all he's got by way of a crowd is a skinny hairy lady, a fat man in a flowered sports shirt, both relatives, and a stranger who has already killed his dog and who is looking at him now as if he's ready to kill him, too. Colley *would* like to kill the son of a bitch. It is Sam Hollip who allowed a vicious animal to roam free in the woods, it is Sam Hollip who smacked him in the face with a shotgun stock. Colley would like to kill him and Myra both; he has not forgotten that Myra stamped up and down on his arm a few times, nice lady.

"Give me that rope," he says to Sam. "Get down off that stool. Will, you come here."

"I didn't do nothin," Will says again.

"Get over here, Myra. With your brother here."

"He's my husband," Myra says.

"Congratulations," Colley says, and hands the clothesline to Will. "Will, I don't have to tell you I want them tied so they can't get loose," he says.

"That's right," Will says, and nods.

"You understand me, don't you, Will? If they can free their hands . . ."

"No, no," Will says, "I'll tie them real tight."

"Good, you do that," Colley says. "I want them back to back."

"Myra, would you step over here, please?" Will says. He sounds very tired.

Colley would prefer doing the tying-up himself, but the fingers on his right hand feel numb, and his arm is bleeding again from Myra's fancy footwork. He thinks maybe the numbness is psychological, but the blood certainly isn't. He does not even want to look at the arm. He will have to do something about the arm, but first things first. He watches as Will ties Sam's hands and then Myra's hands, and then wraps brother and sister-in-law with clothesline as though he is wrapping a pair of back-to-back mummies for burial. "Good and tight," Colley says.

He remembers the times he's been busted, that first time he shot Luis Josafat Albareda in the throat, and then the time he was running away after the tailor-shop holdup and the cops surprised him. Both times they clamped the cuffs on his wrists like they wanted to go clear through to the bone. The way a pair of handcuffs is made, there's a sawtooth edge that slides into the other side of the cuff. You squeeze the cuff onto a person's wrist, the sawtooth edge is engaged and can't be reversed unless you unlock the cuff. Makes it quick and easy for a cop to slam the cuffs on a man, zing, zing. They throw a cuff on one wrist, they whip your arms behind your

back, they squeeze the cuff on the other wrist, you think your
arms are going to break behind your back there, and you
think your circulation is going to stop, you are going to die
of your blood stopping there at your wrists.

They throw you in the squad car like you were a plastic
bag of garbage.

The minute those cuffs are on your wrists, you stop being
a human being. To a cop, you are the perpetrator. Perpetrator is a word out of police manuals. It is not a human being.
You are the perpetrator all the while you are in a police
station, and after they book you and take you downtown to
the Criminal Courts Building to be arraigned, you become
the accused and/or the defendant, and once you are convicted and sentenced, you become the prisoner. When you
add all those things together you are nothing but a plastic
bag of garbage.

"Tighter," he says.

Outside the shack, there are rows and rows of corn and
what looks like cabbage. He has left Myra and her husband
Sam trussed on the floor back to back, and he has locked Will
in the storage shed behind the shack. He is wearing the only
clean clothes he could find in the whole filthy place, a pair
of blue trousers and a white shirt and a plaid sports jacket.
Under the sleeve of the sports jacket, he has wrapped a
pillowcase around his arm. He thinks the blood has stopped,
but he is not sure.

From Sam's bib overalls he has taken the three hundred
and twenty-eight dollars Sam stole from him earlier, and he
has also taken the Smith & Wesson revolver. There are six
bullets in that revolver, and he can fire it very nicely, thanks,
with just his left hand. He would have taken whatever other
money Sam had, but Sam didn't have a nickel of his own. His
brother Will had seventeen dollars and forty cents, and Colley relieved him of the bills but left the forty cents as a tip

for his assistance in tying up Mr. and Mrs. Sam Hollip, newlyweds in Colley's mind, since he's only learned of their marriage quite recently.

The pickup truck is parked near what looks like a pigpen, but there aren't any pigs in it. Sam has promised him the keys are in the ignition. He has told Sam that if the keys *aren't* in the ignition, if he has to come all the way back here again and go through Sam's pockets again for the keys, why, he will just leave Sam on the floor with a broken head. But the keys are here, and Colley starts the truck and feels a sharp pain in his arm, and wonders if he's going to be able to drive the thing. He wants to find a phone booth. He has to get some help for his arm. There was no telephone in the shack, and no directory, and he wants to find one now so he can call a doctor and get some help. He doesn't know what town he's in, except that it's somewhere near the Pennsylvania border, and he doesn't know if it's big enough to have a hospital, but he doesn't want to go to a hospital anyway. That's where he *should* go, to a hospital emergency room, he knows that. But he suspects a hospital would have to report an animal bite, don't they have to call the Board of Health or something? For rabies? He doesn't know, but he can't take the chance. All he wants is a regular doctor, general practitioner. He'll go in, tell the doctor he got bit by a dog, tell him the dog's dead. Doctor wants to report it, he'll do it tomorrow, this is Sunday, no rush. Be different at a hospital, everybody crisp and efficient in white.

Colley puts in the clutch and manipulates the gear shift till he feels certain he knows where reverse and the various drive positions are. He backs around the pigpen toward the side of the shack. The place is silent. Sun is shining on the cornstalks, the sky behind them is blue and cloudless. He brakes the truck, shifts into first, and drives down the dirt road to the highway. At the highway, he turns right, heading north, driving past the diner he held up not four hours ago. There are no police cars outside; the hubbub probably died down a long while ago. He wonders if they've taken Jeanine into custody.

If they've got her in custody, they'll be asking her what Colley meant in the diner when he said "That's my wife." She'll tell them that's all bullshit, she never saw the man in her life, she was sitting out there deciding whether to go in for a hamburger. But they'll search the car, which is their right because a crime was committed and they have good reason to believe she was an accomplice, since the holdup man *did* after all say she was his wife. They'll search the car without a warrant, they won't need a warrant, and they'll find two boxes of cartridges in the glove compartment—a box of 9mm Parabellums and a box of .32 Longs. And they'll already know from Ballistics that the bullet that hit the short-order cook in the shoulder was a 9mm Parabellum, so already there's a connection between the woman who was sitting in the Pinto outside and the man who was in there shooting up the joint.

But more important than that, they will also find in the glove compartment an automobile registration for the Pinto, and it will be made out to one Jack William Wyatt. And if there were any good prints on the gun Jocko dropped in the liquor store last night, and if the New York fuzz got a make on him from the F.B.I. files, why then, a teletype went out describing Jack William Wyatt, alias Jocko Wyatt, alias Jockstrap Wyatt, as he was known in Texas prisons. And if the New Jersey cops are on the ball, then they will know at once that they've got hold of the wife of a man who held up a liquor store and was an accomplice in the crime of murder. It does not take Sherlock Holmes to look at a driver's license. Jeanine Wyatt, it says on her license, they will have looked at her license long before they searched the car. If they can't make a connection from that alone, then they are in the wrong business, they should give up law enforcement and begin selling storms and screens.

He figures she's in trouble.

He does not give a damn. He hopes in fact that they will find Jocko's body and nail her for the murder and lock her up and throw away the key. He does not want to run into her ever again. He can still remember her laugh, and it makes him shiver now. Up ahead, he sees a phone booth on the side of the road.

He has to get help for his arm.

The doctor who opens the door looks a lot younger than he sounded on the telephone. His name is Emory Hughes. He has coal-black hair and brown eyes. He is perhaps forty, forty-five years old and he looks like a tennis player or a skier. Colley wouldn't know a tennis player or a skier if he woke up in bed with one at Wimbledon or St. Moritz, but he's seen actors *pretending* to be tennis players or skiers on television, and this doctor, this Emory Hughes, looks like one of those actors. Usually the actors drink beer afterwards. The beers are interchangeable. Colley can never remember which beer the actors are drinking after they get off the squash court or the sailboat, or after they finish climbing the mountain or jumping out of an airplane without a parachute. He wonders if Dr. Emory Hughes drinks beer. He wonders if Dr. Emory Hughes is an actor pretending to be a doctor, the way he himself is an armed robber named Nicholas Donato pretending to be a tourist named Steve Casatelli. He has chosen the name Casatelli because he is sure that when he talks he sounds Italian. Carter Hewlitt from New Canaan, Connecticut, once told him that the minute he opens his mouth his heritage is immediately apparent. Those were her exact words. That was before she fucked up on the getaway that time. He has chosen the name Steve only because he likes that name, always wished his mother had named him Steven instead of Nicholas. Or Stephen with a p-h, that would have been just as good.

"Mr. Castelli," the doctor says, getting the name wrong.

You give somebody a name ends in a, i or o, they immediately pronounce it wrong.

"Casatelli," Colley says, correcting him, and wondering suddenly if the mispronunciation was a trap. Does the good doctor suspect that this man here with the gnawed arm is not indeed a tourist traveling through the Garden State of New Jersey, but is instead an armed robber who knocked off a diner five miles south of here at twelve noon?

"Excuse me," the doctor says, and smiles. "Let's take a look at that arm, shall we? This way, please."

He follows the doctor through the waiting room and into an examination room. The office is part of a white clapboard house with a white picket fence. Somewhere in the house Colley can hear a baseball game on television. In the back yard there's the sound of children lauging. The doctor watches him as he takes off the plaid jacket. The jacket is winter-weight and the sleeves are a little too long for Colley. He wonders if the doctor is noticing this. Sunlight slants through the curtained window. In a glass-fronted cabinet on the wall opposite, scalpels gleam.

"Would you sit up here, please?" the doctor says, and Colley gets onto the examination table. There is not much blood on the pillowcase he wrapped around his arm. The doctor removes it gingerly, and says "Mmm" when he sees the wound. There is blood caked all over the wound, it looks worse now than it did just after the dog quit gnawing on it. The doctor goes to a cabinet and takes a squeeze-bottle from it, and then wets a piece of gauze and gently soaps out the wound. As he works, it begins to look a little better. There is some fresh blood, but just a little, and he wipes this away and studies the torn flesh and the teeth marks on the arm where the skin has not been ripped.

"Where'd this happen?" the doctor asks.

"Down the road," Colley says.

"Big dog?"

"Police dog," Colley says, and then says, "German shepherd, a German shepherd."

"Mmm," the doctor says. "Where's the dog now?"

"Dead," Colley says. "I killed him."

"Mmm," the doctor says.

"Am I going to need stitches?"

"Not with this kind of injury," the doctor says. "Animal bites, human bites, we leave the wound open. No sutures," he says, and smiles suddenly, looking more like a tennis player than ever. "Don't worry, Mr. Casatelli," he says, getting the name right this time and patting Colley's shoulder reassuringly.

He opens a drawer in the cabinet and searches among a clutter of drug samples, and comes up with a small tube. "This is just an antibiotic," he says, and unscrews the black cap and squeezes the ointment onto a gauze bandage. He puts the bandage over the wound, and then takes out a roll of gauze and begins wrapping the arm.

Colley is beginning to feel better. He likes the way this doctor handles himself, and he also feels very comfortable here in the examination room, with sunlight slanting through the window and children laughing in the back yard and a baseball game going on television. It is like he is in a relative's house. It is like he is a kid again, and he cut his finger visiting one of his relatives, and an uncle or somebody is taking care of it.

But as the doctor bandages the arm, he begins telling Colley about rabies, scaring him half to death. He tells Colley he does not wish to alarm him, and then he starts giving him the symptoms, starting with a pain in the scarred arm, the arm will have healed over by then. This will be about forty days from now, it takes about forty days for the virus to incubate, it is different with a face bite or a leg bite. Colley doesn't want to hear it. He is beginning to sweat as the doctor tells him that *if* he has rabies, and he certainly doesn't want to alarm Colley, why, then the symptoms will start with a pain in the scarred arm, and he'll also have a headache, and he'll feel generally lousy, and he won't have any appetite, and there'll be vomiting, and restlessness, and apprehension, and he'll have difficulty swallowing. Later on there'll be mucus in his mouth and he'll be breathing hard and talking fast, and eventually he'll go into convulsions at the slightest stimulus and will suffer delirium and maniacal attacks, until finally, on the third or fourth day of the acute phase, he'll go into paralysis, coma, and finally death.

The doctor is finished bandaging the arm now. He goes to another drawer, the place is full of drawers, and he takes out a hypodermic and a vial. He pierces the top of the vial with the needle, fills the syringe, and says very briefly, "Tetanus toxoid." He rubs a little cotton ball saturated with alcohol onto the biceps of Colley's arm, and then gives him the shot so Colley can't even feel it. Colley nods.

"Okay?" the doctor says.

"Yes, fine."

"Is that cheek bothering you?"

"No, it's . . . I bruised it when the dog attacked me."

"I wish I knew if that dog were rabid," the doctor says, getting back to the goddamn gruesome subject of rabies.

"He wasn't foaming at the mouth or anything," Colley says.

"Where'd you leave him?"

He can't tell the doctor he left the dog in the woods because then the doctor will want to know what he was doing in the woods and which woods and so on. "By the side of the road," he says. "I got out of the truck to stretch a bit and the dog attacked me."

"Side of the road where?" the doctor says.

"Few miles from here."

"Because if he's licensed, he'll have had his rabies shot, you see."

"Yeah," Colley says.

"If I were you, I'd call the police . . ."

"Well, I'm just passing through . . ."

"Because even if the dog *isn't* licensed, once they find him they can cut off the head and test the brain."

"Well, I don't think he had rabies," Colley says. "He wasn't foaming."

"It's up to you," the doctor says. "But I'd call the police if I were you. It'd be worth the peace of mind. Rabies is not a pleasant disease."

"Well, thank you, maybe I will," Colley says.

"Or I can phone for you, if you like."

"That'd be fine," Colley says. "I'd appreciate that."

"A few miles up the road, you said? Was that north or south?"

"South," Colley says.

"If the dog *should* prove to be rabid, how can I reach you?"

"I'm at 1217 Kruger Avenue," Colley says. "In the Bronx."

"1217 Kruger," the doctor says, writing.

"Yes," Colley says. He knows there is a Kruger Avenue in the Bronx, but he has never been there. He suddenly realizes that he has given the doctor the name of the man who made his life miserable in prison. Kruger. The Kraut.

"How much is that, Doctor?" Colley asks.

"Twenty-five dollars," the doctor says.

Colley pays him, and shakes hands with him, and leaves the office.

Behind him, he can hear the doctor's children playing in the back yard.

He is sure he has rabies.

As he drives the pickup north, he begins to imagine he has all the symptoms the doctor talked about. He begins to believe that his hyped-up, slowed-down condition is a result of the dog biting him. He cannot remember feeling this way before the dog rushed out of the woods and bit him, this feeling of running in place though he is running forward as fast as he can, this sense of impending doom. Apprehension is what the doctor called it. Restlessness and apprehension. He does not remember that this all began the moment Jeanine pulled the red Pinto into the parking lot in front of the diner. The holdup seems centuries ago. He is centuries old and he has rabies and he will go into convulsions at the slightest stimulus and suffer delirium and maniacal attacks. If there is any way he does not want to die, it is from rabies. If he has any choice in the matter, he will choose even death by drowning over rabies. Rabies has got to be the dumbest way in the world to die.

He is suddenly ravenously hungry. The hunger attacks him like another pain, he thinks at first it may be a symptom the doctor forgot to mention. Except for the lecture on rabies, he likes the way that doctor handled himself. He admires professionalism, and the doctor was a real pro. Things were different, these were different times, they'd probably go out and play a few games of tennis together, have a beer afterwards. Jesus, he is starving hungry, he wants a hamburger and a cold beer. He begins looking for a place to eat, but all he can find is a drugstore in a roadside shopping center, with signs in the window advertising specials like eggs with bacon, toast and coffee for 99¢. This is Sunday, he hopes the lunch counter is open. The way he feels, he is going to eat the gear shift if he doesn't get some real food soon.

The day has turned hot and humid; he takes off the wool plaid jacket and throws it onto the seat of the truck. He isn't worried about his bandaged arm being seen; there is no law against getting bit by a dog. He has put the Smith & Wesson in the glove compartment and he leaves it there now, and hitches up his belt when he gets out of the truck, and then walks casually toward the drugstore. He would not walk this casually if he had not killed a man last night. He is exaggerating everything. He does not know why. He is sure it's because he has rabies.

The drugstore is one of those places that sell everything from desk lamps to inflatable whales for swimming pools. He pities a poor guy coming in here to have a prescription filled cause he'd never find where they keep the drugs. Behind the lunch counter there's a waitress wearing black slacks and a pale-blue blouse. Colley thinks of Jill in the diner, the way she came on with that truck driver, dumb fuck with a button on his hat. She'll probably be talking about the holdup for the rest of her life. Tell her children and her grandchildren about it. At the far end of the counter there's an old guy wearing a fedora on the back of his head. He is sucking his teeth and mumbling to himself. The waitress comes over to Colley.

"Hi," she says. She is a girl in her twenties, black hair pulled back in a ponytail, brown eyes, full figure.

Colley figures she's Italian; with that coloring it's eight-to-five she isn't Irish. He feels a little bit safer thinking she's Italian. He's about to get something to eat, and he's alone here in the drugstore with just an Italian waitress, an old guy sucking his teeth, and a cashier sitting there at the checkout counter. The drugstore has a checkout counter like a supermarket, it's really a supermarket in disguise. The drugstore goes into a phone booth, takes off all its clothes, and out flies a supermarket.

"Hi," Colley says. "I'd like a hamburger and a cold beer."

"You can get the hamburger, but all we've got is soft drinks."

"Okay, a Coke then. Put everything you got on the burger, okay?"

"Well, what'd you want?" the waitress says.

"Relish and a slice of tomato and some onions and pickles, everything you got."

"Are you pregnant or something?" the girl asks, and smiles.

"No, I got rabies," Colley says, and returns the smile.

At the end of the counter the old man says, "*Everybody's*

got something wrong with them. There's nobody in the *world* has nothing wrong with them."

The girl taps her temple, indicating the old man is nuts. Colley nods. She goes over to where the hamburger patties are, and puts one on the griddle and then goes to draw his Coke. Colley is thinking he should hide the crew cut. The cops are sure to have questioned Jeanine, and she is sure to have told them who he is and how she cut his hair early this morning. He doesn't expect there's been any big television flash about the diner holdup, that'll wait till the six o'clock news tonight, *if* it gets on the air at all. There's maybe been radio news about it, but he's not worried about that because you can't show what a man looks like on a radio broadcast. What he's afraid of is that Jeanine has told the Jersey cops about him and they have contacted the New York cops, who have sent pictures to the toll collectors at the bridges and tunnels. So he takes a sip of Coke, and while his hamburger is cooking he gets up and wanders around the drugstore, looking for something he can put on his head. He finds a billed cap that looks like the kind of hat his brother Albert used to wear when they went fishing together. That was when they first moved to the Bronx. Albert used to take him out to City Island, and they used to go fishing. The cap is blue, it looks just like the hat Albert used to wear. He tries it on, and then takes it back to the counter with him.

"Where do I pay for this?" he asks the waitress.

"The food here, the hat at the checkout," she says. "What happened to your arm?"

"A dog bit me," he says.

"You *really* got rabies?"

"No, no."

"Cause that's catching, ain't it? Rabies?"

At the far end of the counter the old man says, "There's nobody in the *world* has nothing wrong with them."

"It's only catching if I bite you," Colley says, and smiles.

"You're not going to bite me, are you?" the girls says. She

is looking at him sideways, like a sultry movie queen in an old television movie, sort of from under partially closed lids. She has one hand on her hip. Behind her the hamburger is sizzling on the griddle.

"No, I'm not going to bite you," Colley says.

"How you want this hamburger?" she says.

"Medium rare."

She goes to the griddle, shovels the hamburger off it and puts it on a bun. Then she puts two slices of tomato on it, and some pickles and relish and onions, and she throws a couple of green olives and a piece of celery on the plate and brings it over to him. The hamburger is delicious. He has never tasted anything so delicious in his life. The girl watches him as he eats. It is as if she has never before seen a hungry man eating. She watches each move he makes, she watches the hamburger coming up to his mouth, and his teeth closing over it, she watches him chewing and swallowing, she is making a documentary on what it is like to eat a hamburger.

"You're not a bit hungry, are you?" she says.

"Nobody," the old man at the end of the counter says. "Nobody in the *world* has nothing wrong. Miss?" he says.

"Yes, sir?" she says.

"I would like a check, please."

"Yes, sir," she says, and walks over to him.

Colley watches her behind in the tight black slacks. She knows he is looking at her. She exaggerates her walk. She is wearing low-heeled shoes, but she struts over to the old man as if she is wearing rhinestone slippers with three-inch spikes. As she makes out the old man's ticket, she glances at Colley and smiles. He nods. He is beginning to think he may not go back to New York after all. Where can he go in New York? He goes to his mother's place, the fuzz'll be there waiting. He can't go to Teddy's house, Teddy'll slam the door in his face. And the cops have a dossier on all the guys used to be in the Orioles, they'll be watching Benny's pad, *all* the guys, what's the sense of going back there? Back there is where he killed the cop. At least here in Jersey the cop beef ain't theirs. All they're worried about is the diner holdup. He thinks maybe he will explore this little Italian waitress a wee bit further.

He knows he is very good with girls, and he further knows he is very good-looking. But he is also smart enough to know there isn't a man alive who doesn't think he himself is good-looking. Man looks in the mirror, he says to himself, "Good morning, you handsome irresistible devil." He'd catch guys in prison looking at themselves in the mirror, preening. Ugliest sons of bitches in the world, you ran into one of them in a dark alley you'd drop dead of a heart attack just looking at them. Preening. Good morning, you handsome irresistible devil. So he's smart enough to know that maybe he's mistaken about how good-looking he is or isn't, but he knows he has a pretty fair batting average with girls, and he prides himself on the fact that he's never had to pay for it in his life. That's not to say he hasn't fucked whores, because he has. But he's never paid for it. Never. He is pretty confident that the girl here in the drugstore finds him attractive, and he is also confident that he can make her.

The old man gets off the stool and counts his change. He stares at the change in the palm of his hand and then counts it again. When he approaches the checkout counter, the cashier puts down her confession magazine and looks annoyed because she think's she's perhaps going to have to stop reading and do her job instead. But the old man has paid at the lunch counter, and he jerks his thumb back at the waitress, and the cashier nods and picks up the confession magazine, and he goes through the checkout and out of the drugstore.

The waitress is standing in front of Colley now. She has her hands on her hips. "Will there be anything else, sir?" she asks.

"Call me Steve," he says, using the name he gave the doctor.

"Okay, Steve," she says, and she makes it sound like they have already agreed to spend a month together in Brazil. "Will there be anything else?"

"Depends what you got in mind," Colley says, and smiles.

"Right now, I got food in mind," she says.

"But that's only right now, huh?" he says. She is smiling, too. They are both smiling and looking into each other's faces. "How about later, huh?"

"We'll see about later," she says.

"How about seeing about later now?" he says.

"You want a cup of coffee?"

"I want to talk about later."

"Have a cup of coffee first," she says.

"Okay, I'll have a cup of coffee and also a piece of that Danish back there. Is that Danish?"

"Cheese Danish," she says.

"Let me have a little piece of it," he says.

He watches her as she draws the coffee, and lifts the cover off the Danish tray, and picks up a piece of pastry. He is still watching her when she brings the coffee and the Danish to the counter. She is wearing a smoky sultry look now; she smiles like a harem girl through a gauze mask.

"What's your name?" he says.

"Marie."

"Are you Italian, Marie?"

"French," she says.

"French. Well, well. How old are you, Marie?"

"Old enough, don't worry," she says.

"What time do you get out of here, Marie?"

"Six."

"That late, huh?" The coffee is very hot. He sips at it gingerly and then puts the cup back on the counter. "Six o'clock, huh?"

"Yes." She is looking at him steadily.

"Maybe I'll stop back here later," he says. "What time is

it now?" He looks at his wristwatch. "Almost four-thirty," he says. "That gives me an hour and a half."

"That's right," she says.

"So maybe I'll stop back later."

"If it's *maybe,*" she says, "forget it."

"Hey, wait a minute," he says, but she has already walked away to the end of the counter. She comes around the counter, sits on a stool, picks up the comics from the Sunday *News,* and begins reading Dick Tracy.

Colley sips at his coffee. He is going to give her plenty of time. He puts the hat on his head and looks at himself in the mirror behind the counter. Not bad. He looks a little bit like Albert L. Donato, the noted Buick dealer. He sips some more coffee. He tilts the hat at a more rakish angle. He winks at himself in the mirror and then glances toward where Marie is still reading the funnies at the end of the counter. She is thoroughly absorbed in Dick Tracy. She is lip-reading her way through Dick Tracy there at the end of the counter.

"Marie?" he says.

She turns toward him as if a stranger has entered the drugstore and she cannot locate the sound of his voice. She has heard someone speaking, but she cannot imagine who it can possibly be, since she is alone in the place with only the cashier and Dick Tracy, and this voice from out of the blue has startled her. She locates Colley at last, sighs, gets up off the stool, comes around the counter, and walks to where he is sitting.

"Hi," he says.

She says nothing. She stares at him. She is mortally offended.

"Can I have a check, please?" he says.

She begins writing. She does not look at him now. Her pencil scratches out the figures on her pad. He looks at her hand as she writes. The fingernails are bitten to the quick; he likes tense, nervous girls, they are very good in bed.

"You're a pretty girl, Marie," he says.

She does not look up.

"You want me to come back here at six o'clock?"

She puts the check on the counter face-down, and then she looks up into his face. He thinks she is going to tell him to go to hell. Instead, she says, "Do what you like."

"I'd like to come back," he says.

"Fine," she says.

"Okay, I'll be back at six."

"Fine."

"You live near here?"

"Yes."

"You got a car?"

"I take a bus."

"Cause all I'm driving is a pickup truck."

"That's okay."

"Okay," he says, and picks up the check. "Do I pay this here?"

"Yes," she says.

"Okay," he says, and takes out his wallet, and wonders if he's supposed to tip her. He's just made a date with her, is he supposed to tip her? He pays her the exact amount on the check, and she gives him a look, and he can't tell whether she's still sore because of what he said earlier, or whether she's sore now because he stiffed her. "Well, I'll see you later," he says, and walks away from the counter. At the checkout, he takes off the blue cap and hands it to the cashier. She looks inside it for a price tag, and then rings up the sale. The plate-glass windows at the front of the store are behind her. Through them Colley can see the pickup truck. Alongside the truck is a white car marked NEW JERSEY STATE POLICE.

"That's a dollar forty-seven," the cashier says.

The police car is empty. Colley can see the trooper in the cab of the pickup truck, rummaging around. He can only assume that fat Will Hollip got out of the storage shed and called the state police to tell them a man had shot his brother's valuable and gentle German shepherd and stole a pickup truck besides. Otherwise, why would a trooper be going through the truck now? He will find the Smith & Wesson in a minute. He will thumb open the glove compartment and find the gun. Colley turns immediately from the checkout counter and walks to where Marie is sitting reading the funnies again. She just cannot tear herself away from Dick Tracy, this girl. She has already read four panels of the strip. By Christmas she will have finished the whole page. He imagines being in bed with her. He imagines trying to talk to her afterwards. It will be like talking to a yak.

"Marie," he says, "is there a back door to this place?"

"Why?" she says, and looks up from the comics into his face. Her eyes dart past him to the front door.

Colley turns at once. The door is opening. The trooper is coming inside. He has his gun in his hand. Colley does not know what kind of gun it is, but he knows that the troopers in some states use .357 Magnums, and he knows a bullet from a Magnum can tear off your head. The gun in the trooper's hand is a big one, it could easily be a Magnum. Colley starts moving toward the back of the drugstore. He does not think the trooper has seen him yet. He figures the reason the trooper has his piece in his hand is because he's had a report on a stolen pickup truck, and he's found the truck and there's a weapon in the glove compartment. Which is enough reason for him to proceed with caution. To him, proceeding with caution means having his own weapon in his hand as he enters the drugstore in front of which the pickup truck is parked.

Colley is moving down the center aisle, shelves on his left and right, shelves of perfume, Band-Aids, toothpaste, cologne, razor blades, shaving cream, deodorants, menstrual pads: he is moving between shelves of stationery and monster models, playing cards and boxes of candy; he is moving between shelves of magazines and paperback books. He spots the door at the back of the place, a glass door with a metal push bar across it about waist-high. He tries the door, and it is locked. He glances back over his shoulder. The trooper has moved from the checkout counter to the lunch counter. He is talking to Marie, and she is pointing toward the rear of the store.

The door is wired for a burglar alarm, metal strips creating a border design around the glass. He knows the alarm isn't on, otherwise it would ring every time somebody came in the front door. Besides, an alarm going off would only bring cops, and he has a cop here already, looking toward the back of the store and nodding. In a minute he will come through the store yelling. And maybe shooting. Colley brings back his foot and kicks out flatfooted at the deadbolt lock. The door doesn't budge. He kicks at it again. The cop is coming down the center aisle now. His gun is out in front of him. Colley thinks he has been here before. He has certainly been here before with a cop coming down the aisle at him holding a gun. This cop is not holding the gun in his left hand. This cop is not holding up a shield. This cop is just coming down the aisle very fast. There is also one other difference. Colley does not have a gun.

"Hey, you!" the cop yells.

There are garbage cans and rakes and rubber hoses in the back part of the store, sprinklers, trowels, bags of fertilizer —this is the gardening section of this drugstore that's a supermarket. There are metal garbage cans and plastic garbage cans. He picks up one of the heavy metal cans and hurls it at the glass door, but it just bounces off the fuckin door, the door has got to be made of steel though it only looks like glass. He picks up a rake and swings it at the door, and the wooden handle of the rake breaks in half, and the door still hasn't got a dent in it. The cop is yelling "You, hey you!" and there is nothing Colley can do now but run toward the front of the store again, either that or be taken. There are three aisles in the store, and the cop is running down the center aisle, the gun getting bigger and bigger as he comes closer and closer. Colley breaks for the aisle on the left, and the gun goes off like a cannon, putting a huge hole in the glass door behind him. Colley is sure it is a Magnum now, and he is afraid of it, he does not want to get shot with a Magnum.

He is running up an aisle that has glassware in it, Pyrex dishes and serving bowls and drinking glasses and brandy snifters, this is some drugstore. He knows that when the cop reaches the end of the center aisle, he will come around into this aisle, and he will drop to one knee and steady his firing arm and put a big hole in Colley's back. He has already fired his warning shot, and he is shouting "Halt! Halt or I'll shoot!" as he comes running down the center aisle, Colley going in the opposite direction up the aisle on the left. There is a space above the shelves, an open space, the drugstore has a high vaulted ceiling and the shelves are really only dividers between the aisles. He climbs the divider on his right the way he climbed that fence in the Bronx, only now he is knocking glasses and dishes and cups and saucers to the floor; the entire glasswares department of this fine drugstore-super-market-department store is crashing into the aisle as he climbs the divider and rolls over the top of it as if it is a back-yard fence, and drops into the middle aisle. The blue hat drops from his head. He does not stop to pick it up.

He comes sprinting up the aisle, heading straight for the checkout counter. The cashier has stopped reading her confession magazine, there is a true story unfolding right here where she works, and she is watching Colley goggle-eyed as he runs toward her. For no good reason, she starts screaming. Behind him, the trooper has figured out that Colley isn't in the aisle on the left any more, he has climbed over the divider and is in the center aisle again. But Colley has a good lead on him, and even when the trooper opens fire behind him, he feels confident he is going to make it through the checkout counter and out of the store. The cashier ducks, she is afraid she's going to get shot by accident. Colley runs past her and veers sharply to his left, toward the front door. In a minute he is outside in the parking lot. He does not know whether to keep running, or take the pickup truck, or steal the trooper's car. He wonders if the trooper has left his keys in the car. He doubts it.

He decides to run.

He has always been good at running.

He runs parallel to the front of the drugstore, and then cuts sharply around the edge of the building and into the woods behind it. If the trooper has seen him going into the woods, Colley will still be better off in here than running on the highway, in the open. He is wearing Sam Hollip's blue pants and white short-sleeved shirt, this is the second time in twelve hours he's had on clothes belonging to another man. He wishes the pants and the shirt were green, be better camouflage if the trooper opens fire again. But he does not hear any thrashing in the woods behind him; is it possible the trooper didn't see him coming in here? He tries to remember the kind of lead he had on the trooper, was it long enough so that by the time the trooper came out the front door, Colley would already have been around the side of the building? But wouldn't the trooper have seen him through the plate-glass windows, running toward the right? And wouldn't he have guessed that Colley'd be heading for the woods instead of the highway?

The terrain slopes sharply upward, he is doing more climbing than he is running, but he still doesn't hear anything behind him—is it possible? Is it possible that dumb trooper doesn't know he's in here? He begins to suspect a trap. Maybe the trooper knows a shortcut, maybe he's circling around from another direction, he'll spring out of the woods the way Sam Hollip's monster dog did. But the only sound in the woods is the sound of Colley's own breathing, and the crackle of twigs underfoot as he labors up the incline, and the hum of insects and the occasional voice of a bird. Nothing else. He is getting very good at hearing things in the woods, despite the fact that he is only a city boy. Maybe they will do an article on *him* once this is all over. Put his picture on the cover of a magazine. He does not have much hair on his chest, however.

He has reached the crest of the hill now. The ground is level here, the rock outcropping covered with soil and tufted with weeds. On the other side the ground rolls gently away into a grassy valley. There are wild flowers in the valley, blue and yellow and white and lavender. The sun is shining brightly, and there is a single cloud in the sky; it hangs motionless, a puff of white.

He starts slowly down the gentle slope.

He does not know how long he has been walking. He has forgotten to wind his watch, and it has stopped at four o'clock, and he does not know what time it is now. Ahead of him, beyond a fringe of trees, he hears voices and laughter.

He has come through the valley and into a woods on the other side of it. He has rested more than once in dappled clearings, and he has stopped to drink water from a trickle of a stream deep in the woods. He has crossed a pasture of waist-high grass, butterflies circling, grasshoppers leaping ahead of him, and now he comes through yet another glade, and cautiously approaches the voices and the laughter. He crouches. He peers through the leaves.

There are men and women in bathing suits on a lawn as emerald-bright as the valley had been. The pool beyond sparkles with late-afternoon sunshine. A black man in a white jacket and black trousers is standing behind a table covered with a white cloth. There are whiskey bottles and glasses on the table, a dish with lemon peels and lime wedges, another dish with olives. The black man is mixing a drink for a tall blond suntanned woman wearing a white string bikini. A fat man wearing red trunks and black-rimmed glasses is telling a joke. When he finishes the joke, the circle of men and women around him burst out laughing.

Colley would love a drink. He would love nothing better than to stroll out of the woods and up to the bar, ask the nigger for a gin and tonic. A gin and tonic would hit the spot now. The fat man is obviously the host. He leaves the group of people he's just told the joke to, and wanders over to another group, probably to tell the same joke. If he was any kind of host, he'd ask Colley to come out of the woods and have a gin and tonic. There are great-looking women here, none of them spring chickens, but all of them tall and sun-tanned and wearing hardly any clothes.

There is the smell of money hanging over this place. The black man has set up his bar on a flagstone terrace covered with a striped awning, red and yellow. Behind the terrace, there are mullioned doors leading to a room in shadow beyond. The house is very big, ivy-covered stone rising to turrets and gabled windows, a slate roof, copper gutters, a huge chimney with three green hooded cones sticking out of it. The women are sleek and tan and swift as race horses, and the men ignore them the way only rich men would, talking instead about their investments in oil or soybeans, talking about their clubs in New York, talking about the great squash game they had yesterday, after which they came off the court and drank some beer advertised on television, talking about the business trips they will take to Europe in the fall, and the French girls they are going to fuck when they get to Paris.

Colley envies them and hates them.

He wants a gin and tonic.

He wants the tall sleek blonde in the white string bikini.

He circles around through the trees, toward the diving-board end of the pool, working his way toward the big stone house. It has occurred to him that all these fat rich bastards out here are in swimming trunks. They are out here talking among themselves, ignoring their sleek tanned women, and they are in swimming trunks—which means their clothes are somewhere in the house. Or maybe in a separate pool house.

Colley can't see a pool house. He knows what a pool house looks like because he has seen movies in which people come out of a cabana is what you call them, these pool houses, and then jump in the water or lie in the sun. He has never swum in a private pool. He would like to swim in *this* pool with the tall blonde in the white string bikini. The only pools he has ever swum in are the Boys' Club pool on 110th Street when he was living in Harlem, and the Jefferson Pool on First Avenue, also when he was in Harlem. And then after they'd moved to the Bronx he swam at Tibbetts Brook in Yonkers, and also at Willsons Woods, and once his brother Al took him to Playland and they swam in the pool there. He would give his right arm to swim in this pool with the blonde in the white string bikini. Rabies and all, he would give it. He would give his left arm for a gin and tonic. He would swim armless to the side of the pool and ask the nigger to hold the drink to his lips. The blonde would giggle at his marvelous stunt, an armless man swimming the length of the pool. He would be the first unarmed robber in history.

The trees completely surround the house, he is grateful to the landscaper. The back of the house is all stone, windows slightly higher than his head on the main floor, windows on the second floor some fifteen feet above that; high ceilings. He is looking for a door he can go in through. He keeps circling the house through the trees, and he finds a place where there's a small courtyard, and on one wall in the angle where the walls join, there's a door painted a pale blue. Brass knocker on it. Dutch door, top half open. Inside he can see a black woman puttering around.

He doesn't know if the lady of the house is in the kitchen giving orders to the hired help, but he figures he'll take a chance. He wants to get in that house and find himself some different threads. The trooper back there must have seen he was wearing blue pants and a white shirt. Even if the trooper didn't see it, Marie sure as hell did. Very anxious to help the police officer, old Marie was. There he is, Officer, heading for the door at the back of the store. Thank you, Marie. You cunt. He comes out of the woods and walks nonchalantly across the lawn toward the kitchen door. Inside the kitchen, the black woman is humming. This is plantation time down South. She is probably cooking corn on the cob in a great big pot on the stove and she is humming old slave tunes. He walks right in the kitchen. The black woman is alone in there.

"Hi," he says.

"Afternoon," the woman says, and looks at him.

"I'd like to take a swim," he says, which is most certainly the truth.

"Yessir," the woman says.

"Where do I change my clothes?" he asks. This is the truth, too, more or less. He sincerely wants to change his clothes, or rather Sam Hollip's clothes, for somebody else's clothes.

"Top of the stairs," the woman says.

"Thank you," Colley says, and smiles pleasantly, and walks out of the kitchen into a carpeted hallway.

Everybody's outside, the house is still and empty, there are dust motes climbing shafts of sunlight in the living room. A woman laughs, her laughter hangs delicately on the air and then shatters like broken glass. He climbs the carpeted steps. He has never been inside a house like this in his life. He wonders if the owner of the house, the fat man in the red trunks and black-rimmed glasses, keeps a gun. He would certainly like a gun. Once he gets himself a change of clothes, which he is sure to do in the room at the top of the stairs, the only thing he will then need is a pistol. Guy has a house like this one, he's *got* to have a gun in it someplace, protect the turf. The door at the top of the stairs is ajar, Colley can see into it, can see one angle of the bed, and on it clothes neatly laid out.

He goes into the room and closes the door.

There are only men's clothes in here, the ladies have probably changed in another room. There are trousers and shirts and undershorts on the bed, and on the floor around the bed, lined up in pairs, there are shoes with socks tucked into them. Through the two open windows in the bedroom, he can hear people laughing and splashing and talking outside. He has a crazy idea for a minute—if there's a bathing suit someplace around, maybe in one of the dresser drawers, he'll put it on and go join the party. Stroll over to the bar, tell the nigger he'd like a gin and tonic. Then find the blonde in the white string bikini, tell her she looks very familiar, didn't he once drink beer with her in a television commercial? It was right after they won the stickball game, remember? She will laugh her laugh, it will hang on the air and tinkle like glass.

Most of the guys outside looked fat to him, he wonders now if any of these clothes will fit him. He is beginning to think that he will never again in his lifetime wear his own clothes. When they put him in his coffin in excruciating detail, hands folded over a rosary on his chest, he will be wearing a silk sports shirt and gabardine trousers and stretch socks and patent-leather shoes belonging to some fat rich bastard in New Jersey. He searches on the bed for a pair of pants that seem to be about his size, and he finds a good-looking pair of white slacks, and a shirt made out of a synthetic fabric, polyester and cotton it says on the label, blue-and-green pattern on it, long-sleeved. The long sleeves are good because dear Marie back in the drugstore is sure to have told the trooper the man had a bandage on his arm and was kidding about rabies. He feels a little funny putting on another man's undershorts, used undershorts at that, but he puts them on and then slips on the white pants, Jesus, they fit like a glove. He puts on the shirt then and rolls up the cuffs just two turns. He leaves the shirt hanging out of the pants. The socks are a pale blue, the shoes are white patent leather. The fuckin shoes are too small for him. He goes through the shoes lined up around the bed, looking inside for sizes. His own shoe size is 10½B, he finds a pair of 11's and puts them aside, and then he finds a pair of 10's, and he tries on first the 10's and then the 11's and decides the 10's feel better. They are brown shoes, and they don't go too well with the white pants and the polyester shirt, but that's life, sweetheart.

The door opens.

A woman comes into the room.

"Hi," she says, and smiles.

"Hi," Colley says.

"I'm looking for the loo," she says.

She is wearing an orange beach coat and high-heeled cork-soled wedgies. Long tanned legs, hair like a rust-colored mop. She has brown eyes and she wears orange lipstick that matches the beach coat. There is green shadow on her eyelids.

"Leaving so soon?" she says.

"I just got here," he says.

"I'm Lili Shearson," she says, and sticks out her hand.

"Steve Casatelli," he says, and takes her hand awkwardly.

"I'd love to chat a while," she says, smiling, "but I really have to tinkle. Is that it?" she says, indicating a door, and going immediately to it, and opening it. She sighs in anticipated relief, does a sort of Groucho Marx glide into the bathroom, and locks the door behind her.

Colley leaves the room at once, coming down the carpeted steps into the carpeted hallway. He cannot go out through the kitchen again because he told the black woman he was going to take a swim, and you don't take a swim in white slacks and a blue-and-green polyester and cotton long-sleeved sports shirt. He wishes he could wait for the woman in the orange beach coat to come out of the bathroom to chat with him. He would love to chat with a woman who calls a toilet a loo, and a piss a tinkle. He wonders if the blonde in the white string bikini talks like that. He finds what he thinks must be the front door of the house, and he opens it and steps out onto an oval gravel driveway.

There is a pale-blue Cadillac sitting right in front of the house, the engine running. A woman is getting out of the car on Colley's side, and a man is getting out on the driver's side. A kid in blue jeans and a striped T-shirt is holding the door open for the woman. She smiles at Colley as she gets out of the car. He smiles back nervously. The man comes around the car and says "Hi" to Colley, and Colley says "Hi" back. The kid in the blue jeans says, "Be with you in a minute, sir," and the man says to Colley, "Roger Lewis," and sticks out his hand. "Steve Casatelli," Colley says, and shakes hands with the man. "My wife Adrienne," the man says. "Nice to see you," the woman says. They both nod and smile and then go into the house without ringing the doorbell. Colley starts walking up the driveway.

The kid is parking the blue Cad on the road that runs past the house. There are a half-dozen cars parked in the oval driveway, and another dozen or more on the road. Colley figures he can drive away from here in style if he is willing to add a grand-larceny auto to what the cops already have on him. Counting the diner this morning, they have him on two separate counts of armed robbery, one in New York, the other in Jersey, and they have him on what they will probably call murder one, though it was actually self-defense, and they also have him on assault one in New Jersey, for shooting the cook who came at him with the cleaver, though *that* was self-defense too. So he figures adding the grand-larceny auto to all the rest isn't going to make a hell of a difference, one way or the other. He has the feeling, in fact, that since nine o'clock last night, when he returned that cop's fire and shot him dead in self-defense; since *that* minute and *that* second, nothing he's done and nothing he's about to do is going to change the situation in the slightest. He isn't particularly worried about this, he figures *Que sera, sera.* So he continues walking up the driveway, knowing he is going to steal a car. When he was a member of the Orioles, they used to steal cars all the time, but only for joy-riding, dump them in the city

someplace after they were done with them. It was easy stealing cars back in those days, but not as easy as it is going to
be today. Today he is going to be handed the car of his choice
on a silver platter. The kid is running up the driveway to
meet him. "Yes, sir," he says, "which one is it again?"

"The brown Mercedes," Colley says.

The kid frowns, looks at him as if he's wondering if this
is the same guy who drove up in the brown Mercedes. But
Colley stares him down, and the kid turns and runs to where
the Mercedes is parked right at the head of the driveway. By
the time Colley reaches the big brick pillars flanking the
drive, the kid has the car started and is standing outside it,
holding the door open on the driver's side. The kid still looks
puzzled. He is probably certain now that Colley isn't the man
who drove up in this car, and he is probably also beginning
to wonder if Colley is the man who was earlier wearing the
white slacks and the polyester shirt. But Colley hands the kid
a buck, and the kid says, "Thank you, sir," and smiles, and
keeps holding the door open until Colley is inside and fastening the seat belt. He closes the door then and stands back a
few feet, watching Colley as he eases the car out into the
road.

The car smells of real leather. It is a rich smell, he luxuri-
ates in it. He has not driven a car since he got out of prison.
He began breaking parole a month and four days after his
release from Sing Sing, but the one thing he has not done in
that time is drive an automobile because he does not want to
get stopped by a cop on a traffic violation and be unable to
show him a driver's license. The car he is driving now is a
280SL, a '63 or a '64, he's not sure which, but a discontinued
model either way. Probably cost eight or nine thousand dollars new, bucket seats in beige leather, stick shift on the floor,
AM/FM radio—he turns on the radio now, stabbing at one
of the buttons and getting a rock station, and then pushing
in another button and getting a station playing an opera. He
remembers his grandfather going to the opera in Brooklyn

all the time. The car has a convertible top, he is tempted to lower the top and drive along with the wind in his crew cut and the sounds of the opera flooding the countryside. It is a beautiful countryside he drives through. He forgets for the moment that he is running from the law. He feels instead that he is out for a late-afternoon drive. He looks at his watch, sees that it is still four o'clock, and remembers that it's stopped. The dashboard clock reads 6:10.

In a little while it will be dark.

He desperately needs a gun.

Before this he has used guns only aggressively, to force people into doing things he wanted them to do, to force people into giving him things he wanted from them. Now, at 7:48 P.M. on the dashboard clock, he wants a gun only for defense. He is afraid that something terrible is going to happen to him if he does not get his hands on a gun soon. He knows that there are probably two very angry people back there at the pool party, the one whose clothes he stole and the one whose car he stole—unless they are one and the same person. He knows the police have undoubtedly been called by now, and he knows they are probably looking for the stolen car this very minute, but he is reluctant to get rid of it until he has a gun.

All that remains of the afternoon sun is a thin line of vibrant purple behind the silhouetted hills. As he drives northward and eastward, the sky and the hills blend into one. There is a moon, a slender silver slice hanging against the blackness. His headlights have meaning now, they pierce the darkness ahead, picking out shops, and roadside stands, and gasoline stations, all of them closed—this is Sunday. He glances at the fuel gauge. The tank is a quarter full. In the glare of the headlights he sees a phone booth on the side of the road, and he pulls in alongside it, and then steps out of the car and walks quickly to the license plate at the rear. The plate is a Jersey plate, pale yellow and black, the police undoubtedly have the number. There is a clean pressed hand-kerchief in the hip pocket of the slacks he stole, and he takes that out now and tents it over his hand and gingerly unscrews the bulb illuminating the license plate. He throws the bulb aside, and then steps into the phone booth.

If this was New York City, there'd be no telephone directory in the booth. Also, the phone wouldn't be working. Also, somebody would have pissed on the floor. But this is Jersey, and when he closes the door of the booth the light comes on, and there's a directory on the end of a chain and the booth is clean and he figures if he wanted to make a phone call, he would stand a very good chance here in this booth. In New York City the odds are thirty-to-one you will never get to make a phone call from a public booth. It is nice of the police to have a special number to call when you want to report a crime. Trouble is, you go into a booth the phone is always out of order. Colley sometimes thinks there is a bunch of guys just like himself running all over New York City fucking up the phones. So if later they're committing a robbery or a burglary or mugging an old lady in the street, nobody can pick up the phone and dial 911.

He opens the directory to the yellow pages at the back of the book. There are two pages with the heading GUNS at the top. One of them reads GRAVEL-GUNS and the other one reads GUNS-HAIR. The listings start near the bottom of the first page, under the heading GUNS & GUNSMITHS. There are four listings on that page, and six on the following page. Colley rips both pages out of the phone book. Then he puts a dime in the slot and dials the operator. When she comes on he tells her he is on the highway someplace, and doesn't know exactly where he is, and could she please give him the location of this phone booth, what town it's in. She tells him where he is, and he thanks her and hangs up, and then goes to sit in the car with the interior light on, to study the ten listings for GUNS & GUNSMITHS.

There is only one listing for this town. A place called Richard's Gun Rack, Inc. The address is 76 Rock Ledge Road. He snaps off the overhead light, puts the car in gear, and begins driving north again. Probably going in the wrong direction, Rock Ledge is probably someplace behind him. He passes two closed gas stations, an Exxon and a Mobil. He passes a closed diner, looks just like the one he held up this afternoon, except it doesn't have those big aluminum poles out front with the OPEN 24 HOURS sign. Finally, he comes to a shopping center with everything closed in it but a tavern.

The juke box is playing a country-western song when Colley walks in. He takes a stool at the bar and waits for the bartender to discover him. At the other end of the bar, there is a man wearing a pinkie ring that sparkles even in a place as dim as this. A girl wearing a black dress is sitting on the stool next to him. She almost fades into the background except for her frizzy blond hair. The bartender nods at something the girl says, and then comes over to Colley.

"I'm looking for Rock Ledge Road," Colley says.

The bartender nods. "Keep going north till you come to the third stop light," he says. "That's Main, goes straight through the middle of town. You make a right, you'll go two more stop lights, and then you'll make another right, that's . . ."

"What are you telling him, Lou?" the guy with the pinkie ring says.

"He wants Rock Ledge. I'm sending him down Main."

"He's better off taking Lakeview."

"Too complicated."

"Shorter, though."

"You go the way I'm telling you," the bartender says to Colley. "Third stop light, you make a right, then you go two more lights and make another right. That's Pointer Street. You go four blocks on Pointer, that's Rock Ledge. What number did you want?"

Colley hesitates, and then lies. "One-oh-four," he says.
"You'll have to make a left, I think. Where's one-oh-four Rock Ledge, Andy?"
"Down around Osborne, I think," the guy with the pinkie ring says.
"Yeah, you'll have to make a left. That's mostly stores on Rock Ledge," the bartender says. "You're not looking for a store, are you? Cause this is Sunday, you know."
"No, it's not a store," Colley says.
"There's houses, too, on Rock Ledge," the guy with the pinkie rings says. "Tony from Newark used to live on Rock Ledge."
"Who's Tony from Newark?" the bartender says.
"Tony from Newark, what do you mean who's Tony from Newark? Tony from Newark."
"You mean Tony who lives on First Avenue?"
"Yeah, Tony who lives on First Avenue."
"You telling me he used to live on Rock Ledge?"
"That's right, he used to live on Rock Ledge."
"It's mostly stores on Rock Ledge," the bartender says to Colley, and shrugs.
"Well, thanks a lot," Colley says.
"He don't know who's Tony from Newark," the guy with the pinkie ring says to the girl. The girl lights a cigarette and says nothing. On the juke box, there is a click, a pause, and then Sinatra comes on singing "My Way." Colley thanks the bartender again and goes outside.
The car starts immediately, he is beginning to like this sweet little wagon. His mother always tells him he has expensive taste, and she is right. She is not right about too many things, his mother, but she is certainly right about his taste. There is nothing he would like better than to live in the kind of house he stole the clothes and the car from, swim in a pool with a blonde in a white string bikini, take her to the Copa afterwards, show her off. Drive up in this sweet little wagon, doorman'll say, "Good evening, Mr. Donato," give the guy

a five-dollar tip, go inside and show off the blonde. Wear a big diamond on his pinkie, like the one the guy in the bar was wearing just now. Flash it around. Colley doesn't care much about clothes, but jewlery, yeah, and good food, and expensive liquor, yeah, he could enjoy that kind of life, all right. Maybe when this is all over, when the heat cools about the cop, he will do a big one someplace. Maybe go West, knock over a bank in a hick town out there. Not Texas, those Texas Rangers are cocksuckers. But someplace out there. Some hick town. Maybe in Kansas someplace. Walk in, shove the piece in the teller's face, you probably could knock over one of those hick banks with a cap pistol. Cops out there wouldn't be like New York cops, fuckin bastards. Cops out there'd be sitting with their feet up on the desk, fanning themselves with a cardboard fan. The phone rings, somebody tells them the bank's just been held up. "Yeah?" the cop says. He's probably a sheriff. "Yeah?" he says, and swings his feet off the desk, and looks around for somebody he can make a deputy—was that the second stop light just then, or the third? Colley's thinking about holding up a fuckin bank, and he's losing track of the stop lights. He hopes it was only the second one. There's another one up ahead, and if that's where he's supposed to turn, it'll say Main Street.

He peers through the windshield, sees the street sign on the corner—it's Main, all right. He makes the right turn, and starts counting stop lights again. At the second light he makes another right turn and that's Pointer Street, just like the bartender said. Four more blocks to Rock Ledge, there it is, there's a FULL STOP sign on the corner. He brakes the automobile, he looks in both directions, he is being a perfect little driver in this sweet little wagon, and he is beginning to feel as cheerful as a whore on payday because he is about to find Richard's Gun Rack, and he is about to break into it and steal himself a deadly weapon. A death machine. Maybe a P-38 like the one he emptied into the dog. Or maybe a .45 automatic, he likes that gun, too.

He discovers in a minute that he's heading in the wrong direction. The number on the corner was 125 and the numbers are moving *up* instead of *down,* he has reached 137 before he discovers he's made a mistake. Not *his* mistake, actually, he's only following the bartender's directions, it's the bartender who made the mistake. He drives to the next corner, the streets are almost empty even though it's only eight o'clock by the dashboard clock, eight o'clock on a Sunday night in a hick town in New Jersey, there probably won't even be an alarm system at Richard's Gun Rack. The light on the corner is red, he waits it out, he is doing everything by the book. He is just a law-abiding New Jersey resident out for a drive in his brown Mercedes-Benz, cruising Rock Ledge Road in search of an open pizzeria. He makes a right turn, circles the block, comes down to Rock Ledge again, and makes a left. The numbers are dwindling now, 118 and 116 and 114, he passes the corner, he is in the 90 block now and then the 80 block and finally he comes into the 70 block.

76 Rock Ledge Road is in the middle of the block.

GUNS the sign says.

It is a big white sign over the entire front of the shop. GUNS.

There are two plate-glass windows flanking the entrance door of the shop, and there is nothing on either of these windows but the single word GUNS again, lettered in gold leaf on each window. There is nothing about this being Richard's Gun Rack. Guns are what the man is selling and that's what it says on the big white sign in black letters, and that's what it says in gold leaf on each of the plate-glass windows: GUNS.

Colley has come to the right place.

He continues on past the place, though, because if the cops in this hick town stumble onto the hot Mercedes, he wants them to find it outside a paint store or a beauty parlor and not outside the place he is in. He parks the car in the 60 block, in front of a store selling radios and phonographs and television sets and stereo equipment. The television set is going in the front window. Owner probably left it on over the weekend because there are millions of people milling over the sidewalks here in this thriving little metropolis. A night baseball game is on. It is the Mets and some other team, Colley can't make out the uniform. He watches for a minute, and then starts back toward the gun shop.

The sidewalks are deserted.

There are rifles in both windows of the shop, with cartridges spread all around them as if they were gold coins spilling from a pirate's chest. Colley searches the plate glass for the metallic strips that will tell him the place is wired. He cannot find any, nor are there any burglar-alarm stickers on the windows. He wishes he knew more about burglar alarms. He knows guys can tell you exactly what kind of alarm is in a place just by taking one look at any exposed wire. Some systems, it doesn't matter if there are exposed wires hanging all over the outside walls, because if you cut a wire the alarm goes off anyway. But he doesn't see any strips on the windows here, and as he circles the building, going through the alley on the side of the store and around to the back, he can't see any wires or bells or anything that would indicate the place has an alarm system. He can't believe it, a gun shop that isn't wired. There's a door on the back of the shop, glass panels in the upper half of it, a deadbolt showing on the outside. That's in case anybody smashes the glass, they can't simply reach in and turn a bolt and open the door. This kind of lock, you need a key to open it even from the inside. No metallic strips on the glass here, either. Is it really possible?

He tries a flatfooted kick at the deadbolt, hoping to spring the lock, but the door doesn't budge an inch. This is what he hates about this kind of shit. When you're doing a robbery, you just walk in the front door and throw a gun on the man, and that's it. Here you have to go fooling around with locks and trying to break into a goddamn place, anybody'd go into burglary has to be out of his mind. He doesn't know what to do. If he breaks the glass panels, he won't be able to unlock the door because of the deadbolt. And even if he breaks out all the glass *and* the wooden frame, the opening will still be too small for him to crawl through. There are *guns* inside this fuckin shop, he can *taste* them.

He comes through the alley again, looking for a window, and he finds a small one high up on the wall, probably a bathroom window. Loo, she called it. I'm looking for the loo. If he can open that window, he can get inside the shop. He goes around back again to where he saw a garbage can alongside the door, and he carries the can into the alley with him and stands on it, and tries to open the window. He can see the street at the end of the alley. A single lamppost illuminates the sidewalk, but the alley itself is in darkness. There is no traffic on the street. In the darkness, in the silence, he works on the window, trying to raise it. He wishes he had a screwdriver or a knife, but he has neither. There are probably tools in the trunk of the Mercedes, he should have thought of that, but he didn't know he was going to have to open a window. He's half thinking of forgetting the whole thing. But there are guns inside there.

He climbs down off the garbage can, and then takes the lid off, and turns the garbage can upside down, and climbs onto it again. There is garbage all over the alley floor now, but it's not rotten food, it's clean garbage—little cardboard boxes that cartridges come in, and newspapers and gun-company brochures, crap like that. Colley plans to smash the window with the lid of the garbage can. He will smash the upper pane of glass just above the inside latch, and then he will reach in and unlatch it. He is afraid that maybe the place is wired, after all, maybe with one of those new sonic alarms where they put microphones around and if a door or a window is opened or anything is smashed, whoever's listening picks up the noise and calls the police. He is afraid that when he smashes the window a bell will go off. He is also afraid that when he smashes the window he will get glass splinters in his eyes.

But there are guns inside there.

He brings back the lid of the garbage can. He is holding it like a shield, and he smashes it flat against the glass and the glass shatters, making a racket he is sure they can hear all the way in the Bronx. There is no bell, only the sound of the glass shattering, but his heart begins to beat wildly anyway. He waits in the darkness. He is sure someone has heard the breaking glass. He is sure someone will yell Hey, what are you doing there? "There's houses, too, on Rock Ledge," the guy with the pinkie ring said back there in the bar. Colley waits. A shard of glass falls from the window frame and shatters on the alley floor. It sounds like a cannon going off in church. He waits and listens. Nothing. He reaches in and turns the latch. He opens the window, crawls in over the sill, and comes through the bathroom into the shop.

There are guns everywhere.

He has never seen so many guns in his life. There are rifles and shotguns in racks on three walls of the shop, and there are handguns in cases along two of the walls and also in a center case that has an aisle on either side of it. Light from the lamppost outside splashes through the two plate-glass windows, glinting on blued steel barrels and walnut stocks. On both plate-glass windows, Colley sees the word GUNS backward. He reads it as SNUG, and he smiles. Yes. Yes, he feels snug and cozy inside this shop, he could stay in this shop forever. The shotguns and rifles in the wall racks stand like soldiers at attention as Colley inspects the revolvers and automatic pistols in the cases. There are Remingtons on the wall, and Springfields, and rifles and shotguns he cannot immediately place. But he knows each and every handgun in the cases.

He can never remember the names of all the seven dwarfs, but he knows all these guns by name. Silently, he rolls the names on his tongue. The names echo sonorously inside his head. Lovingly, like a poet reading his own work, he recites the names in silent reverence—Colt and Llama; Bernadelli; Smith & Wesson, Crosman; Ruger and Savage; Steyr & Derringer; Hi-Standard; Iver Johnson. He knows the models, he loves *those* names, too—the Buntline Special and the Buntline Scout, the Commander and the Agent, the Chiefs Special and the Centennial Airweight, the S & W Terrier and the Sidewinder, the Trailsman and the Python. There is a Walther P-38 in one of the cases, identical to the one he used to kill the dog, and there is a .357 Magnum—Jesus, it is a monster gun. He would be afraid to hold that gun in his hand, afraid it might go off accidentally.

He takes his time deciding which gun or guns he will finally choose. He is like a child in a toy shop on Christmas Eve, and his father has said to him he can have any toy in the shop. He can hardly remember his father, he wonders why he thinks of his father at this moment. But he does feel childlike here in the midst of all these pistols of varying sizes. The cases are locked. With the stock of a rifle he smashes the glass on the case in the center, and then reaches into it and begins trying various pistols for grip and heft. He has carried many of these guns in the past, but some of them are new to him, and he examines each with care and discernment. Here is the pistol he shot the cop with last night, he does not want *that* hoodoo jinx of a gun again. And there's the gun Jocko was using, and there's the .32-caliber Smith & Wesson that Colley left in the glove compartment of the pickup truck. He passes a boxed pair of Number 4 Derringers, be a nice gun for Jeanine, she could tuck it in her G-string, fire off a shot with every bump and grind. He wonders where she is. Fuck her, he thinks.

He keeps coming back to the Magnum.

It is some gun, bigger than any of the others in the case —well, bigger than any of the *real* guns. Some of the target pistols and early Western reproductions have longer barrels, but the Magnum, a Ruger Blackhawk, has got to be what—

ten or eleven inches overall length? Has to be at least a
six-inch barrel on that weapon, *has* to be.

He is afraid of picking up the gun. He guesses it isn't
loaded, but he has never held such a huge weapon in his
hand, and he's fearful of it. He moves down the case to the
Walther, and he picks it up, the heft is familiar, he knows this
gun, it saved his life this afternoon when that fuckin hound
was chewing on his arm. The arm feels pretty good now, he
is beginning to think that maybe he won't die of rabies, after
all, even though the doctor told him it would take forty days
for the first symptoms to appear. He has already forgotten
what the first symptoms will be. Doc, Dopey, Sleepy, Happy,
Droopy, Dumpy and Doc, he thinks and bursts out laughing.
He is beginning to feel very giddy and silly here inside the
gun shop with the light shining through from the lamppost
outside. He doesn't think he wants another Walther, maybe
he'll take the Government Model Colt. But he keeps drifting
back to the Magnum.

That is some big gun.

He picks it up. Blackhawk is some name for a gun. It
sounds like an Indian. His hand is trembling as he picks it
up. It's a heavy gun, it weighs a little more than two pounds.
It's got a walnut grip with an emblem on it just behind the
trigger, looks like a bird in flight, must be the Ruger trade-
mark. He hefts the gun. He rolls out the cylinder to make
sure it is not loaded. Then he rolls the cylinder into the gun
again, and pulls back the hammer with his thumb, and
squeezes the trigger.

Click.

It is as if he turns on a red light. He squeezes the trigger,
and he hears the *click* and the red light goes on. It takes him
a second to realize he has not caused the sudden red illumina-
tion, it is not his squeezing the trigger that makes the light
go on. The light is coming through the plate-glass windows
of the shop. The light is red, the light is flashing, the light
is the dome light on top of a state trooper's car.

The first thing Colley thinks is Yes, the place is wired, it is one of those sonic jobs, and then he thinks No, it is probably a neighbor who heard the glass smashing, and then he realizes it doesn't make a damn bit of difference, they have got him cold inside here, he is standing here with a huge pistol in his hand, but the pistol is empty, he is standing here naked. The trooper who gets out of the car is a big black bastard. He is wearing the trooper hat and the trooper boots, and he is coming toward the front door of the shop. He has his gun in his right hand and a long torchlight in the other hand. As he approaches the door, a second car pulls into the curb, and then a third one. Two of the cars are state police, the other one belongs to the local fuzz, this is a three-alarm fire here. Colley can see through the two plate-glass windows, and it looks like a movie taking place on two big screens that have the word SNUG written on each of them.

"Watch it, there he is!" one of the local cops yells, and the trooper who got out of the second car throws his light through the window into the shop. The second trooper is white. Colley sees this the instant before the light comes on. He also sees that the black trooper is taking aim along the length of his arm. It is just like the liquor store last night: the bastards are going to start shooting at him, and he is going to have to kill one of them in self-defense. But the gun is empty. The gun in his hand, the big fuckin gun that can tear off a man's head, has no cartridges in it.

The movie screens up there are splintered with light now, everybody is throwing light onto the glass and it is splashing all over the shop, there are guns everywhere. There are guns inside the shop, on the walls and in the cases, and there are guns outside there on Rock Ledge Road where two state troopers and two local cops are waiting to shoot him dead, he wonders if they know he killed a cop last night. Light is bouncing all over the shop, he can see only guns and light, the plate-glass windows splintering first with light and then splintering with the impact of the bullets that come leaping out of the darkness. The glass shatters, he has never heard such noise in his life, the sound of the guns going off outside and the sound of the glass shattering and then the sound of something angry buzzing past his ear, he must do something, they are trying to kill him.

Instinctively, he fires back with the empty pistol. He hears a *click* and another *click,* and he keeps squeezing the trigger, and he sees the big fuckin gorilla nigger cop taking steady aim again, and he thinks No, you don't! and fires the empty gun at the trooper, and then sees a flash of light from the muzzle of the trooper's gun, and hears the explosion, and wonders if the trooper is firing a Magnum same as he's firing, *click, click,* and the trooper's shot takes him in the face.

In the last instant of his life he wonders what they will tell his mother, Jesus what will they